BOOK 2

GHOST HUNTRESS
the guidance

MARLEY GIBSON

G

Houghton Mifflin
Boston   New York   2009

*Library of Congress Cataloging-in-Publication Data
is on file.*

ISBN 978-0-547-15094-9

Manufactured in the United States of America

EB 10 9 8 7 6 5 4 3 2 1

ACKNOWLEDGMENTS

For those who have provided *me* with guidance:

To Deidre Knight, the best agent evah, who is always there when I need her. I appreciate your knowledge, support, and, most of all, your friendship. You were there, it happened!

To Julia Richardson, an amazing editor, who graciously went on a ghost hunt with me and saw what it was all about. You're the best at what you do and I'm privileged to work with you. And to the entire team at Houghton Mifflin Harcourt for all of their support and efforts.

To Maureen Wood . . . these characters wouldn't exist if it weren't for you. 'Nuff said.

To Jessica Andersen and Charlene Glatkowski, who are just an e-mail away anytime and always pick me up no matter what. Thanks for the confetti cannon.

To Wendy Toliver and Jenn Echols for their insightful critiques and for making me feel like I was writing something *really* special. Read all of their books . . . they're amazing!

To my special *chicas* who need no explanation as to why they're being thanked here: Kristen Painter, Melissa Francis, Gena Showalter, Maria Geraci, Louisa Edwards White, Elaine Spencer, Pamela Harty, Roxanne St. Claire, Kresley Cole, and Jill Monroe. Love you guys! Mean it!

To my awesome friends in the paranormal community who have shared so much of themselves with me: Patrick Burns, Chris Fleming, Jason Hawes, Grant Wilson, Michael and Marti Parry, Mark and Debby Constantino, Scotty Roberts, Bill Murphy, Chip Coffey, Tim Dennis, John Zaffis, Donn Shy, Kathryn Wilson, and Ron Kolek.

To my boss, Matt Raynor, for too many things to list, and to all the folks at work who support and encourage me and lend me their names for characters. To the real Rebecca Asiaf, for her amazing friendship, memorable lunch hours, and being *the* first fan of this series.

And, as always, to Mike Gibson, for who he is and all he's done.

To DarknessRadio.com's Dave Schrader, my own personal paranormal cheerleader: Thanks for the support and friendship.
When can we go UFO hunting?
And to his daughter, Keila Schrader,
for being such a sweetheart.
You both rock!

For what is faith unless it is to believe what you do not see?

—*Saint Augustine*

CHAPTER ONE

ONLY TWO MONTHS IN TO BEING A GHOST HUNTRESS, and I do believe this current case takes the freakin' cake.

I'm sitting in the living room of one Mrs. Millicent Lockhart of 859 Crow Lane here in Radisson, Georgia. Mrs. Lockhart called my team and me in to help find her deceased husband. And I don't mean, like, to connect with him spiritually—although, as a still budding psychic, I'm able to do that—she wants us to physically find his missing body. Literally. I'm not exactly sure how she lost him, but anyway, here we sit in the very prim and proper living room of an old carriage house on the grounds of a sprawling mansion.

Talk about it being the best of investigating times and the worst of investigating times . . . No, no, no, Dickens already used that line. We'll have to figure this one out on our own.

"More lemon tea bars?" Mrs. Lockhart asks, nudging the crystal serving plate toward me. Even with a deceased and misplaced husband, she's still a Southern lady and the quintessential hostess with the mostest.

"No, thank you, ma'am," I say politely. My friend, neighbor, and fellow ghost huntress Celia Nichols rolls her eyes, but then she reaches out for another one of the tart treats. It's her third. This isn't a tea party, though. It's a ghost investigation. Or at least it's supposed to be.

"These are delicious," Taylor Tillson says. She sits daintily with her ankles crossed and her long golden tresses perfectly in place. Taylor always looks like she just walked off the pages of a magazine, even when we're in full ghost-hunt mode. She wipes her hands on the starched linen napkin and continues. "I just have to make sure I don't get any of the *bonté délicieuse* on my camera when I start taking pictures."

Two years of French. What are you gonna do with her?

Rebecca "Becca" Asiaf lets out a long sigh and taps her foot impatiently. Her digital recorder is poised in her left palm, and I can tell she's ready to get this puppy going. Her silver-ringed thumb, with its black nail polish, waits to hit Record. Obviously, she's as eager to get on with this investigation as I am. Niceties with our hostess aside, we've got work to do.

But this feels more like a social obligation with a great-aunt or something. The four of us are seated on Mrs. Lockhart's crushed-velvet Victorian sofa like perfect little debutantes, sipping our tea and hoping to get more details of her tale of woe. It's important to get as many facts about the dearly departed as possible before we fully begin examining the case at hand, which, in this instance, is File GH-0018—Delaney Lockhart.

Yeah, we're up to eighteen cases!

See, a couple of months ago, my family—Mom, Dad, and little sis, Kaitlin—moved here from our beloved Chicago when dear old Dad took the job of city planner for Radisson. A town that I feel is out where God lost his shoes. The closest metropolis, Atlanta, is an hour's drive. As if leaving behind everything you've ever known in your life isn't hard enough, I am also going through my "psychic awakening." That's according to Loreen Woods, my friend, mentor, and the owner of Divining Woman, a metaphysical store on the Square.

Yep, I can see, hear, and talk to spirits . . . ghosts, the recently and not-so-recently deceased.

Let me tell you what: it's been a busy couple of months for me, Kendall Moorehead. Once word got out about how my team of ghost huntresses had helped a 150-year-old spirit that was trapped in city hall pass into the light, well, everyone and his brother has stopped us with a ghost story or two to tell. Being official ghost huntresses has made me and my friends—Celia, Taylor, and Becca—the talk of the town, and we've garnered a ton of attention. (Not all of it is positive, especially the dirty looks and ill treatment from school beeyotch Courtney Langdon and her flock of followers. However, I think that has more to do with the fact that I'm now dating her ex-boyfriend—and Taylor's twin brother—Jason Tillson.)

It's sort of hard to have a boyfriend when all of your weekends are filled with visits to Radisson's most historic—and often haunted—locations, the mustiest and dustiest of basements, and the homes of some lonely and weird townspeople. Like the one we're in right now.

I shift on the antique couch and clear my throat to ease the tension in my tight chest. I don't think that Mrs. Lockhart is one of those weirdoes we've been running into lately—the kind who wear tinfoil hats and sleep in their bathtubs for fear that things are watching them—because she was a kindergarten teacher in Radisson for years and schooled all three of my friends. However, the woman is definitely broken-hearted and forlorn. The sadness radiating from her is palpable, and I can feel it in the depths of my being like the heat from a well-stoked fire.

I nudge Celia in her ribs with my elbow, and she knows that I'm ready to get down to business.

"So, Mrs. Lockhart, can you tell us again everything that happened with your husband?" Celia says in a very grown-up, professional manner. She flips open her notepad and twirls her Bic between her long fingers.

Becca clicks on the digital recorder and places it on the marble coffee table. She's our sound expert on the team, trying to capture EVPs, electronic voice phenomena. EVPs are the coolest thing ever. I mean, I can hear the spirits' voices in my head, but the digital recorder can actually pick up disembodied voices that answer questions or make statements during our investigations. What we capture can totally back up what I've said. Taylor nods at me and then moves over to where she has the video recorder set up. She's a whiz-bang at anything photography related. That's why she's on the team. Some of the pictures she's captured with the infrared camera and the night vision are a-freakin'-mazing!

Sitting forward, I fold my hands together and listen as Mrs. Lockhart explains why we're here. The older woman dabs her wrinkled eyes with the corner of a lace handkerchief. She sniffs hard and then takes a deep breath.

"Delaney and I went out to Scottsdale last week to visit with our younger daughter, Veronica—our older girl, Evelyn, lives in the main house—and her boys. They're such good boys, those grandsons of mine. Derrick is on the soccer team and Spencer has learned to ride his bike—"

"Yes, ma'am. Now, about Mr. Lockhart, please," I say, trying not to be rude.

"Certainly. As I was saying, we were having a ball at Veronica's. Even to the point where Delaney said he would consider moving out there. I never thought he'd want to leave Georgia. But the weather out in Arizona is simply amazing." Mrs. Lockhart moves behind her ear a stray lock of salt-and-pepper hair that has escaped the tight bun at the base of her neck. I feel a tension at the back of my own neck and wonder if it's empathy with what she's going through or if I slept wrong last night.

She continues. "Delaney loved the putting greens and courses out there and was spending most afternoons golfing and relaxing. He'd been so stressed lately, what with the economy and all and watching our retirement accounts dwindling.

But on Saturday he didn't come back from his golf game, and Veronica and I got worried. Someone from the country club called and told us that he'd had a . . . a . . ." She trails off and then begins to cry. My heart goes out to her, knowing she lost the love of her life. I mean, literally lost him.

"It's okay, Mrs. Lockhart," I say, hoping it sounds soothing. It would probably be a good thing for me to get up and go sit with her. Taylor nods at me from across the room as if she's reading my mind. I slide off the couch and move to our client's side, taking her frail hand. Immediately at the connection of skin to skin, I'm stung with grief and pain and a deep, deep loneliness. In my mind's eye, I see Millicent and Delaney as a young couple, walking hand in hand down by the Spry River here in Radisson. So much in love, with the rest of their lives ahead of them. Children . . . two girls. Years flash past me like cards shuffling until I see her weeping in her daughter's arms. "Can you finish the story you told Celia on the phone?"

Mrs. Lockhart fists her free hand against her mouth and nods. "He . . . he had a h–h–heart attack on the eleventh hole and was more than likely taken straight to Jesus with no pain or suffering." She blots under her eye to catch a wayward tear. "The man he was playing with said he'd just gotten a hole in one," she adds with a slight laugh.

"Man, golf's a rough sport," Becca mutters. Taylor gives her a nasty look.

Celia jumps in to cover Becca's comment. "Tell Kendall the

part with the airlines, Mrs. L." Celia looks at me. "This is the most important part."

The woman keeps going. "Oh, very well. It seems that Southeastern Airlines kind of—well, how do I say this—misplaced my Delaney."

"They what?" I ask incredulously.

She tugs a piece of paper out of the pocket of her housedress and passes it over to me. It's got a bar code with a number and is marked ATL, the airline code for Hartsfield-Jackson Atlanta International Airport.

"Is this a claim ticket?"

"For his coffin," she says.

Holy crap!

"Just a second. You're telling me—" I begin.

Celia finishes, "That she checked him into Baggage in Phoenix, but when Mrs. Lockhart landed in Atlanta and went to claim him, Delaney was missing."

Mrs. Lockhart sniffs into her handkerchief. "I was so distraught; I didn't know what to do. Evelyn had to drive over and talk to the supervisor. Poor child was grief-stricken herself, losing her father, and she had to go through all of the airport's bureaucratic red tape."

"What can we do, though, Celia?" I raise my eyebrows and bite my bottom lip as I consider what it is exactly that I—that we—can do to help locate the body. Not really the type of investigation we're used to.

Mrs. Lockhart grips my hand tightly in hers. "You've got to use your powers to find him."

"I don't really have powers." I'm not a comic-book or movie character like Superman, Iron Man, or Wonder Woman. "I locate *spirits* of the deceased, not the deceased themselves."

"Have you talked to the local coroner?" Becca asks.

"He was no help. But y'all will be, right?"

"I-I-I don't know—what exactly can I do?"

Her eyes light up. "Oh, but that's just it. I feel Delaney here in the house. Evelyn said she's sure he's around too. She's even felt him over at her house. Surely you can try to contact him. He would know where his body is, wouldn't he?"

Celia shrugs. "I suppose."

Taylor lets out a long sigh and says, "*Une telle tragédie.* Such a tragedy."

So, let me get this straight. I'm to make contact here in the house with Delaney, and he's going to tell me where we can find his body so Mrs. Lockhart can get him home for the funeral he deserves to have. A final resting place. As ludicrous as it sounds, I guess we can help out with that. Honestly, I don't think the guys on *Ghost Hunters* have ever had a case like this one.

I release the older woman's hand and drag my palms down the sides of my jeans as I stand up, not sure which one of us is responsible for the nervous sweat. "I'll give it a try."

She's on her feet too. Gratitude paints her wrinkled face.

"I'm going to need assistance though," I say to my posse.

"We're here, Kendall," Taylor pipes up.

"Ditto" from Becca.

Celia nods and smiles.

I push my wavy brown hair behind my ears and then rub my hands together. "I appreciate that you guys are here, but I'm going to need even more help."

"Emily?" Celia asks.

My turn to nod.

And just like that, my spirit guide, Emily—who first came to me as a voice in the white-noise machine in my new bedroom—is with me, ready to give assistance. She's only visible to me at certain times, and I mostly just talk to her in my head. Yeah, I know . . . throw a net over me. That's what my mom's threatening to do anyway.

I walk through the old carriage house, trying to get a sense of who Delaney Lockhart was before he passed. Since I've only lived in Radisson a couple of months, I don't know everyone's business, like most people in town seem to. Taylor told me that Mr. Lockhart had worked at the First National Bank, and Celia knew him to be an avid lake fisherman who always shared his catch of the day with people down at the Methodist church. Now, as I sit in the worn Barcalounger in the den, I'm seeing a slide show of images in my head. Delaney was tall. He'd lost his hair. He cut his fingernails in this spot while watching TV. (Eww!) He was a stern father but loved to spoil his grandchildren. For the last twenty years, he snuck Swisher Sweets cigars out in the backyard. I'm sure that had something to do with his heart problems.

Focus your energies to the right, Kendall . . .

Emily directs my attention toward a door. "Where does this go?" I ask.

"To the basement," Mrs. Lockhart answers. "The laundry room is down there. Other than that, we mostly use it to store extra belongings from the main house. When Evelyn got married, we moved out and let them have it."

"That's okay. We're not here to rifle through your things," I assure her.

"It's a mess. I don't think you girls should go down there. Especially if you have allergies."

Hmmm . . . and me without my Claritin.

I hear Emily whisper, *Goooo . . .*

If she says so, then I must.

"I *have* to go down there." I turn the handle, and immediately the smell of dust and mold and dampness attacks my nostrils. Celia flicks the light cord that's dangling in the doorway.

"This doesn't look very good," Taylor says.

Becca snickers. "Don't be such a girl, Tillson." And then she passes all of us and heads downstairs.

"I'll stay up here," our hostess says.

It's probably better that way.

Emily whispers to me: *Laundry room.*

The four of us pick our way through boxes of Christmas ornaments, winter clothes, and toys for the grandchildren, back to where the washer and dryer sit. My chest begins to tighten in a deep ache. The atmosphere is dense in this section, and I'm finding it hard to get a good breath of air. It's like I want to pant but there's nothing to suck into my lungs.

"Are there any spirits here with us?" Becca asks as she holds her digital recorder out in front of her. "Is the spirit of Delaney Lockhart present? I have a recording device in my hand that is able to pick up your voice if you have the energy to speak to us. We can play it back and see what you had to say and try to help out."

While Becca's doing her EVP work, my chest continues to throb. My heartbeat accelerates to *Speed Racer* levels and I try to tell myself that this isn't really happening to me, per se—it's just that I'm empathetic and can often feel what the spirit might have experienced.

I hear Emily plainly in my head. *He's here . . .*

"Play back your recorder, Becca," Celia says before I can.

After a quick rewind, we hear Becca's question and then a garbled swooshing turning into a voice that says, *"Leeeeeeeeeeefffffffff behind."*

"Did you hear that?" Becca says with excitement. "Score!" She loves getting EVPs, and I must admit I get a real rush out of it as well.

Then, a little further into the recording, we hear, *"Miiiilll-lllie."*

He called her that, Emily tells me.

I take out my rose quartz pendulum that I use for dowsing. It's really cool because I can ask it yes-or-no questions and have a two-way conversation with a spirit. I'm absolutely sensing a presence here in this basement. However, I have to make sure it's Delaney Lockhart. We've run into so many street ghosts in our investigations lately—random spirits that inhabit Radisson, people who lived a long time ago, before the interstate to Atlanta cut through or the town was wired for cable.

As I hear Taylor clicking away in the background with her digital camera, I'm still experiencing the emotional choke of extreme heart pain. Is this from Delaney's cardiac? It feels more like a broken heart than blocked arteries. Not that I'm a doctor or anything. There just isn't that sense of blood stopping and not filling the chambers of the heart. I'm picking up something much more forlorn.

"Are you Delaney Lockhart?"

I watch as the pendulum dangling from my thumb and forefinger swings back and forth, from left to right. This is how I get the answer no.

Hmm. "Are you a female spirit?"

The pendulum confirms another no.

"Are you a male spirit?"

"Duh," Becca says with a snicker.

"You know we have to explore all options," Celia snaps.

My pendulum begins to swing in a circle, clockwise, which signifies a yes answer.

"Check this out!" Taylor shouts. "I just took a series of pictures of that corner."

Sure enough, there's a mist in the bottom right corner that

gets larger in each frame until it takes on a shape. A very distinct human shape.

Taylor points. "That looks like a soldier's cap. Like someone from the Civil War."

We do have a lot of Civil War history in this town. Local legend has it that General Sherman visited Radisson on his infamous March to the Sea. He and his men were so enamored of a townswoman here that they didn't burn the place and left many historic antebellum houses in their original condition, like the mansion that Celia and her parents live in on the street behind my house.

Turning to Celia, I ask, "Did Mrs. Lockhart say anything about a ghost in her house before Delaney's death?"

She shakes her head, tossing her short black bob back and forth. "Never before, although she claims her daughter Evelyn's house is haunted. That was one of the reasons she and Mr. Lockhart gave it to her and moved out here into the carriage house."

"You're some kind of street ghost, aren't you?" I call out. "You sensed what was going on here, that we were looking for a spirit, and you butted in. If that's what you are, you need to leave, please. You don't belong here. Go back to where you were or let me help you cross into the light."

Before I can say another word, I feel a piercing pain so bad that I have to clamp my hands over my ears to stop it. All I hear reverberating through my head is this wicked, evil laughter, sinister almost, echoing off my cerebral matter. I scream inside, telling him to bugger off. He's not wanted. I clutch my chest and then I feel an insane twinge in my head.

He's trouble . . .

Like I need Emily to tell me that.

I fall to my knees from the intense throbbing in my temples. Taylor drops next to me. "Jason should have come with us tonight," she says. "He's going to be inconsolable if anything happens to you."

Yeah, my boyfriend still doesn't exactly like that I do this on a regular basis.

You'll be fine. Ride it out, Kendall.

I reach for Taylor's hand and hold on tightly as the pain begins to subside. I just wish the soldier would stop it with the evil laugh, like he's taking pleasure in seeing me this way.

Suddenly, a man appears before me in plaid shorts, a white Titleist shirt, and a Nike visor. Oh, this has *got* to be Delaney Lockhart. He glances down at me and smiles. Then he tosses a glower to the corner where the soldier is standing. Inside my head, I hear him tell the other man to be gone and leave me alone, to "go back to Evelyn's." Great, we're going to have to come back and clean out her house as well.

The soldier disappears, just like that.

Celia and Taylor help me up. I cock my head to the left. Celia's EMF detector flashes like the lights on a state trooper's car. *EMF* stands for "electromagnetic field," and the detector reads levels of energies. It's widely thought in the paranormal community—*yes, we're a community*—that spirits use energy to manifest. And since everything in the world is basically made of energy, you never know where a ghost may appear or how it'll do it. Let me tell you: I've got a manifestation, all right.

"Mr. Lockhart?" I ask out loud.

Celia and Taylor spin in the direction my voice is aimed. Becca follows along behind me.

I hear him plain as day, as if he's really standing before me. Well, he *is* standing before me, only no one but me can see him.

Mr. Lockhart smiles. "I'm sorry about that soldier. He's been nosing around here trying to get attention and cause trouble. Are you okay, dear?"

"Yes, sir," I say, catching my breath. All of my physical symptoms have eased. "You know why I'm here, right?"

Becca lifts a dark brow at me and then positions the digital recorder toward where I'm speaking. Taylor snaps away on the camera, and Celia stands by, taking all sorts of measurements. They've all seen this before and know to go with the flow and not freak out that I'm seeing an entity . . . and having a conversation with it.

"They left me behind," he says. "Those idiots at the airline. I sat on a conveyor belt for at least two days. Good thing I was embalmed before they put me in the casket. Otherwise"—he waves his hand in front of his nose—"that would be a horrific smell, don'tcha think?"

I snicker at the ghost's joke about his own demise. I have to be serious though, since I don't know how long Delaney will be able to manipulate the energy for me to see and hear him. "Where are you?"

He takes off his visor and scratches his head. "I don't rightly know."

My body sags and I exhale noisily. "You have to remember something. A detail? A sound? A smell?"

"Nope. The formaldehyde sort of masks everything else."

"Ask him about the airplane," Celia instructs. "Is there anything he can remember about it? Particularly the color?"

"Sure, sure," he says, hearing Celia's question. "I remember going into this big ol' gold plane."

"Gold," I say to Celia. "He says it was gold."

She runs her hands through the top of her hair and I can almost hear the wheels of thought turning. "Mrs. Lockhart said she was on Southeastern Airlines. Their planes are blue and silver. The luggage handlers must have loaded him onto the wrong flight."

"Who has gold planes?" Becca asks.

Of course, Celia, knower of all things trivial and seemingly unimportant—seriously, the girl could win the adult *Jeopardy!* tournament—snaps her fingers. "Journey Airlines has gold planes. I've seen their ads on television."

"Do they fly into Atlanta?" Taylor asks.

Celia shakes her head no. "Their hub is Memphis."

The energy shifts in the room and becomes almost staticky. My own oomph is starting to fade; I know Delaney's been pulling off my psychic abilities to talk to me. He smiles and waves and blows a kiss. *We'll get you home,* I say in my head.

You did well, Emily notes to me.

We rush upstairs to tell Mrs. Lockhart. Well, I don't. Becca has to help me up the stairs and over to a couch to regain my strength. Man, connecting with spirits like that just wears me the hell out. I need a massive nap now.

Celia dials up Journey's toll-free number on her cell phone and gets the proper customer service person to help out. We listen to the one-sided conversation as she relays the information. Mrs. Lockhart stands holding Taylor's hand as she awaits the verdict.

"Yes, she's right here and can give you all of the information." Celia breaks into a wide grin. She passes her cell phone to Mrs. Lockhart. "They have your husband."

"Thank you, Jesus!" she sings out. "And you girls! Thank you, thank you! This wouldn't have happened without you. Now my Delaney can come home for a proper burial. Evelyn and Veronica will be so relieved." She puts the phone to her ear and begins giving her personal information.

"Yep, just another typical day for the ghost huntresses," I say with a contented sigh. Taylor and Becca high-five and Celia leans over for a fist bump.

Why am I still feeling a bit kerfuffled though?

You haven't seen the last of that soldier . . .

And along with Emily's sweet voice, the sinister laugh is back.

Yeah, I have a feeling our paths will cross again.

CHAPTER TWO

"YOU WERE HOME EARLY LAST NIGHT," Mom says the next morning, pouring Rice Krispies into a bowl for me like I'm not almost seventeen and can't do it myself. She's such a . . . mom. "Were you able to help that woman out?"

I pour the fat-free Lactaid—no real milk in this house due to Mom's intolerance (to milk, among other things)—into my cereal and listen for the familiar snap, crackle, and pop that I've loved as long as I can remember. "Her husband's coffin was picked up by the wrong airline and sent to Eugene, Oregon, by mistake."

Across the table, my thirteen-year-old sister, Kaitlin, screws up her face. "Ewww . . . that's gross, Kendall!"

"Kaitlin!" Mom fusses.

"She asked me!" I shout back to Kaitlin. For some reason, Kaitlin's bratty tendencies make me react to her in the same immature manner.

Mom sighs. "Kendall. Really."

Dad walks in and smacks Kaitlin gently on the head with

the morning paper. "No squabbles first thing in the morning, girls." He pours a stream of hot coffee into his WGN mug and sits at the table with us. "What about a missing coffin?"

I put several spoonfuls of sugar on my cereal and fill everyone in on the ghost hunt last night at Mrs. Lockhart's, leaving out the part about the laughing soldier. No need to acknowledge his antics any further. Dad nods his head and listens, seemingly impressed with my abilities and how I was able to obtain the necessary information from Delaney to find his body. "The airline told us he should be here in Radisson by the weekend." I spoon in a mouthful of Krispies and munch delightedly.

Mom wipes at an imaginary spot on the counter while one of my cats, Buckley, weaves around her legs. The other two cats, Natalie and Eleanor, are under the table, waiting for my bowl of cereal milk that I've been spoiling them with lately. I can see Mom's still having a hard time with my . . . *abilities*. After all, it's only been two months and it remains a hard pill for her to swallow. See, she's really strong in her religious beliefs and doesn't quite grasp that I'm able to communicate with the dead. Not that I'm not a spiritual person. I am. Even more so now. Mom just thinks it's wrong and even evil and defiant of God's directives in the Bible. Thanks to Dad's patience and open mind, she's trying to accept me. I'll give her that. However, there are vestiges of tension between Mom and me.

"Well, I think that's fascinating, kiddo," Dad says with a smile.

"I think it's retarded," Kaitlin says with a Krispy hanging off her bottom lip.

I ignore her and continue to vacuum cereal into my mouth. Gotta get to school soon.

From behind me, Mom clears her throat. "Remember our deal, Kendall."

Oh yeah . . . the Deal.

Mom let me develop my psychic abilities under the tutelage of Loreen Woods—a really awesome lady who *gets* me and what I'm going through because she's psychic too—and go on ghost investigations with my girls as long as, in return, I agreed to see a psychiatrist. Mom's a nurse and always has to rule out medical conditions as the first-response answer. She's afraid I've got something abnormal going on in my brain that's causing my psychic headaches or, worse, that I'm schizophrenic and that's why I'm seeing strange people and hearing voices.

I gulp down hard; the Rice Krispies nearly stick in my dry throat. "Yeah, Mom, I totally remember the Deal."

Dad reaches over and pats my hand. "We have to make sure there's nothing physically wrong with you, Kendall."

"I know, Dad." I put off the visit to the psychiatrist as long as I could, but the appointment is set for the Saturday after next. "We're going to spend a fun-filled day in Atlanta."

Kaitlin perks up. "Do I get to go? I want to go to Six Flags. Penny and me want to ride the Mind Bender."

Mom clicks her tongue. "It's Penny and *I* want to ride the

Mind Bender, and no, you can't come to Atlanta this time. Kendall and I are going together."

I want to roll my eyes, but out of respect I don't. I know Mom's worried about me and only wants to make sure I'm not suffering from some mental ailment. Hell, I sorta want to find out as well. You know, just for confirmation.

Dad winks at me from behind his glasses. "I wish I could come. Just too much going on with the Mega-Mart project."

Part of Dad's job as city planner is to oversee the development of a huge area being created around Mega-Mart's new distribution center. It's going to include affordable housing, a school, and tons of jobs for Radissonians. Celia's dad, Rex Nichols, is the owner of Mega-Mart—Celia's a rich girl, although you'd never know it—and the development played a major part in our first investigation at city hall. A ghost was messing around with my father, and even hurt him pretty bad. So Dad knows I'm for real and that the battery of psychological tests awaiting me is more for Mom's benefit than anyone else's.

"That's okay, Dad," I say with a resigned sigh. I bend down and set my bowl on the floor. Soon Natalie and Eleanor are nose-butting each other to get at and slurp up the sugary milk.

He reaches for my hand. "But everything's going to be okay, Kendall. Your mother and I both love you greatly, and we'll continue to support you no matter what."

I return his squeeze and try to cram down the emotions rising from my stomach and clenching in my throat. I'm not too thrilled about being poked and prodded, but I did make a promise.

I just wish I could see what's in store for me in Atlanta.

Monday morning's classes whiz by, thankfully. Celia and I shove our books into our respective lockers and head to the caf to meet up with Taylor and Becca and, of course, Jason. I haven't had nearly enough Jason Tillson time.

Ever since our group helped the belligerent spirit at city hall find peace and go into the light, our website (www.ghost-huntress.com) has been getting pummeled with hits. Word about us teenage ghost huntresses spread throughout Radisson and even into surrounding towns. Because of this, my weekends have been full of investigations, research, and honing my psychic skills, not so much honing my Jason skills. That's going to change this weekend, however. Friday night we're going out on a bona fide date, like normal high schoolers.

"Hey, Kendall! Celia!" Sean "Okra" Carmickle calls out to us in the cafeteria line. He's one of the stars of our football team, only he's nursing a broken leg right now. And he's one of the most popular guys in school. Behind him is Jim Roach, Student Government Association president, and Kyle Kadish, president of my class; they nod and smile at us too. A group of girls wave, wide-eyed. It's truly weird how many people at Radisson High School seem to know about and be in awe of my psychic abilities. I guess word got out. Celia and her big mouth.

"Well, wha'd'ya know," Celia notes. "Is this what it feels like to be popular?"

I signal at the girls. "I guess so. Who knew?"

Back in Chicago, I was happy to be just another face that blended into the crowd. The main thing I wanted here at Radisson High School was to get by and fit in. It's strange to have attention for this reason. I certainly didn't ask for this gift, and I wouldn't have requested it had I known everything it would entail. Loreen says it's God's plan for me, so I try to go with the psychic flow, learning about tarot and dowsing and reading up on divination and other people with psychic abilities. Being the new kid in school is hard enough without the whole talking-to-and-seeing-ghosts thing.

The cafeteria lady glops on my plate a pile of mashed potatoes, some green peas, and a formed meat mound that they dare to call "Grandma's Meat Loaf." My Grandma Ethel is rolling in her grave right now at the thought of someone pushing that gray crap as anything she might have made. It's weird that I can see almost every Tom, Dick, and Harry spirit here in Radisson, as well as Emily, my spirit guide who lives in my house, and yet I can't connect with Grandma Ethel, which would be the ultimate in cool. Loreen says it means she's at peace.

Celia motions her head toward a table. "Taylor already got us a seat. I told her to bring the pictures from Mrs. L.'s so we can decide which ones to put up on the website."

I'm about to answer when I hear, "Hey, Ghost Girl!"

I turn my head in the direction of the insult and do my best to plaster on a smile.

"Boo!" the girl yells and then laughs like it's the funniest thing ever said. "Did I frighten you, Kendall?"

This is followed by cackles and giggles from the girl's fellow cheerleaders and followers Farah Lewis, Megan Bremer, and Stephanie Crawford.

You'd think I'd be used to this after a couple of months of juvenile harassment from the likes of Courtney Langdon and her flock.

Courtney doesn't let up. "You know, I have an excellent tailor who could fashion a stylish straitjacket for you, Ghost Girl."

Whatever, beeyotch.

"Get over yourself, Courtney," Celia—suddenly my alpha wolf—says in my defense.

"Like I'm so scared, Nichols."

Courtney's clique giggles more as Celia and I try to pass. They follow us, making weird noises. Ugh. They're so imma-ture. Well, except for Stephanie Crawford, who looks rather un-comfortable going along with the herd. I tune in to Stephanie's thoughts and pick up a sense of embarrassment for Courtney's behavior. Deep down, Stephanie thinks it's cool what I can do. She even admires me. Wow . . . that's righteous. I smile in her direction to let her know I don't lump her in with the others.

There's really no point in giving Courtney the time of day, let alone the satisfaction of knowing that she continues to hurt my feelings. A lot of kids at school stop me in the hall or talk to me at lunch and share their own ghostly encounters. But not Courtney Langdon. She's your stereotypical high school bitch: cheerleader, blond, skinny, head of the RHS ruling class. I know good and well that she's been making nonstop nasty-ass comments behind my back, so I do my best to take a deep breath and hold my head high.

"I don't know why she hates me so much," I mutter.

Celia snorts. "Hello. You're psychic and you don't know? First off, you're stealing her thunder. She's supposed to be the most popular girl in school, but suddenly you are."

"I'm not—"

"And, dude, you're dating her ex-boyfriend."

True. That was more than likely the cause of the friction. Jason and Courtney had dated about a year ago, until he called it off. Or came to his senses, as Taylor likes to say. However, my psychic senses tell me there's more to Courtney's hatred than merely a cute boy. (And what a cute boy he is!)

Speaking of said cute boy, Jason slides up to me in all of his blond, blue-eyed gorgeousness and takes my tray from me. "Celia's right, Courtney. Get over yourself and leave Kendall alone."

Not missing a beat, Courtney bats her eyelashes. "I don't know what y'all are talking about," she says in a Southern simper.

"I heard you," Jason says in an authoritative voice. "Just piss off, okay?"

She stamps her Steve Madden–booted feet. "I won't have you talk to me like that, Jason Tillson. You don't own me anymore!"

"Thank God for small miracles," Celia mumbles to me.

Courtney signals to her posse that they're leaving now. "Don't be fooled, Jason. She's just using you."

His eyebrows lift in a mischievous manner. "How so?"

"Just to get popular."

There's that word again.

"Whatever, Courtney. Come on, Kendall. Let's go eat," Jason says with the brightest smile on his face. Those Dasani-bottle-blue eyes of his literally make my knees weak. I can't believe a guy this fine is with me. It's worth it to put up with the Courtneys of the world if I get to spend time with Jason.

"She's a fake, you know," Courtney tosses over her shoulder. "She's just playing at being a psychic to get attention. It's all a ruse."

Taylor joins the fray all of a sudden, and, boy, is she ticked off. "Leave my friend alone. She's the most genuine person I know. I can't say the same for you."

Courtney dismisses Taylor with a flip of her hand, which only makes Taylor's resentment boil more.

"She's not worth it, Tay," Jason says to her.

To complete the circle of friends, Becca Asiaf walks up in her black sweater, camouflage pants, and combat boots and plants herself directly in Courtney's path. "Shouldn't you be on your way to the bathroom instead of bothering my friend?

You don't want to accidentally digest any of your lunch, now, do you?"

It's a well-known fact at RHS that Courtney chooses to splurge and purge on most days, although it's the great unsaid. I love that Becca metaphorically punched her in the face with that one.

But Courtney steels her gray gaze at me so hard that I can feel the energy of her disdain bouncing around like radio waves. "All y'all can kiss my perfect little ass."

With that she turns around and dashes out of the caf, Farah and Megan in her wake. Only Stephanie shrugs an apology before running off to catch up with her friends. There's something in her eyes that reads like a light sadness. If she reached out to me, maybe I could help her.

We sit down in silence to eat. I'm trying not to tremble over the verbal assault. Quite frankly, I'd rather have a ghost try to take over my body than deal with another scene like that. Thank heavens the school day's almost over and I can avoid her, for the most part.

Jason holds my hand under the table and leans close. "I think you're awesome, Kendall Moorehead."

"Me too," Taylor pipes up.

"Ditto" from Becca.

"Yeah," Celia says with a mouthful of mashed potatoes. "Besides, you have a much better ass than hers, hands down."

And with that, I almost pass out from laughing so hard.

———

Physiology class.

The good thing is I love the teacher, Ms. Pritchard, who's young and hip and really makes the subject interesting. I mean, I want to be a city planner, like my dad, so the human body and how it works is the farthest thing from my academic interest, but Ms. Pritchard is a great teacher and makes the class actually enjoyable.

The bad thing is Courtney Langdon takes physiology with me. (She does sit all the way across the room though!)

"Good afternoon, y'all," Ms. Pritchard begins. "We're starting a new project today that we'll be working on for a few weeks. It will make up forty percent of your final grade for the semester. It's going to entail completely dissecting a fetal pig and cataloging all of the parts."

Ewwww . . .

"All right!" one of the guys shouts from the back.

"That's jank!" another says.

"That'll play havoc on my manicure," Courtney quips.

Yeah, it's going to be really gross, but I'll just concentrate on the same mental exercises I use for tuning in to my intuition and try not to see the baby pig as something that was once living and is now a science project. Even though I deal with the dead, they *were* people once and still are. What if the pig has a spirit that won't like what we're doing to it?

Kendall, you're just being silly now, Emily whispers in my head.

It's like having my mother with me twenty-four/seven sometimes! *Emily, be quiet!*

Ms. Pritchard grabs a sheet of paper and continues. "You'll be working in pairs on the assignment. I'll just go down the class roster and match you up alphabetically."

As she's calling out pairs of names, I quickly run through the ABC song and want to do a Homer Simpson "D'oh" when I realize that *L* and *M* are next-door neighbors. (Okay, that's how Mom always said it.) *Oh no, say it's not so. Pleeeeeeease!*

"Langdon and Moorehead," the teacher says.

Son of a . . . well, a bitch. What else is there to say?

Courtney glares icy gray eyes across the room at me. Like I planned this!

I don't know whether to move my stuff over to Courtney's area or wait for her to join me. I'm sure it'll be a cold day in hell before she makes the first move, so I decide to be the bigger person.

Plopping my backpack down at her lab table, I force a smile. As if anyone could be pleased to be matched up with her. "So, we're partners on this, huh?" I say, sitting on the stool.

Without acknowledging my presence, she sings out, "Such a freeeeeak . . . such a freeeeeak."

"Look," I say, wanting to touch her arm but afraid of how she'll react. "We're going to have to work together, so you might as well call me by my name. It's not Boo. It's not Ghost Girl. And I don't remember seeing Freak on my birth certificate either. It's Kendall. Got it?"

My leg quivers on the high stool a bit. I can put up a good front with difficult people when I have to. (Oddly enough, I don't have any problem dealing with aggressive spirits.) Loreen has been teaching me lately about auras that come from our chakras. According to yoga principles, the human body has seven centers of energies, or chakras. It's a whole metaphysical thing that I can't really explain right now. Since I'm new to reading auras and not completely trained yet, I'm mostly seeing white hazes around people. However, suffice it to say that Courtney is emanating an amazing red glow that signifies possible anger (duh), a high emotional state (double duh), or conflict in the air (*ding, ding, ding* . . . we have a winner!).

"I don't care what your name is." Her voice is laced with venom. "You're obviously delusional and you've got this whole town thinking you're something special. You're not, though. You're just some outsider who wormed her way into my boyfriend's life with this little scheme of yours. Why don't you go home and take your meds?"

Courtney's words hit hard, stabbing me in the chest with the sharpness of their delivery because they're so similar to ones uttered by my own mother. I pick up more from my enemy, though, as I sit here with her. The rest of the class adjusts seats to pair up with their new partners—no big deal. Courtney's threatened by all the positive attention I'm getting. Like it's taking something away from her?

It's lessening her popularity, Emily tells me.

Geez, conceited enough?

I really don't want to start thinking of my abilities in any negative light. It's taken me a couple of months to accept and embrace what's going on with me. Not that I've fully embraced it or understand, but I'm doing my damnedest. Instead of playing into Courtney's hands, I close my eyes and take a few deep breaths to calm my nerves. I'm mentally in Chicago, standing on the edge of Lake Michigan, smelling the air and listening to the birds squawk as they circle overhead. This is a happy place for me. A place where no one—especially Courtney—can hurt me. I also think of the lessons I've learned from my parents about loving your enemy and treating people the way you want to be treated. Father Massimo Castellano at the Episcopal church has reiterated the same mantra to me in his own guidance of my gift.

So, fine. I'll kill Courtney with kindness.

"Look, I'm really good in science and you're a wicked smart girl, right? We can easily ace this assignment if we work together."

She tosses her long blond hair over her shoulder then turns her attention to an apparent chip in her fingernail polish. "Whatever."

I look at the handout Ms. Pritchard gave each team. "So, what do you want to do first . . . I mean, once we get the fetal pig?"

Courtney leans across the lab table and points her index finger at me. "Don't think that because I'm forced to work with you in this one class we're all of a sudden going to be all palsy-walsy and BFFs. *You* are the enemy."

"Of what?"

"Me. Everything I know. You're nothing but a sicko who wants attention. I'll be damned if you get any from me."

I hear Emily laugh inside my head and I'm tempted to join in. Instead, I smile and say, "Whatever you say, Mean Girl."

I think I won this round.

CHAPTER THREE

WHEN THE LAST SCHOOL BELL RINGS, I borrow Celia's Segway—she's going to catch a ride home with Taylor after a science club meeting—and motor the few blocks to Divining Woman to see Loreen. She's been a godsend through this whole awakening thing, primarily because she went through it herself as a teenager. Now she's in her midthirties and is the owner of this cool metaphysical catchall-type bookstore on the Square in downtown Radisson.

The over-the-door bell clinks as I make my way inside. Spicy cinnamonlike incense dances in the air, along with the smell of sage, juniper, and vanilla. Each scent has a special meaning and is used to help center the mind and relax the body and soul. I should know; Loreen—horrible saleswoman that she is—has practically given me one of everything in the store these past couple of months.

The place seems empty though.

"Loreen?"

There are lit candles on the bookshelf. Surely she wouldn't

go anywhere and leave those burning. I move to blow them out when I hear a rustling from the back of the store.

"May I help you?" she calls out. Rounding the corner of a table full of various tarot cards stacked up high, Loreen sees me and her smile broadens. "Oh, Kendall! It's you, sweetie. I'm with a client."

I muffle my laughter as I take her in. She's about Mom's height, with short, curly strawberry blond hair that just touches the neck of her novelty T-shirt, which reads "Ghosts Were People Too." "I'm sorry to interrupt. I can come back later."

"Pish-posh," she says, swatting at me. "I'm just finishing up a tarot card reading. You can sit in."

"I really sh—"

"No worries." Loreen pulls me through the store and slides the makeshift curtain to the left, revealing a small, round table covered with red crushed-velvet material and a Rider-Waite tarot deck spread out in the Celtic cross formation. An impeccably dressed woman in a smart navy blue suit and pink blouse sits at the table with her fingers laced together. "Evelyn, you don't mind if my protégée Kendall joins us, now, do you?"

"Why, of course not." The woman extends a slim hand forward, free of any rings or jewelry except a silver watch. "Evelyn Crawford. So nice to meet you, Kendall. Loreen thinks the world of you. As does my mother."

"She does?" Do I know her mother? I shake her hand.

Evelyn blinks at me. "Mother had you over to the house the other night, looking for Daddy."

The realization hits me. "You're *that* Evelyn! Mrs. Lockhart's daughter. Geez, I'm so sorry about your father."

The lovely woman forces a smile. "It was quite a shock. More so was the fact that the airline lost him. Terrible thing for a family to go through."

"Any news?" I ask.

She nods. "He's been sent to Memphis and they're driving him home. He should be back this weekend so we can have the memorial service." She takes my hand. "I'm so grateful for your help. If there's anything I can ever do for you, Kendall."

"Wanna do my physiology project?" I say with a nervous giggle.

We all laugh as I pull up a chair and sit next to Miss Evelyn.

She pats her perfectly coifed dark brown hair. "You'll have to come check out my house sometime. I swear, we've got ghosts," Evelyn says. "Honestly, Loreen, is there a residence in Radisson that *doesn't* have any activity?"

I think back on the soldier I'd thought was a street ghost. Mr. Lockhart had hinted to me that he was attached to his daughter's house. Perhaps he was right. Do I tell her I saw one of the spirits from her house? Hmm . . . probably not on our first meeting.

"It seems like it these days. Kendall and her team have done about twenty investigations in the past couple of months," Loreen says with pride. "They wouldn't be solving—and de-bunking—cases without Kendall's psychic abilities."

I feel a blush coming on. "Well, that's not altogether true. Each member of our team brings something to the table." I want to give credit where credit is due.

"That's just fantastic," Evelyn says.

Loreen quirks her mouth to one side and I can tell she's got an idea.

"What?" I ask, my eyes wide.

"Why don't you try doing a psychic reading for Evelyn?" Loreen looks to her customer. "You wouldn't mind, would you?"

Evelyn shifts in her seat to face me. "Just the opposite. I'd love to see Kendall in action."

I bite my bottom lip as I think this through. I've only been practicing this on Celia—like she has anything to hide from me—and have never done it for a stranger.

"Emily's not with me right now," I admit.

"Who's Emily?" Evelyn asks.

I pop my knuckles to relieve the stress from dealing with Courtney earlier. This is exactly the type of mental focus and relaxation I need. "Umm . . . Emily's sort of my spirit guide. I don't know much about her other than she died young—maybe twenty—and she wears what looks like a hospital gown all the time. Turns out, I've known her all my life. She used to be my imaginary friend until I was told to stop talking about things like that. Now Emily gives me clues to what other spirits are doing or thinking. Like I said, though, she's not with me right now, so I don't know how much I'll get right, Miss Evelyn."

Loreen pats my hand. "That's okay, sweetie. Try it on your own. You don't always have to rely on Emily."

She's right. I have to keep developing my own intuition, and I can't always depend on Emily as my CliffsNotes to the paranormal realm.

I clear my throat and sit up straight. "Okay, well, first I'll need something personal of yours."

Evelyn reaches down, gets a very large Louis Vuitton bag, puts it on the table, and withdraws a matching tan and gold wallet. "Will this work?"

"Sure." *I think so.*

Miss Evelyn hands over the wallet, and I turn it over and over in my palms, feeling the soft leather and listening to the change rattle within. I breathe deeply and try to see the contents. Many quarters, a lot of pennies, and a stack of five, no, six Benjamins. Wow. I didn't know anyone walked around Radisson with six hundred dollars burning a hole in her pocket. Must be nice.

Must. Focus.

Then Loreen screws up her face.

"What?"

"That's nice that you're seeing what's in the wallet," she says. "But you need something with some metal in it to help you pick up on Evelyn's energy—like jewelry or keys."

"Oh! You're right. What was I thinking?"

"Here, dear," the woman says. "Try this."

She hands over a heavy knob of various keys that jingle and swing from a double-C Chanel chain.

"That's more like it," Loreen says. "Keep going."

I start my breathing and concentration again. Immediately, I pick up on the vibrations of energy from Evelyn Crawford. In my mind's eye, I see it all so clearly. "I'm traveling down a long path, lined with tall cedars on either side. A large white house sits at the end of the drive. There are—one, two, three—four large columns on the outside, and the shutters are painted black."

I hear a sharp intake of breath. Evelyn's, I assume. "That's my house. On Crow Lane."

"Oh, right, near Mrs. Lockhart's."

The woman nods. "Mother and Daddy live in the carriage house on the south end of the property. Well, I suppose it's just Mother now," she says with a sniff.

Loreen pats Miss Evelyn's hand and signals for me to continue.

I mentally wipe away the fog and cobwebs of the image to try to describe further what I'm seeing. "There's a woman on the porch in an old-timey dress."

"How old-timey?" Loreen asks. "Be more specific about the style, Kendall."

"Right," I say. "She looks like an extra from *Gone With the Wind,* with, like, an apron and petticoats and a parasol. She's a babe, too," I tack on with a laugh. "She's got this chestnut brown hair that's piled on her head in all of these crazy curls and twists and stuff. Man, that must have taken hours!"

"Kendall . . . ," Loreen fusses.

I peek with my left eye. "Well, it's true."

Suddenly, it's like I'm leafing through a family-history book. Information flies at me. Words scroll by, telling their story. Conversations dotted with laughter and arguments, colored with tears. There is much passion in the house surrounding this beautiful antebellum-times woman. I'm absorbing it as quickly as possible, hoping to remember every tiny detail in order to share. After a moment, I force the sequence to stop so I can relay what I've seen.

Opening my eyes, I look at Miss Evelyn. "This woman on the porch. She's related to you?"

"Possibly," she says.

"I'm hearing the name Larry. No . . . Harry. No . . . Airy?" I shake my head, tossing my hair about with frustration. "Why can't I get this?"

"There's a *p* sound that I'm getting," Loreen chimes in.

I nod my head. "P-P-P . . ."

"Could it be Parry?" Evelyn asks.

"Yes! That's it. Not Larry or Harry. Parry. Is that a name in your family?"

Evelyn's smile brightens. "It is indeed. My great-great-grandmother. She was—"

My hand lifts to stop her. "Please. Don't tell me anything.

Let me see what I can get." I concentrate again, squeezing the keys even tighter in my fist. "I'm getting an *A* name and I'm getting"—I listen for it, waiting for the sound to come to me—"Ada? The name is Ada," I say with much confidence.

"Amazing," Evelyn shouts out. "How did you know that?"

It's sort of hard to explain. I could see Adam Bostwick from my calculus class up at the chalkboard. He'd written "No *m*" over and over and over again for me to see—which leaves Ada. Not that Adam ever did that in class, just in my vision. I can't really tell Evelyn how I came to learn the names. "I just knew" seems the easiest explanation.

Following several more minutes of deep breathing and concentrating, I see this Ada Parry standing on the front porch, speaking to many people. "Ada was important in Radisson. A lot of folks really liked her and thought she was smart and pretty and the kindest person ever. Took good care of her sick father . . . and her little . . . sister?"

"All true," Miss Evelyn says.

Then the vision morphs. "I see she's very sad, though, while she's talking to a Union soldier. He's powerful, 'cause he's got a lot of bling on his shoulders."

Loreen snickers. "They didn't call it bling back then."

I scrunch up my nose. "I don't really know rank and stuff, but he's got to be one of the guys in charge. He's not General Sherman, is he?" I ask Loreen.

"I can't see what you're seeing, sweetie," Loreen tells me.

Evelyn points a finger in front of her. "Ada was around

when General Sherman and his troops were here. She and several of the ladies in town did all they could not to fight the Yankees; actually, they rolled out the red carpet and welcomed them like the fine Southern women they were, hoping Sherman wouldn't burn Radisson as he had other towns," she explains.

Celia had told me a similar tale. In fact, the mansion that she and her family live in was the mayor's house back during the Civil War. And it was a woman who kept Sherman from burning it to the ground. Girl power, baby! Even back then.

"I think this guy is a major or something. At least, that's the impression I'm getting. He's dressed in Union blue and he's got that little cap on."

It's at this moment that the keys literally heat up in my hand. At first, I think it's just my palms sweating over the on-the-spot reading. But no. It's not just a warm sensation. The keys suddenly seem fiery against my skin, scorching so much that I have to let them drop to the floor. That's when I see the face of the Union soldier, and the look in his eyes nails me to the seat.

"Kendall?" Loreen prods. "Are you all right?"

I turn to her, sure that my face is ashen. "I swear, he looks familiar to me."

"Have you seen him somewhere in your investigations?"

I bend down to retrieve the keys, which are a normal temperature now. He could be one of the soldier apparitions I saw in the Radisson cemetery a couple of months ago. Heaven knows, they all sort of look alike to me with their scraggly beards and war-worn faces. There's just something so, so . . . sinister about him. Talk about the heebie-jeebies.

My right eye begins to twitch, and my stomach hurts like I ate dinner too late and then went straight to bed. The nausea rolls around, making me dizzy, when I begin to hear the sinister laugh that I heard last night at the Lockhart house. Is that same ghost appearing in my current vision just to mess with me, or was he actually around during the Civil War?

"Kendall, you've gone pale," Evelyn says. "Maybe you should stop."

"I guess I kind of overdid it or something," I say weakly. I don't want to scare Evelyn if it's only a spirit mucking around with me. But it did seem like this soldier was *in* that time period.

Loreen hands me a bottle of water. "Very good, Kendall. You'll get better and better with more practice."

I give Evelyn her keys back. "Thanks," I say to both of them. "I'm sorry I couldn't get more."

"No, that was very impressive," Evelyn says. "You got my great-great-grandmother's name, Ada Parry, you described her house—which is my house—and you knew she was involved with Sherman and his troops. Very impressive indeed, young lady."

Gulping the liquid into my parched throat, I smile and again say, "Thanks."

Miss Evelyn returns the keys to her bag and stands up. "Well, I should get going. Loreen, it was a pleasure, as always. Thanks for the advice."

"I'll be praying for you, your mom, and your sister," Loreen says.

Nodding, Evelyn turns back to me. "And Kendall, if you want to visit my house, I have a lot of memorabilia from Great-great-grandmother Ada. You're welcome over any time."

This may be just the research I need to nail down who this laughing soldier spirit is.

"That's totally awesome," I say exuberantly. "I mean, thanks."

She smiles at me, a brilliant white smile. "That's okay. I have a teenage daughter. I'm used to the lingo."

I listen for the tinkle of the front-door bell to let me know that Loreen and I are alone, and then I sprawl out on the chair. "God, that was exhausting. And I barely got any information!"

I feel Loreen tug on my hair. "You're still learning, Kendall. I'm so glad to see that you're testing new things and trying to help people with your skills."

Suddenly, the rush of anxiety over the Courtney situation floods back. My apprehension picks up, as does the crazy rhythm of my overanxious heart. I'm short of breath, and I can't stop replaying the ridiculous scenes with her over and over, like it's some sort of sick DVR recording that won't delete from the queue. Her words are like pinpricks, each one taking a nip at my psyche, at my soul. It's like being pecked to death by baby ducks. Evil, devilish, bitchy baby ducks.

Loreen reaches for her ceramic teacup and then takes a seat on the couch. She folds her jeaned legs up underneath her and looks at me worriedly. "Tell me what this Courtney person has done to you," she says.

I love that I don't have to bore her with a lot of the backstory of my high school drama. She simply *knows* it.

I give Loreen the 411 on what happened in the caf today and also how Courtney and I got matched up to work together in physiology in some kind of weird after-school non–*High School Musical* way.

"I'm telling you, Loreen. The things she has said to me. No one has ever talked to me like that in my life." I scratch at my eyelid, feeling the sting of a fresh tear that wants to escape. I won't let it though. "She's accused me of all sorts of terrible things, like being a fake and a liar. I'm not either. She said I stole Jason from her, but they were already broken up!"

"What does your intuition tell you?"

"Are you kidding me? That she's an effing bitch."

Loreen snickers. "Besides that."

Sitting up, I wave my arms about. "That she thinks I'm a . . . a . . . freak. That I need medical attention. That I need medication."

Loreen shifts on the couch to make room for me. I slog over to her and collapse on the cushions, resting my head on a crocheted pillow. "This is more than merely some snotty-ass cheerleader at school with an eating disorder. This has to do with your mom too. Am I right?"

"You didn't have to be psychic to figure that out," I say with a harrumph.

There's a twinkle in Loreen's hazel eyes. "Two years of child psychology in college helped."

"It's just that Mom's still convinced that I have a chemical imbalance or a medical condition. *She* thinks I need medication as well, so to hear some shithead—sorry!—like Courtney say the same thing, it kicks my feet out from under me."

Loreen puts her tea down and takes my hand. "You know your mom has seen a lot of cases of people suffering in her career, especially when you lived in Chicago. Didn't you tell me she was an ER and ICU nurse before working in a doctor's office? Besides, you're part of her. She doesn't want her baby to turn out like those unfortunate people she wasn't able to do anything for. I can see it, Kendall. They were lost, confused, no friends or family. Sarah's only trying to protect you because she loves you so much."

In reality, I know this is the case. In actuality, I still have to go through the motions of making my mom happy by going to the doctor. I promised I would when she allowed me to begin ghost hunting. "I've put it off as long as I could."

"I know."

"Can you go with me?"

Loreen shakes her head.

"Yeah, that was a stupid question."

"I'll be with you in spirit though. And I'll send Reiki energy your way."

"What if . . ." I play with the zipper on my hoodie, running it up and down on the track. Then I glance at Loreen. "What if this battery of psychological tests shows that I'm a big schizo and I need considerable amounts of medication? They're going to poke and prod me and I won't be—"

"Okay. Enough of that. You're working yourself into a froth for no reason, Kendall." She shifts in the seat and stares off at a faraway place for a moment. Then she turns back to me. "You know, I underwent the same thing . . . when I was younger. I was twelve years old, and my parents were scared shitless over my awakening, reacting in a crueler manner than Sarah is reacting to you."

"How so?"

"Well, they didn't believe that my headaches were from visions or that I was hearing things that they couldn't. They told me to stop pretending at first, but after a while, when I continued to tell them about the people and pets parading through our house wanting my help, my stepmother and Daddy were convinced I had a tumor. You know, that it was pushing against my brain and making me have these hallucinations."

Hand to my mouth, I say, "Oh, Loreen, that's so terrible!"

I can see into her mind, how she's living this over again. "I had blood tests and X-rays and you name it. They even had me so doped up on meds, I could barely function. I was hardly able to get out of bed, get dressed, and go to school."

That's just wrong on so many levels. "That's no way for a little kid to live."

"Certainly not. Or even an adult."

"What happened?" I ask anxiously.

"I refused medication and then eventually started keeping my visions and sightings to myself. I played the perfect teenager for them because I knew they didn't want to hear it." Loreen closes her eyes for a moment, and I hear a little catch in her throat when she begins to speak again. "I kept my true self hidden until I turned eighteen and left home. They never accepted me as I was . . . as I am."

I reach over and hug Loreen tightly, letting a few tears slip out.

"Did you ever see them again?" I can't imagine leaving home and not going back.

"About ten years ago, I wrote them a letter, filling them in on my college studies and travels. I worked my ass off to pay for school, and I wanted them to see how I'd succeeded."

"You have."

She agrees. "One day, my daddy walked into the store and hugged me like I was still his normal little girl. We cried our eyes out and I could see he was genuinely remorseful for not supporting me more. It was probably my stepmother's influence over him. He was sorry that he didn't stand up for me when I got picked on by kids at school." She sets me away from her. "So you see, the world is full of Courtneys. They don't matter. Your family, that's what matters. And your mother loves you so much, Kendall. Humor her by going through the tests. You'll just prove yourself in the end, which I wasn't able to do."

"I'll do it, Loreen," I say with a sniff. "For you, for me, and for people like us . . . everywhere."

CHAPTER FOUR

THIS DAY HAS SUCKED ASS.

It's Wednesday afternoon, and I'm sitting on the bumper of Jason's Jeep, waiting for him to finish playing basketball.

I'm not going to cry. I'm not going to cry. I'm not going to cry.

I look down at the front of my light blue Billabong T-shirt that's stained and still a bit wet and sticky with the Mott's pomegranate-flavored applesauce that Courtney "accidentally" spilled on me in the caf. Sure, pomegranate is a great source of antioxidants (I pay attention to advertising); however, it's going to take a whole bottle of detergent to get the color out of my shirt.

It didn't help that Courtney said, "It looks like you've been slimed by one of your little ghosty friends, which you should be used to since you enjoy crawling around cemeteries on your hands and knees like the freak of nature you are, looking for dead things to talk to. As if!"

I had no comeback in the caf because I was too dumbstruck by the fact that I had purple applesauce cascading betwixt my boobage. Of course, her minions cackled, pointing at me and high-fiving Courtney for making me look the fool. Too bad Becca was home from school today with cramps. Otherwise, I'd have had her kick a little cheerleading badonkadonk for me.

"Hey, you been waiting long?" Jason shouts out. His sneakers squeak on the pavement as he comes to a stop in front of me, arms spread for a hug. His usually short blond hair has grown out these last months into something resembling an Ashton Kutcher shag. It's all plastered down on one side, obviously from running his hands through his hair. He flashes those amazing, hypnotic blue eyes my way and beckons me forward with a sexy little wiggle of his eyebrows.

"Not that long."

I should push him away 'cause he's covered in boy sweat, but I needs me a little Jason time, which I have been greatly lacking of late. I nuzzle a bit on his T-shirted chest, taking in the odor of Right Guard and salt mixed together. I try to stuff down the tears that threaten to fall. You shouldn't cry in front of your boyfriend, especially when he technically remains a *new* boyfriend. We're still in that stage where he hasn't seen me without my makeup—although I only wear a little bit, on my eyes—nor has he heard me burp (or worse!), and we both get those crazy roller-coaster climbs and dives whenever we're with each other. At least, he told me he does. What can I say? I'm waaaaaaay smitten.

He lifts my head with a finger on my chin. "Everything okay?"

"Yeah. Just a long, ri*donk*ulous day."

His blue eyes crinkle with laughter. "Huh?"

"It means being ridiculous to an exceedingly preposterous degree. Like today."

"Good word. I'll have to use that."

Jason steps away, unlocks his Jeep, and then tosses his gym bag and books into the back seat. "Sorry I missed lunch today. I heard from Roachie that it was quite a show."

Roachie would be Jim Roach, one of Jason's best buds. I spread my hands out in Vanna White fashion to show off Courtney's handiwork. "This is nothing compared to what she did in physiology class."

Jason raises an eyebrow. "Do I even want to hear this?"

"Oh yeah," I say, almost with a laugh. "We got our fetal pigs and were supposed to come up with a game plan for the dissection and everything, right? Well, Courtney takes the poor pickled little thing and holds it like it's a puppet or something and says, 'Nooooo, I don't want no crazy beeyotch touching me!' Can you believe that?"

"Did you pop her one?"

This time I do laugh. "I wish. Fortunately, Ms. Pritchard saw what she was doing and gave her the stink eye. After that, we worked on the to-do list the teacher gave us. Do you know how hard it is to sit with someone you're supposed to be teamed up with if she won't even carry on a decent, normal, convo with you?"

"I'm sorry, Kendall." Jason hugs me again, crushing me to him with his protectiveness. "I'm sorry I can't do anything other than stand up for you."

Jason's definitely the shielding type. Alpha male, all the way. He does this for his sister, Taylor, because their dad left them and moved away to Alaska to be a park ranger. I can see why Jason wants to take care of Taylor so much; their mom is sort of reliving her twenties, and it's left Jason as the unofficial head of the household. A lot to ask of a seventeen-year-old guy who just wants to play basketball, run track, and hang with his girl-friend. I admire the hell out of him for all he's doing to keep his family knit together.

"You don't need to fight my battles for me," I say. "Even though Courtney is your ex and I'm sure most of her hatred stems from the fact that we're together." The tears well in my eyes again, blurring the image of Jason before me. God, when did I become such a weak female? I lean against the driver's side of the Jeep, not wanting anyone to see me. I'd be totally ripped if Courtney or any of her flock witnessed me close to tears. I don't ever want that little bitch to know she's gotten to me.

"Hey, y'all." I hear a familiar voice from behind us.

Jason moves in front of me, then relaxes and waves. "Yo, Nichols, Price."

Celia Nichols bounds up with Clay Price in tow. He's a cutie pie in his own right, and he and Celia make *the* most adorable couple. They're both nerdy and geeky in a completely endearing way.

"What's up?" Clay asks.

"Oh, you know," I say, steadying my voice. Sure, Celia's my best friend, but I know she'd read me the riot act for getting upset over Courtney. "I've barely seen you today, Celia. How ya doin'?"

"I'm hangin' in like a hair in a biscuit," she says, her grin stretching from ear to ear.

I can't help but screw up my face. "A what? Eww . . ."

Clay hugs her to him and ruffles her bobbed black hair.

Jason squints into the glaring sun. "What are y'all so happy about?"

"I just saw Principal Trumbell talking to Courtney in the office," Celia reports. "He had a finger in her face. I think he was giving her what for about the applesauce incident."

I dab my knuckle in the corner of my eye to make sure my mascara hasn't run. Phew! Good to go. "I don't want to talk about Courtney anymore."

Celia agrees. "She's not worth your breath. Besides, I got an e-mail today from this guy in Riverdale and he wants us to do an investigation of his barn the Friday after this. Says something's spooking his cows. I was thinking we could try out the new trifield meter that I got from Ghost-Mart.com, as well as the K2 meter that's been showing promise as a divination device, using lights for yes and no answers—"

"No way," Jason says, looking at Celia and then at me. "You promised, Kendall."

I bite my bottom lip. "No ghost hunting that weekend,

Celia. We're going to the football game that Friday night with our boyfriends, and then we're going to the bowling alley like normal high school juniors."

Jason grunts his approval next to me.

Celia seems disappointed. "But . . . I just got this new meter and I wanted to—"

"Nope," I interrupt. "Normal. Teen. Agers."

Clay bumps Celia with his hip. "So, I'm really your boyfriend?"

She rolls her eyes, first at him and then at me. "What*ever*."

Jason and I laugh while Clay wraps his arms around her tall skinny body. "You like me! You like me!"

Celia's knocked off balance by his playfulness. "Oh my God. Grow up, Clay!"

He smacks a big wet kiss on her neck and that settles her down. I love seeing them together, and I'm happy that Celia's got someone who understands and appreciates her just the way she is. It makes me feel less guilty for having a boyfriend of my own.

Looking at Jason and me, Clay shakes his head. "Man, what were you thinking, dating Courtney Langdon?"

"Yeah, seriously, Tillson," Celia chimes in.

"Cut me some slack," he says. "She actually used to be sort of nice. She's just high maintenance, you know? Her parents both travel a lot and she doesn't have much parental guidance on matters."

Celia flattens her lips together. "And now Kendall's getting the attention you used to give her. And a majority of the school and the town are giving our ghost-huntress group more recognition, and I bet it's eating Courtney alive."

I snort. "If that's true, then the girl sincerely needs to get over herself."

Jason squeezes me again. "I'll make her get over it if I have to."

"Speak of the devil . . . ," Celia says, looking behind me.

My pulse begins to speed up at the idea of another melee with Courtney. I'm just not strong enough for it right now. But my intuition tells me it's not my nemesis, so I pivot to see which one of her cheerleading minions is approaching.

Stephanie Crawford smiles shyly, shielding her eyes from the sun with her left hand. "I know we don't really know each other, but can I, like, talk to you, Kendall?"

I turn my head in either direction at my friends. "We don't have any secrets from each other."

"Sure, that's cool. I can respect that."

I brace for more RHS snottiness from one of the ruling princesses, but instead, Stephanie offers an apology.

"I'm really sorry about what Courtney did to you at lunch today. That was classless," she says.

I reach out toward her with my feelings to make sure she's for real. Her large hazel eyes sparkle genuinely to match her smile. Her shoulder-length goldy-brown hair is pulled away from her face with a rhinestone headband, and she's nervously awaiting my response. Her spirit seems honest, true, kind, and trustworthy, and it makes me wonder why someone like Stephanie hangs out with a skank like Courtney.

As if reading my mind, Stephanie says, "I wouldn't blame you for hating me for associating with Courtney. She and I aren't even that tight. We're just cheerleaders together. I don't follow along with everything she does like some other people do."

I give her a smile of my own. "The applesauce incident wasn't your fault, Stephanie. You have nothing to apologize for. But in any case, it's proper of you. Thanks."

She appears to be quite relieved when she reaches a tanned arm out to me, her hand extended. "I'd like to be friends."

Celia shifts her eyes from Stephanie to me, and I can tell she's wondering what the catch might be. There is no catch. Stephanie truly wants to make peace. I take her hand and shake it up and down a couple of times. Very grown-up of us. Then Jason holds out his fist to her and she bumps his back.

"Cool," she says, letting out a long breath. "I wanted to tell you that I believe in your abilities. Especially after what you did to help find my grandfather. I'd never have the guts to go on a ghost investigation or anything like that."

I crease my eyebrows together. "Your grandfather?"

Celia knocks me with her elbow. "Delaney Lockhart . . . remember?"

"Oh! Your grandfather! Right. That was a hard case. I'm glad we were able to help your grandmother," I say.

Stephanie's face lights up at my recognition. "She was so

appreciative," Stephanie says with her hand to her heart, and I know she means it. "Y'all'll have to come to the memorial service on Sunday at McWhorter's Funeral Home."

"That would be nice," I say. Part of me worries about what I'll encounter at a funeral home. Will it be full of lost souls wanting my help?

Stephanie's eyes are open wide, vivid with life all of a sudden. "Hey, I've got a great idea! Kendall, why don't you do psychic readings at my Halloween party? My mother raved about the one you did for her, and it would be awesome to have something like that."

Quickly, I put two and two together and remember the lovely woman from Loreen's shop. "Oh, right. You're Evelyn Crawford's daughter." Man, I should have seen the resemblance.

"That's my mom! Would you be willing to do that for me?"

I glance at Celia and then over my shoulder at Jason, who shrugs his approval. "Why not? That'll be fun. Wicked cool, even."

"Wicked cool it is. I like that," Stephanie says happily. She points at Celia and Clay. "Of course, y'all are invited as well. Everyone's going to be there. Jason, tell Taylor and Ryan to come too."

"And Becca Asiaf?" I ask. We leave no ghost huntress behind.

Stephanie hesitates for a minute and then says, "Yeah, sure."

Right then, another one of Courtney's flock, Megan Bremer,

bounces up next to Stephanie and sneers at me. "Are you coming with us, Steph? We're going to Reuben's Deli."

"Absolutely," she says, but I can hear the hesitation in her voice. "It was great talking to you, Kendall. Don't forget the party." She heads off with Megan but then flips back around and waves.

"Wow . . . invited to Stephanie Crawford's party," Celia says with a smirk. "'Now go we in content / To liberty, and not to banishment.'"

"Thank you, *Celia,*" I say with a snort.

She and I both double over laughing.

"I don't get it," Jason says.

"Celia . . . get it? That's a quote from Celia in *As You Like It*. See, Celia quoting Celia—" The look on Jason's face reads blank as a fresh notebook. "Never mind."

"It's a Shakespeare thing, Tillson," Celia says. "You wouldn't get it."

I stand tall. "Well, I get that I'm doing readings at Stephanie's party and becoming friends with her, so maybe Courtney will finally get over her problem with me and start being nice."

Jason pulls me back to him and kisses me on the head. "Aww, Kendall. And maybe that dead pig you're dissecting will resurrect itself and fly too."

I quirk my mouth to the side. "Stranger things have happened."

Celia looks at Clay and then says, "And probably will."

CHAPTER FIVE

"*THIS WAS ON MY LOCKER,*" I say at lunch on Friday as I slam the crinkled photocopy on the table.

I startle Celia, who grabs the paper and smooths it out. "Ahhh, last year's Valentine's Day dance." Cuddled together in the picture is Jason, in a nice suit, and Courtney, in a blood-red formal holding a bouquet of pink roses.

"She put that on your locker?" Taylor asks.

I breathe out noisily. "For everyone to see. Like she's got a claim on him just because they once dated. How juvenile is this? I'm tired of her shit."

"You and me both," Celia mutters. "Someone needs to put her in her place. You're never going to get her to leave you alone. Either punch her or do something else. This has to end."

I contemplate how it would feel to connect my knuckles with Courtney's right cheekbone, but that's so not me. The only person I've ever hit was Kaitlin, five years ago, when she pulled my Barbie's head off and split her face right in two. I hauled back and smacked her into the middle of next week.

Course, when she went running to Mom, I got the worst tongue-lashing of my life, followed by a couple of wallops to my hindquarters from Dad's bedroom slipper. Something tells me if I take a swing at Courtney Langdon, I'll end up spread-eagled against the wall in Principal Trumbell's office while he has batting practice on my rear. Deservedly so.

"What sort of revenge can I take?" I ask instead.

"Copy a bunch of pictures of you and Jason making out and plaster them all over her car," Celia says with a smirk. "Oh, I know—speaking of her car, we could Oreo it."

I shake my head. "Do what?"

Celia sits up. "You get a few packs of Oreos, twist them apart, and stick the icing side to the car. It's a bitch and a half to get them off, and if you go through the car wash, it just looks like total crap. It takes three or four washings to get it clean."

"You sound like an expert in this field," Taylor notes.

I giggle at the thought, but it wouldn't be very Christian-like of me. "Revenge doesn't belong to us."

"True," Celia says sadly.

I crumple up the picture again and chuck it over toward the nearest garbage can. "Something has to break though, before I do."

"I suggest an *offre de paix* with Courtney," Taylor says calmly. She's painting her nails with a frosty OPI color that makes it look like she has diamond dust on the tips of her fingers.

"A what?" Celia asks. "I knew taking German was a mistake."

"A peace offering," I say, even though my language curric-
ulum of choice is Spanish. "You're saying that *I* need to make
nice with the campus wench?"

Taylor purses her lips and then blows on her fingernails.
"It seems like you need to be the adult here and take the high
road."

Celia crams a fish stick into her mouth and mutters, "Kendall
hasn't done anything. What high road does she need to take?"

Patting my hand carefully—not wanting to mess up her
fresh paint job—Taylor says, "Kendall, I just hate seeing you so
upset all of the time."

"I'm not upset *all* the time."

Celia snorts.

"What?"

"Dear, we're so worried about you," Taylor says.

"Don't be. Courtney will find something else to interest
her soon enough," I say with confidence. Truth be told, I am
in a complete and total funk, but that has nothing to do with
Courtney. I have problems that don't revolve around her and
her one-woman mission to ruin my junior year. The sand in
my hourglass is running out. In a week and a day, I'll be lying
on the shrink's couch, discussing my feelings and my childhood and my relationship with my parents and heaven knows
what else in an attempt to "cure" me of my psychic abilities.
Not. Looking. Forward.

Courtney is merely the cherry on top of the nervous sun-
dae. (God, what a horrible analogy.)

The Oreoing of the car is starting to sound pretty good. Just kidding.

"Look," Taylor starts. "I'm an expert at hiding my true feelings. I mean, my *father* left us, moved to Alaska, and is dating a flight attendant for Icelandic Air. And my mother, well . . . there's a lot going on with her that I don't necessarily want to discuss or let be known to the general public. Y'all already know she's considering a boob job for this Delta pilot she's been seeing."

"What *is* it with your parents and airline personnel?" Celia asks, trying to lighten the conversation. "Is it that expensive to fly?"

Taylor flattens her lips. "It's not my business. I have to go on with my life. The parents have become the children, and the children have taken the high road. See, Kendall. The high road."

I put the spoon to my chocolate pudding down on the tray. "And just what *is* this alleged high road?"

Eyes lighting up, Taylor says, "I was thinking if you show Courtney what you can do, you know, not read her mind or anything, but really try to show where you're coming from, she might understand you more."

"Yeah, tell her to check out the pictures and sound files on our website," Celia says.

Your friend has a good idea . . . , Emily says to me.

"I suppose I could do that."

Not suppose . . . it's a good point, Kendall. . . .

"Let her know how many case requests we have in our system. Cases from people in other towns who really trust us to come help out." Taylor sports a satisfied grin, like she knows that my spirit guide has just validated her suggestion.

I hold my hands up. "All right. I'll do it. Anything to bury the hatchet once and for all with this chick."

Celia wipes her hands on the paper napkin. "If that doesn't work, we can always have Becca's boyfriend, Dragon, beat the shit out of her."

I nearly snort Diet Coke out of my nose, and Taylor almost ruins her self-manicure.

"No need to resort to that yet," I say. "I'll see what I can do."

That's my girl . . .

I've only been to one funeral: Grandma Ethel's. It was the saddest day of my life, looking at my formerly vibrant grandmother lying supine in a gold fiberglass box with satin sheets and pillows around her. She was so . . . still . . . and my heart was broken. Even then, I think I felt the presence of spirits, although I was unable to acknowledge it. I remember hearing whispers all around me but chalked them up to other funeral guests.

I hear these same whispers now as I stand in line with Celia, Taylor, and Becca to pay our respects to Delaney Lockhart, who has been delivered home safe after his whirlwind tour of America.

The funeral home is dimly lit and smells of mums, carnations, and roses. It's packed with Radissonians who've come to see Mrs. Lockhart and her daughters, Evelyn and Veronica. They're standing at the front of the room, next to the open casket draped with a blanket of dark red roses. I gasp when I realize I can see Mr. Lockhart's forehead peeking out of the coffin. I talk to the dead all the time, yet somehow seeing his body like that skeeves me out.

"You okay?" Celia asks.

I swallow hard and shrug. "It's just that the dead are usually more animated for me."

She smiles. "Well, this is how the rest of us see them."

We move forward and I can see Becca's almost as uneasy as I am. Her eyes dart about the room, never stopping too long on any one object. She won't look at Mr. Lockhart or the casket. Everything about her screams that she's just waiting for the right moment to bolt out the door, hop on her motorcycle, and blow town.

"Oh, look, it's the ghost hunters who helped us," Mrs. Lockhart sings out.

"Huntresses," Celia corrects.

Mrs. Lockhart waves her lace handkerchief at us and draws each of us into her bosom for a smothering hug. "If it weren't for y'all, my Delaney would have been lost forever."

Miss Evelyn hugs us all as well. "So nice of you girls to come."

Stephanie finishes speaking to the older woman ahead of

us and turns to me. She's not a Courtney clone; rather, she's a supernice girl who's lost a very important person in her life. I sense she's lost more than merely her grandfather. Her father left her recently as well. Not passed, but her parents had divorced. Mr. Lockhart was the only male figure in her life and Stephanie misses him desperately.

Wanting to help, I stretch my arms out and hug her to me. It's a friendly exchange, and I feel her slump a little as she whimpers. "I'm so sorry about your grandfather," I say.

"Thanks," she says as she pulls back. "I'm gonna miss him tons. We used to go fishing together." She turns and motions toward him. "I put his lucky lure in the pocket of his suit. Something to remember me by."

"That's really sweet of you, Stephanie. I know wherever he is, he appreciates it."

I glance about the room, wondering exactly where Mr. Lockhart is now. Was he reconnected with his body once it arrived back in Radisson?

Celia nudges me. "My EMF detector is going crazy."

Horrified, I whisper loudly, "You brought an EMF meter to a funeral? Celia!"

"What? It's a great place to do research."

"I never."

As Taylor and Becca pay their respects, I move aside with Celia and say a quick prayer for Mr. Lockhart.

"I'm getting a reading in the sevens," Celia mutters.

"Stop that!"

"Aren't you curious as to what it is?"

I spin to face her, but there's someone between us. He's wearing a blue suit, a white shirt, and a red-striped tie. His hair is powdery and his cheeks are sunken in and pale.

"May I help you, sir?" I ask quietly.

Celia freezes. "Who are you talking to?"

The man looks at me. "Lucky bastard. He's got a full house. I'm in the other parlor in there, and it's just my two ex-wives, my two ex-mothers-in-law, and my obnoxious son, who can't wait to see how much money I left him. This man's turnout tells me he was a great guy."

"Were you not a great guy?" I ask. Celia continues to wave her meter around, knowing that I've picked up on the spirit's energy. Thank God she's turned the meter's sound off and it's only flashing red instead of beeping for all of the Lockharts' guests to hear.

"I reckon I wasn't so great," the man says, scratching his chin. "Had a heart attack 'cause I didn't eat right and was over-weight. My doctor tried to get me to take those there Zocor pills for my cholesterol, but I never liked taking medication."

"Why haven't you gone into the light?"

"I ain't seen it yet."

From behind me, I hear, "Maybe we can go together."

It's a good thing I don't frighten easily anymore. Right next to me is Delaney Lockhart, still in the golfing attire he wore on the day he died. He smiles at me. "Hey there, girlie."

"Hey, Mr. Lockhart."

Miss Evelyn pushes over to me. "Kendall, did you say you see Daddy?"

"Yes, ma'am." I hope she doesn't freak out on me.

She lifts a hand to her lips. "He's here right now?"

He chuckles. "I just wanted to check out the service before I skedaddled."

I repeat what he said to Miss Evelyn, and she laughs with tears in her eyes. "That sounds so much like Daddy. Please tell him how much I love him and that I'll take care of Mother."

Mr. Lockhart lifts a hand to Miss Evelyn's face and strokes her cheek. Too bad she can't feel it. "Tell her I know."

"I will," I manage to get out.

He turns to the man standing next to him. "Wha'd'ya say we get out of here?" He points over to the left corner of the room. "See it?"

I look over myself, but since it's not my time, the bright light is invisible to me. At least these guys recognize it. Before I know it, the two of them disappear into nothing, and my heart feels as if it will burst from the joy radiating in their wake.

"He's passed into the light," I whisper to Miss Evelyn.

She wraps an arm around me. "Thanks for everything, Kendall." She looks to Celia, who's finally put the damn meter away. "Let's just keep this between the three of us, okay?"

"Sure thing."

Then I hear the creepy laughing again. That soldier is here.

In my head, I try to contact him. *Why don't you follow them into the light?*

Ain't no light for me . . .

I'm going to have to find out who this guy is and get him to move along. And fast.

Monday afternoon I'm armed with the peace offering Taylor suggested. After the brush with the men at the funeral home— and the laughing soldier—I realize life is too short to be miserable. Since Courtney makes me miserable, I've got to be the one to try to mend the fence.

Courtney uses the scalpel and pokes our poor pickled pig in the chest.

"Do you want me to do it?" I ask impatiently. We've been sitting here for ten minutes staring at this thing like it's going to jump up and crunk out for us. Everyone else in the lab is working quietly, getting along, and making progress.

She snaps at me. "I said I'd do it and I'm doing it!"

Something tells me that the girl who seems afraid of nothing doesn't have the courage to make the first cut. I can't help but snark off. "Today would be nice."

Ice-cold gray eyes slice over my face, raising the hairs on the back of my neck. The energy surrounding Courtney right now is black and damn near dismal. She's not a happy girl. A negative haze envelops her like a miasma of shifting darkness. For some reason, I get the sensation that Courtney's hatred for me, for Jason, for our ghost-hunting team, and, most of all, for the attention we're getting has opened her up to—for lack of a better phrase—the dark side. Not like I think Darth Vader and the Emperor are going to strike out from within her, but there's an evilness radiating from her. A door to her soul has been left wide open because of her unease, jealousy, and ill will toward me.

Taylor's correct. I have to make things right with this girl.

I reach over and carefully take the scalpel from her. She opens her mouth to snap at me, then stops. It must be the intensity in my eyes and the way I'm looking at her. Almost pitying.

"What is your problem?" she finally asks, the words punctuated with venom.

Be nice. "I'm worried about you, Courtney."

She laughs derisively. "*You're* worried about *me?*"

"Something's not right about you."

"Oh, and you're an expert on who I am, I suppose," she says. "You've been in this school, what . . . two months? Get over it, Ghost Girl."

I wrinkle my face. "That's just it. My name's Kendall, Courtney."

"Whatever."

"No, it's not whatever. I'm a person. I haven't done anything to you. You have no reason to hate me."

She rocks back on her stool, stunned and speechless for once.

"You've got other things to worry about," I continue. "That C minus you got in trig might get you in trouble with the cheerleading squad. Instead of focusing all your energies on hating me, you should get your grades back up. You're a smart girl, you know?"

The last thing I expect from her is a snide smirk. "What, did your geek sidekick Celia hack into the school's computers so you could read up on me and use that?"

I roll my eyes. "No. Give me a break. I can read your thoughts. They're practically neon signs flashing above your head."

She drops her eyes down, not meeting my stare. I also pick up that her parents are fighting and her allowance has been cut. She's worried that she won't be able to keep up with the latest fashion trends if she doesn't have money to buy clothes and accessories. She has a rep to uphold. Seriously? *This* is what's worrying her? Man, I wish I had her problems.

Here comes the olive branch.

"Look, Courtney," I say as I twirl the scalpel in my fingers. "It's mentally and physically exhausting worrying about someone completely hating you for no reason. I can't go on like this. I have a proposition."

She sneers at me. "Sorry, you're not exactly my type."

"Yeah, right. Don't flatter yourself." *Be nice. Be. Nice.* "We are stuck doing this project together that's, like, a big part of our grade. Can we put aside whatever differences we have and work through this? At least for one hour a day?"

Courtney folds her arms across her chest and furrows her brow at me. I know she's concerned about grades too, so maybe this is the carrot I need to dangle.

"I'm not trying to usurp your popularity or status here at

RHS," I assure her. "I just want to do my thing and let you do yours. Which means stop calling me names and doing stupid shit like spilling food on me in the caf."

"I do need to score well on this," she says, relenting, but her thoughts still mirror the evil mist of true abhorrence swirling around her.

Time to try another route. I tug a book out of my backpack and slide it across the table. Loreen, who's been worried about this feud as well, thought the book might come in handy for dealing with nonbelievers.

"What's this?" Courtney asks. She picks it up and reads, "*So You Think You're Psychic: Now What?*"

"It's a really great read that explains psychic awakenings and what people go through. It even tells you how to recognize the signs, so you'll know someone's not faking or anything."

Tossing the book to the table, Courtney asks, "What am *I* supposed to do with this?"

"Read it," I say. "It might help you understand what I'm going through. That I'm a teenager just like you." Okay, I don't, like, throw up everything I eat, like she does, but that's a problem to solve another time. "I'm in a new place, trying to make friends and fit in, and I've got this really extraordinary thing happening to me that allows me to help people in a way I never thought I could. We're all born with psychic ability. It's whether or not we decide to recognize it and make use of it. That's all I'm doing, Courtney. Not trying to run your clique or rule the school."

She reluctantly takes the book and tucks it in her bag. "Fine. Whatever."

At least she took it. That's got to be a step in the right direction.

I pass the scalpel back to her. "Wanna take a crack at this again?"

Courtney holds the instrument, mustering up her nerve.

"'Screw your courage to the sticking-place/And we'll not fail.'"

"Huh?"

"Sorry, Celia and I do it all the time. It's from *Macbeth,* act one."

"Like the play *Macbeth*? What the hell does that mean?" she asks with a slight lift in her voice.

"It means, do what you need to do to get the job done."

And with that, Courtney Langdon, head cheerleader, my nemesis, and school beeyotch, slices down the middle of the pig and then looks up at me . . . and smiles.

CHAPTER SIX

"IT'S FRIDAY NIGHT. Can I get a big woohoo?"

Emily sits across the room from me in the rocking chair—literally sitting on my stuffed bear, Sonoma—and watches as I Snoopy-dance next to my bed.

"I've got the football game tonight and then a date with Jason, which I haven't had in a really, really long time," I tell her. I don't necessarily have to talk out loud to Emily, since she can hear my thoughts and I can hear hers. Sometimes, though, I just like talking to her as if she's a regular—*i.e., alive*—person.

"Are you and Jason going to be kissing a lot?" Emily asks.

My face burns, knowing that Emily has witnessed most of the make-out sessions between Jason and me. "Umm . . . duh," I say with a laugh.

"I think you two kiss too much."

I roll my eyes at her and then dab mascara on the tips of my lashes. "You know, my mother is *downstairs*, thankyouvery-much."

"I'm only looking out for you, Kendall."

I spin around to sort of glare at her. "I appreciate it, Emily, but it's not like Jason and I are getting married tomorrow. We're in high school and simply having a good time."

She frowns, as much as a ghost can. "I worry."

"About what?"

"That you're too close," she says quietly.

I don't understand. "Too close how?"

Her eyes are distant, as if caught up in a memory. "I was close to a boy like that once."

Intrigued, I say, "Oh yeah? When was that?"

"Before your time."

I have so little to go on about Emily's past. She wears something resembling a patient's gown, which makes me think she passed away in a hospital. What did she die of? It's so foggy around her, and I'm unable to pick up anything. She's so pretty . . . so young. How tragic that she died when her life was only beginning. "Was he your boyfriend?"

Emily nods, her flowing hair shifting around her face.

"What was his name?"

"It doesn't matter," she says dismissively. "We're talking about you. You and Jason. All that kissing. Things are moving too fast with him, and it worries me."

I run my fingers through my long, wavy brown hair that's looking pretty stylish tonight, if I do say so myself. "You don't have to worry."

A sigh escapes from her. The doorbell rings throughout the house.

"Keeeeeeeeeeeendall!" Kaitlin screams up the stairs. "Jason's here!"

I grab the black military jacket off the bed and layer it over my Kill City gray hoodie. Then, I snag my Betsey Johnson shoulder bag. (A score off SmartBargains.com.) Emily watches me and I can almost hear the *tsk, tsk* in my head. Stopping at the door, I say, "Can you please give me some alone time tonight with Jason, Em?"

She stands in front of me with her hands on her hips.

"Seriously," I insist. "I appreciate everything, I really do. I just want to be as normal as possible tonight, hanging with my friends and going out with my boyfriend. Please promise?"

After what seems like three years, Emily nods, blows me a kiss, and then quietly disappears.

Tonight's all about having a good time. Fun and friends and some semblance of *normal*. Tomorrow, Mom and I head to the ATL for my appointment with the shrink, who'll be ready to analyze me to death and possibly diagnose me with all sorts of afflictions.

Go be with your friends, Emily says, although I can't see her anymore. Yet somehow I know she's with me, like she has been my whole life.

Jason shuffles me out the door of my house and toward his Jeep, where Taylor's waiting for us.

"Your sister's coming on our date?"

He shrugs. "She's just riding with us to the football game

and then she'll hook up with Ryan and go with him in his car to the bowling alley later. You know, once he's showered and stuff after the game."

Ryan MacKenzie has been Taylor's steady for these past couple of months. He plays on the RHS football team, so I shouldn't be too bent to have her tailing along with us. Besides, it's not like I'm going to attack Jason on the way to the stadium, whether Taylor's in the back seat or not. Puuuuuhleeeeze!

At the stadium, we meet up with Celia and Clay, as well as Becca and her boyfriend, Brent "Dragon" Dragisich, a kind of biker dude who runs with the rougher crowd at school. More of Becca's rebellion from whatever's eating her. We all get along swimmingly though, and we enjoy watching our team kick a little ass on the gridiron.

RHS wins a rollicking defensive game of matching field goals, and then we all head off to Radisson Lanes to bowl some balls. It doesn't hurt that they have *the best* local attempt at Chicago pizza. The owner, Brendan McDonough, is a transplant from Chicago himself and knows how to make a mean pie.

We order a pitcher of Coke Zero (for the boys) and Diet Coke (for the girls) and a large pizza with sausage, pepperoni, mushrooms, and extra cheese. Jason and Clay secure two side-by-side lanes, and we all slip on the ever-so-attractive (not!) bowling shoes that have been sprayed with that alleged sanitizing spray.

Taylor holds her black, red, and white loafer and scrunches

up her face. "I always wonder what kind of possible diseases reside in these."

"I had a buddy get a plantar wart from 'em once," Dragon says with a crooked grin.

Taylor's mouth drops open in horror.

Becca smacks him on the forearm. "You're such a liar." She turns to Taylor. "Ignore him. He's an ass."

Ryan slips into the seat next to Taylor. "No bacteria would dare attach itself to you, Tay."

She melts into his hug and smiles in the most ridiculously cute and contented way. Next to me, I can sense Jason relaxing, knowing his sister is relatively happy for the first time since their dad walked out the door. I can't exactly pick up on his thoughts like I can other people's, but I know what a relief it is for him to just be himself and not constantly worry and watch over her. Like Emily does for me.

Celia stands up and wipes her hands on her jeans. "Who's on what team?"

"Guys against girls?" Jason suggests.

"Not a chance," Becca chimes in, although she's a ringer when it comes to bowling. The girl has a left hook that would make professional bowlers blush. "Me, Dragon, Clay, and Celia against y'all," she says, pointing at Ryan, the Tillsons, and me.

Jason keys all of our names into the computer system while Celia and Becca polish off the pizza. The place is really jumping tonight with RHSers and older kids hanging out by the pool tables. The energy inside the building crackles in a static-filled way. Laughter floats in the air above the zooming of the balls on the hardwood floor and the eventual *kkk-whacccck* against the pins.

I sense a pair of eyes on me, so I scan the crowd, not knowing what to expect. Cold, steely gray orbs glare at me from nine lanes over, where Courtney Langdon, Stephanie Crawford, Farah Lewis, and Megan Bremer are with Jim Roach, Kyle Kadish, Sean Carmickle, and some other guys from the football team. Stephanie sees me and waves. Courtney turns her nose up at me like I've just committed a mortal sin. I wave back and smile. No reason to be rude or lower myself to her level. I can't believe that after my concerted effort to get on her good side, she still disses me. I don't get this girl. Maybe I never will. Maybe she's destined to be my sworn enemy from now through eternity. Wow . . . dramatic much?

Jason's warm hand slides over my waist, and he pulls me against his chest. "The hell with her," he whispers in my ear, and then kisses my hair. It's the sexiest thing ever and I feel loved and protected. With Jason around—choosing me over *her*—nothing can hurt me.

"You're up, Kendall!" Celia yells.

I nab a seven-pound swirly-design emerald green ball and jam my fingers into the holes. Something's not right though. A tingling sensation pulsates under my palm. Sweat rolls down my neck, making my hair feel heavy. My breathing deepens, and my head begins to hurt. It's the psychic headache I've been experiencing on and off since moving to Radisson. The same one that makes my mother lose sleep, worrying that I have a brain tumor or worse. Searing pain crawls up my right arm, and I can barely hold on to the marble ball. Blood courses through my veins, making them bulge and roll. It's like I'm fighting off something . . . an infection? An injury?

"You gonna throw it or not, Moorehead?" Becca teases.

I take two steps and make a valiant effort to toss the ball down the lane. However, it slips right off my hand, bounces hard three times, and then slides gracelessly into the groove.

"Gutter ball!" Dragon yells triumphantly.

His laughter is swallowed up by the ringing sound in my head. I fall to my knees, unable to bear the immense hurt in my right arm, or the pounding of my temples as a terrible scream rips through my brain. Not mine. Someone's.

The lights in the alley flicker and go out. The '80s Hall and Oates tune playing overhead comes to a slow stop. The electronic boards controlling everyone's score suddenly sputter and then wipe clean.

Clay pounds his fist on the seat. "Oh, man! There goes my perfect score."

Jason's at my side, ever my rescuer. "What's going on with you, Kendall?"

"I'm not sure," I say and accept his hand up.

Mr. McDonough yells to get everyone's attention and apologizes for the power outage. "Sorry about that. We've got a computer glitch up here. I'll comp everyone one game to make up for it."

"That'll cost him a pretty penny," Celia mutters.

There's more to it, though. It's not simply a computer glitch. "There's a spirit here," I tell her and Jason.

His face falls. "Come on, Kendall. Not tonight. You promised."

I search his eyes, trying to find understanding. "It's not something I can turn off, Jason. I can *feel* him. He's here." I stare down the lane, toward where the pins are swept away. "He's back there."

Celia's smile hikes to one side. "And me without my ghost-hunting equipment."

"Are you okay, Kendall?" Mr. McDonough asks. "You didn't fall down, did you?"

"No, sir," I say. "I just . . . Mr. McDonough, do you know if anyone ever died here at the bowling alley?"

He scratches his head for a moment and then bobs it. "That's right. You're those ghost huntresses everyone's been talking about."

Celia gives a thumbs-up.

"You think I got a ghost?" Mr. McDonough asks.

"Did anyone die here?" I press.

"Actually, the guy who owned the place before me was killed in a freak accident. Saddest story too. The feller was trying to reset the pins, and he crawled up underneath the mechanism at the end of the alley to work loose the jam. Edgar Moncrief, who works over at the firehouse, told me the machine clicked on and crushed the guy's arm, then ripped it clear out of the socket."

"Gnarly!" Dragon shouts out. Becca smacks him in the stomach.

Mr. McDonough finishes up. "Poor bastard died of blood loss before the paramedics could get to him."

I grip my upper arm, acknowledging the red-hot pain in my joints. "That would explain it." My whole body involuntarily convulses, just thinking of the guy caught up in the pin resetter and losing a limb like that. And he's still here. I know it.

I ask, "May I take a look?"

"Well, sure thing, little lady."

The six of us follow Mr. McDonough down the lane. He crawls into the gutter and slips behind the pins into the rear pathway. I follow him, as does Celia and Taylor. Taylor pulls out her BlackBerry and starts snapping pictures as I walk around getting a feel for the place. I breathe in deeply, smelling the musty dustiness coupled with the dank smell of a cleaning mop. Closing my eyes, I zero in on the spirit that's been teasing me with a *tap, tap, tap* on my brain. I see him clear as a bell. Curly hair. Crooked smile. Small scar between his eyes. An old sailboat injury, when the jib hit him. His name is . . .

I look at Mr. McDonough. "Was the man's name Rob Breslin?"

He chortles. "Damn, you're good! That was his name."

And just like that, Rob Breslin appears before me, as vivid

as Celia, Taylor, and Mr. McDonough. He's wearing dirty khaki pants with a bit of green paint smudged on the left leg. A Grateful Dead T-shirt adorns his chest, and he's missing his right arm. Dried blood is encrusted on the sleeve of the shirt.

"Do you see my arm?" he asks me. "I can't find it anywhere."

I flick my eyes over to Celia and nod that the spirit is here. She stretches her hand out to feel for any changes in the temperature. Goose bumps dance up and down her arm as she comes in contact with the area where Rob Breslin is standing. She's found a cold spot! Celia cocks her head to the side, indicating to Taylor that she should take some pictures.

I focus on Rob though. He can't be over forty. What a disastrous way to die—having a limb jerked from your body.

"I've got to find my arm," he says.

"I don't know where it is," I say to him.

He runs his remaining hand through his hair with great frustration. "I've been looking for it since the accident. It's got to be here. I mean, you don't just leave an arm lying around."

His smile is heartbreaking, and I want nothing more than to find his limb for him. It's impossible, though. Through my psychic vision, I see that the appendage was so badly damaged by the machinery that there was nothing really to bury with him. I've got to do everything in my power to help him cross into a better place.

"Rob, do you see the light?"

"Sure I do. It's been around for forever, but I gotta get my limb back."

"You need to cross over into the light, Rob."

"Not without my arm."

Celia and Taylor watch with great interest.

"He won't go into the light without his arm."

Celia turns to where I see Rob. "You know, if you go into the light, you'll be whole again," she says. Girl's damn smart.

"That's right," Taylor says, agreeing. "They say we're all healed up and whole and everything when we get to heaven. You should totally go."

"You'll find peace there," I add. "You don't want to hang around a dirty old bowling alley forever, do you?"

Mr. McDonough lifts his eyebrows at me, but I wave him off, since my comment wasn't meant as an insult. I mouth *sorry,* and he seems to understand.

Rob glances past me. "The light is spectacular. I've wanted to check it out for a while."

"Your arm will be there for you . . . in the light."

With that, he walks toward me, through me, almost. Although I feel a jolt like my entire system has been shocked, it soon turns to a warm sensation. I'm consumed by his joy and relief; he feels so loved and welcomed. He radiates tranquillity.

"Thanks, kid."

I smile. "You're welcome."

And with that, he's gone.

I double over, my hands on my knees, as I catch my breath.

I don't get *as* winded talking to spirits as I did at first, but it still takes a toll on me.

"Check this out," Taylor says. She holds up her BlackBerry, and there on the screen is a wispy mist swirling around where I saw Rob standing. "*Très* exciting!"

"Is he gone?" McDonough asks.

"Yes, sir. He's crossed over."

I crouch down to fill Jason and Becca in on what just happened and see that we've drawn quite a crowd. Celia slides out and shouts, "Kendall just crossed over another spirit! She rocks the house!"

People clap and cheer as Jason pulls me out of the crawl-space and into his arms.

Not everyone is cheering though.

I glance over people's shoulders to a small group gathered on the fringe. Courtney Langdon has been watching.

And she's pissed.

Jason pulls his Jeep into my gravel driveway and yanks up the emergency brake. I can tell he's not particularly pleased with me over tonight's turn of events. What was I supposed to do? Just let that Breslin guy wander around for eternity, looking for his missing limb?

The connection with Breslin completely drained me of my energy, but I'm trying not to let that show. I promised Jason a night without ghosts or ghost hunts, and it hasn't turned out that way. Then there was the nuclear death stare from Courtney.

My life seems to be spiraling into a pathetic mess that I can't do anything about.

Well, I can do *something* . . .

I reach over and lace my fingers through Jason's. He's got such large, tan, strong hands. Mostly from working construction last summer—before I moved here and even knew who Jason Tillson was. Or what ghost hunting was all about. Man, talk about life-altering occurrences in the past two months: a new town, a new school, new friends, a boyfriend . . . oh yeah, and becoming psychic. Most teenagers would go crazy with a list like that.

But I'm not crazy. And tomorrow, I'm going to prove it.

Jason curls his hand around mine and tightens his grip. I draw strength from just being around him.

"Don't let how Courtney acted tonight upset you," he says softly.

"Courtney's ass in a coffeepot," I say back.

"Huh?"

I giggle. "Sorry. It's one of my dad's stupid sayings. I have no idea what it means."

Jason's smile is illuminated by the streetlight. "I think it means who gives a shit what she thinks."

"Unfortunately I do, because at the present time, she's making my life a living hell."

"Don't let her," he says, so nonchalantly.

I nearly snort. "Easy for you to say. You're a guy. The one that dumped her. You don't have to deal with the repercussions of her nasty attitude. It's always easier for a girl to pick on another girl. Especially one who's already put herself in the spotlight by being 'different.'"

"You're not different, you're special," he says.

Awww . . . heart melt . . .

"Yeah, but you don't buy into all of this stuff that's going on. You're the skeptic on our ghost team, remember?"

He lifts his blond eyebrows and moves his eyes back and forth. "I'm supporting you, Kendall. And my sister. You both believe in this stuff."

"You've seen and heard the same evidence as we have. What about what happened tonight at the bowling alley?"

Jason moves his hand in the air, gesturing, unable to come up with words. "I don't know. What do I know about the afterlife? Do I believe you connected with something tonight? Yeah, seems like you did. Was it a ghost? I don't know. I didn't see him."

I do get where he's coming from. "Do you believe in God?"

"Of course I do!"

"And in the devil."

"Sure . . . so?"

"Well, then there have got to be other entities in this world that we can't see. We can't physically *see* God, yet we have faith that he's there."

"That's different," Jason says.

"How so?"

"It just is."

"Great argument," I say with a laugh. "I'm only saying that part of faith is believing what you can't see. You can't actually *see* love, can you? But you've felt love in your life," I nearly plead. It's so important to me that Jason gets all of this. I'm determined to make a believer out of him. "Love isn't tangible, except in things like a kiss, or holding hands, or like my dad doing the dishes so my mom doesn't have to."

Jason tilts his head back against the car's headrest and closes his eyes. "You're right. I get what you're saying."

Feeling cheeky, I say, "Then you believe in ghosts?"

"Nah."

"Spirits?"

"Nope."

"Not even angels?"

He shakes his head. "No way."

I smile at him in the dim light. "Then how do you explain me?"

Jason laughs so hard, the Jeep nearly shakes. "Ahhh . . . a technicality."

He leans in, so close that I can feel his warm breath on my face. I love it when he makes his move like this. I know what's coming next. Sure enough, his lips touch mine, and the familiar electrical current surges through me, igniting my insides and making my heart skip a beat. I don't care what happens in the future or who I eventually end up with when I'm eighty and rocking on the porch; I will *never* forget Jason Tillson's kisses. The boy's got talent.

I dissolve into his arms and put my free hand on his shoulder, pulling him closer to me as he deepens the kiss. There's nothing as secure as having Jason's arms around me, protecting me in a way that no one else can. Not that I need protecting. It's just good to know he's here if and when I need him.

Jason ends the long kiss and then feathers lighter ones on my cheek, eyelid, and forehead, like he's truly worshiping me. It's . . . un-freaking-believable. And it wipes out all—well, most, anyway—of the apprehension and anxiety over what tomorrow will bring.

As if he's psychic himself, Jason lifts my chin with his finger and asks, "You're thinking about your appointment in the morning, aren't you?"

I shrug innocently, not wanting to ruin our moment. It's not often that Emily gives me alone time with Jason, so I definitely want to take advantage of it.

"You don't have anything to worry about," he says. "At least your mom lived up to her end of the bargain, taking you to a doctor familiar with kids who have gifts like yours."

"This coming from the eternal skeptic."

"I'm not skeptical about *you,* Kendall. Just the whole existence of spirits and what have you. I still need to see things for myself. It doesn't mean that I don't believe you see things."

I let out a long sigh and relax into the bucket seat. "Now you sound like Mom."

He tugs me back to him. "I'm only saying that this doctor is open-minded."

Yeah, maybe so. "It still means he's going to be checking for all the signs of crazy and wack."

Our fingers find each other again. "You want me to come with you?" he asks. "I was gonna play basketball with Roachie, but I can come to Atlanta instead."

I lay my head on his shoulder and smile. "You're the sweetest, Jason. I've got to do this on my own though. Besides, I need the time with Mom so she can really listen to the doctor and to me and understand that what's happening inside me is not something psychotic or evil."

Jason touches his forehead to mine. "I'm proud of you, Kendall." Then he kisses me again. Like the kind from the movies, when the music swells, crescendoing to a magical height until it bursts into fireworks and the moon begins to sing. (Okay, so I've watched *Moulin Rouge* one too many times.)

"Thanks, Jase," I mutter between kisses.

"And, I . . . you know."

"Know what?"

His blue eyes shimmer. "You know. I love you, Kendall."

I bolt upright. "You do? Whoa!"

He laughs at me, and I can see his face is red from ear to ear. Holy craptastic! Jason Tillson just told me he loves me!

"I love you too, Jason," I say, bringing his sexy self to me again.

"I believe in love 'cause I *can* see it. I'm looking at it right now, Kendall," he says before kissing me again.

After we make out for a while—nothing too porno—I

finally gather my wits about me and break apart from him, promising to call him when I get back into town. I float into the house, past Dad, who waves from the den where he's watching David Letterman, and collapse face-down into the fluffy quilt of my bed. It's hard to put into words the satisfaction of helping Rob Breslin cross into eternal bliss, and it's coupled with the fact that Jason *believes* in me sooooooo much. And he frickin' loves me!

"Did you have fun tonight?"

Emily's in my rocking chair, making it move ever so slightly. I don't even get frightened anymore when she shows up.

"I don't know," I say with a grin. "Did I?"

"I kept my promise, Kendall. You were on your own."

Rolling onto my back, I scoot to the pillows and prop myself up. "It was . . . interesting." I fill her in on what happened at the bowling alley, and she seems pleased. "Most of all, I got to spend time with Jason, and that was awesome." A satisfied sigh escapes from me. "He loves me, Emily. Like, said it and all. Do you know how much that means to me?"

"You're very loved, Kendall. You should know that."

I clutch one of my throw pillows to my chest. "This is like *real* love, though. Not like the love between parents and their kids. Parents have to love their kids. This is someone who picked me out from all the rest and *chose* to love me. That's . . . wicked amazing."

Emily appears to gnaw on her lip, biting back words she

seems to want to say. "Your parents love you that way too. That's why you're going to see that doctor tomorrow."

I toss the pillow across the room at Emily, knowing that even if it hits her, she won't feel it. "My mom wants to prove that she's right about my awakening, that it's all in my head."

"You should be grateful that she's so protective and cares what happens to you. Not everyone has that in their life," she says wistfully.

"Was your mom not protective of you, Emily? Is that why you died?"

She waves me off with a flick of her hand. "This isn't about me, Kendall."

Following a long pause, I reassure her. "I do realize that I'm loved and cared for. I'm not stupid. I just want to get this over with, prove myself, and get back to my life. I don't want Mom running the meeting or telling the doctor what he should think about me."

"She won't."

"Yeah, she will. But I understand."

"For what it's worth, Kendall," Emily says, "I'll be there for you too."

My heart pounds hard, like it did when Jason said he loved me. Because I realize that in her own way, Emily loves me too. "That means the world to me, Em."

CHAPTER SEVEN

I GRAB THE SISSY BAR—or in this case, the "oh, shit!" handle—over my head as Mom takes the exit for I-85 off I-20 like she's Kyle Busch pulling in to have his tires changed. "Whoa, Sarah!" I say, only half kiddingly.

Mom shakes her head. "I knew we should have left Radisson earlier. I don't want to keep the doctor waiting."

As a longtime nurse, Mom thinks it's incredibly rude for patients to keep the medical staff waiting when they have set appointments. Of course, she has no defense for how patients always seem to have to sit in the doctor's waiting room for weeks on end, reading year-old *Redbook*s and back issues of *Sports Illustrated*.

"We've still got a half-hour to get there."

"Atlanta traffic is always a nightmare."

"It's Saturday," I say.

"We'll still barely make it downtown." Mom switches her Volvo into the left lane and guns it past a rickety old pickup truck doing its best to keep up with the early-morning interstate traffic. "Did you deliberately try to make us late so you wouldn't have to do this?"

My brows knit together as I stare at her over my sunglasses. "Uh. Wha—I can't believe you think that! I said I'd do this, and I'm doing it. Geez."

Mom bites her bottom lip and reaches over to touch me on my blue-jeaned knee. "I'm sorry, Kendall. I'm just nervous about this meeting and what we might find out."

That your daughter's really psychic, Emily says in my head.

I mentally wave her off. "I'm not trying to be the bratty kid, Mom, you know that. Kaitlin has that role down pat. I want this over and done as much as you do."

In no time, Mom zigzags through the I-85 raceway, exiting swiftly downtown and turning onto Peachtree Street. This is really the first time I've been to the city. I'd love to have a chance to explore the Underground, go and visit Coca-Cola World, see the Carter presidential library and Martin Luther King Jr.'s grave, take in a Braves game, or even see my beloved Blackhawks play the Atlanta Thrashers (High-Stickin' Chickens, more like). Maybe Jason and I can visit the city together one weekend when I'm not ghost hunting. *If* I still get to ghost hunt.

We park in the office-complex garage and make our way into the building. It smells of antiseptic cleaner coupled with a Febreze-like odor. It's times like these that I wish I didn't have that clairsentient ability where I'm able to pick up spirits through my sensitivity to smells. Not that there are any spirits here. Are there? No, it's a pretty recently built building and it's not like it's a hospital, where people die and stuff.

I need to get a grip on my thoughts. Especially since some quack is about to start dissecting them.

"Sarah and Kendall Moorehead to see Dr. Kindberg," Mom says to the receptionist. "We have an appointment."

The nurse checks us in and tells us to wait. Great. Mom drives like a bat out of hell to get here, and they make us wait. Whatever.

My BlackBerry sings that I've received a text message, so I pull it out of the case.

>Patience 4 the patient.

Huh? Who's this from? There's no number to text back.

Mom tsk-tsks me. "Do you have to do that now?"

Another beep.

>I'm here if u need me. E

How did you do that, Emily?

Just then, the door to the inner sanctum opens and an older man steps out. He's wearing a light blue dress shirt with the sleeves rolled up and no tie. He's sporting a crewcut, like he's just finished a tour in the Middle East with the Eighty-second Airborne. His khakis don't look institutional or anything, so maybe this guy doesn't have a stick up his ass after all. "Mrs. Moorehead? Kendall? Why don't y'all come on in?"

I follow behind Mom into the nondescript medical office. Plants in one corner, a large brown suede chair in the other.

The standard couch is against the back wall, facing an outstanding view of the Georgia Dome.

"I'm Dr. Ken Kindberg. Nice to meet both of you."

Mom shakes his hand and introduces me.

"Hi there," I say politely.

He spreads his arms wide in welcome. "Have a seat anywhere you like and let's get to know one another."

"I presume the couch is for me?" I try not to be snarky. This dude's just doing his job.

"Is that where you want to sit, Kendall?"

Oh dear God. And we're off. Honestly, I've watched enough TV medical dramas to know when a psychiatrist is psyching you out. I want to be true to my word to my parents, but do I have to put up with him trying to get all, well, psychological on my ass?

Calm down, Kendall . . .

Knowing that Emily's with me, I breathe a little more easily. Instead of taking the couch, I plop into the gigamonic suede chair.

Dr. Kindberg grabs a legal pad and a pen from his desk and scoots his chair around. That leaves Mom sitting on the couch, which is ironic, considering how she might need some counseling when it's proven that I'm not sick or faking.

After the beginning mindless shitchat about moving from Chicago, how I like Radisson, if I'm making friends and stuff, Dr. Kindberg clicks the end of his pen and laser-beams his eyes at me. "So, Kendall, your mother tells me that you've been experiencing restless sleep, headaches, and tingling sensations in your extremities."

"Yes, sir, I—"

Mom sits forward. "You know, Dr. Kindberg, I'm a nurse and I've been doing a lot of research on Kendall's symptoms. The insomnia could certainly be a reaction to the move and being in a different time zone. However, the headaches are so severe and are causing these"—she slices her eyes over to me and lowers her voice—"visions that she claims to have."

"I don't *claim* anything, Mom. I have them." God, I sound like Kaitlin. I have to remain calm and not act like a baby.

She's got your best interests at heart, Emily pleads.

"I'm concerned that Kendall may be in the beginning stages of dementia or, heaven forbid, schizophrenia," Mom diagnoses.

Dr. Kindberg is making notes. "Do you have a history of either of those diseases in your family?"

"No, but—" Mom stops and glances out the window for a moment. "Neither my husband nor I have family members who have suffered from either."

"Kendall, I'm going to ask you some very personal questions and I need you to answer honestly," Dr. K. says.

"Sure." I mean, why not? I'm an honest person.

"Are you taking any medications?"

"Besides popping a Claritin every now and then because of the pollen?"

"No, dear," Mom says. "He means prescription medications."

I shrug. "You know I don't."

"Yes, but maybe you've gotten something from someone at school," she says in a voice that I can't believe is coming from my mother.

"Are you kidding me? I'm not some OxyContin addict, nor am I buying Ritalin off kids at school!" What is this garbage?

"Kendall! I'm exploring all avenues here."

"You know me better than that, Mom. Honestly!"

Dr. K. stands. "Mrs. Moorehead, perhaps it would be best if Kendall and I meet alone to go over these questions."

"I have a right to know what my child is doing."

"I'm not *doing* anything, Mom. Please believe me." We're not going to get anywhere with her running this meeting instead of the psychiatrist. "Let me just talk to him."

Mom picks up her purse and reluctantly heads toward the door. "I still think I need to be here with you."

"Don't worry," the doctor says. "After Kendall and I talk, I'm going to have her take some tests that can be used to determine if she's truly having psychic encounters."

"I don't know—"

"I'll be fine, Mom. There's a Starbucks in the lobby. Why don't you go give them all of your money on that Dolce Cinnamon thingy you like so much?" I flash a confident smile toward her so she won't see how scared shitless I really am. I want her to sit and hold my hand and merely listen and not think the worst of me. But I've got to do this on my own. I've got to prove that what I'm going through isn't psychotic, a sickness, or anything evil.

When the door closes, Dr. K. retakes his seat. "Okay then . . ."

"Okay," I echo. I fidget with the fringe on the edge of a throw pillow. I should stop before he starts taking notes on my squirming.

"So, do you deal with kids like me a lot?"

He peers over at me. "Psychic kids?"

"Yeah."

"Sure. That's why you're here. I have a lot of clients who are going through the same sense of awareness that you're possibly having. We just need to answer more questions and do some tests and rule out everything medically possible so I can set your parents' minds at ease."

I cross my Timberlanded foot over my knee. "Fire away with the questions."

Over the next fifteen minutes, Dr. K. asks me about everything: my drug usage (if any), if I smoke, if I drink, if I'm I sexually active (Jason and I *just* started dating!), if I take birth control, if I sniff glue (WTF?), about my menstrual cycle (I could *not* be more embarrassed), if I've ever been abused, if I force myself to throw up (I'm not Courtney, thank you), if I've ever been pregnant or had an abortion (see aforementioned no-sex answer), you name it. By the time he's done, I feel completely violated and mortified. Maybe Mom *should* have stayed in the room.

He clicks his pen again. A nervous habit, or just thinking? "Very well, Kendall. Thanks for your honesty. Please understand, all of that is merely standard, and I mean no disrespect with any of it."

"It's cool, Doc."

"Like I said, Kendall, I deal with a lot of kids who are experiencing what they believe to be paranormal activity or connections with spirits that have passed. Often, children have overactive imaginations or are trying to get attention from their parents or it's related to stress caused by some change in their lives. Didn't you just recently leave all of your friends and classmates behind in Chicago to move to"—he thumbs through my file—"ah yes, Radisson. Lovely little town."

I hold my hand up. "Dr. K., I understand what you're doing. I really do. Yes, it sucked royally having to leave Chicago to move out to East Bumblebutt, USA—"

He interrupts me with a sincere chortle. "That's a good one. I'll have to remember that."

"But seriously, with this awakening, I haven't had time to miss home or cause mischief. I just want to fit in the best I can. You know, being normal, or as close to normal as I can."

"What do you consider *normal*, Kendall?"

I quirk my mouth. "Umm . . . not talking to the ghost in my house or seeing deceased Civil War soldiers all over town.

Not hearing the thoughts of others or knowing how people died." I stop for a minute. "Though maybe this *is* normal for me now. My friend Loreen Woods tells me that I've probably had this gift my whole life and am only now experiencing it full-blown."

"Loreen Woods?"

"Yeah, she's sort of my mentor," I say. "She's helping me develop my abilities."

"How do your parents feel about that?"

I roll my eyes. "How do you think? Mom's like really religious and is having a hard time with the fact that I'm practicing divination in my room. She's marked passages in the Bible with Post-it notes on how divination is wrong. She ratted me out to my Episcopal priest, but fortunately he's open-minded and has experience with gifted people and tells me it's God's plan for me."

"I see," Dr. K. says. "Well, one step at a time, Kendall."

Now I bite my lip. "What do you have in store for me?" Visions of extra-long needles sucking fluids out of me while I'm strapped down to a gurney in a straitjacket cross my mind. This is definitely my imagination in overdrive.

Dr. Kindberg stands and opens a door to an adjoining room. Ahhh, the torture chamber. Or maybe not. "First off, I have several tests I'd like to do with you. Nothing intrusive. Some mind exercises to see how good you really are. I like to test for precognition and extrasensory perception. It's a good way to gauge if a patient is faking for the sake of attention, has a severe medical problem, or really does possess the skills you think you do."

I don't *think* I possess psychic abilities; I *know* I do. And I also know something else that Ken Kindberg, MD, PhD, doesn't know. I have Emily with me. My ace in the hole.

"Let the games begin," I say with a smile.

"Okay, Kendall. I want you to breathe, relax, and concentrate." Dr. Kindberg sits across the table from me and shuffles an ordinary-looking deck of cards.

"Watch out," I say with a grin. "I'm killer at blackjack."

He laughs and lays out five cards in front of me, face-up. "These are Zener cards. We use them in a guessing game to test if a patient might have extrasensory perception. They were invented by a well-known psychologist named Karl Zener. There are twenty-five cards, made up of these symbols."

I glance down at the cards laid out.

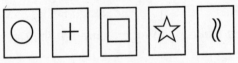

"These are the cards I want you to concentrate on," he informs me. "I'm going to shuffle more and then take a card out of the deck one at a time. You won't see the face, but I'll ask you to identify the symbol on the card. And we'll keep going through the deck until you've had enough or are tired."

Dr. K. reaches for a clipboard with some sort of score sheet on it. Geez, what if I can't do this and I fail? Then he'll think

I'm a fraud and not really experiencing these conversations with spirits. As he turns over the first card and looks at it, my pulse accelerates. How will I know which symbol to pick? Will it be right? Wrong? Holy crap! This is worse than calculus!

"Relax, Kendall," he repeats. "Focus on the card. Trust your instincts."

I open my mouth to speak, but he stops me.

"There's no rush."

I close my eyes, picturing the rows of cards: circle, cross, square, star, squiggly thing.

"Squiggly thing," I say.

Not saying a word, Dr. K. makes a mark on his chart.

"Well?"

"I'll go over the results with you when we're done."

I slump a bit in the chair, wanting immediate gratification. Guess I'll just have to be patient. I try to relax and control my breathing so I can see the cards in my mind's eye. He picks up another one and holds it up, the design facing toward him. It's not like I can make anything out through the thickness of the card.

"Star."

Another card.

It's a square, Emily whispers to me.

Ugh! I wish she wouldn't tell me. "Square." What? She already told me.

"Circle," I say for the next one, after a few moments.

This one's a cross . . .

Put off, I smack my hands on the table. "Would you stop?"

Dr. K. widens his eyes. "We just started."

"No, not you." I close my mouth before I say too much. "Sorry. Go ahead."

We go through the entire pack with me reporting each geometric shape. Over a hundred, at least. Emily gave me only a handful of the answers. Though doesn't that prove I talk to spirits, if one is helping me out?

Last card. I'm exhausted. It's like my mind's been on a treadmill or something. I don't think I have the strength to make another guess.

You're tired, Kendall. It's a circle . . .

"Emily! I told you not to tell me!"

Dr. K. slowly looks up at me. "Who's Emily?"

I panic. "No one."

"Kendall, you have to trust me with the truth."

Tell him . . .

I swallow hard. "Emily is the spirit who lives in my house and . . . helps me out."

"I see," he says. "Is she helping you out now?"

I fold my hands together on top of the table, trying not to wring them together. "Yeah, I'm sorry. I only listened to a few of her answers. I really wanted to do this on my own."

He doesn't seem fazed by this at all. Then I remember he deals with kids like me all the time. I only hope I'm one of the ones he actually believes.

"How many answers did Emily assist with?"

"About a dozen," I say.

Swiftly moving his pen across the score sheet, Dr. Kindberg tallies up my results. "You're either very lucky or Emily was giving you the correct answers."

"Seriously?" Why do I feel like dancing? "So how'd I do?"

"Very impressive," he tells me. "You scored in the very high range, Kendall, showing significant psychic ability. Mind you, this is only one measure and we still have a lot of testing to do." He gathers up the cards, straightens them, and places them back into the cardboard container.

My intuition tells me that he sort of thinks I'm full of shit.

"You don't believe me, do you?"

He reaches up and scrubs his left hand through his crewcut. "I'm not here to judge, Kendall. I'm here to test and diagnose and talk and decide the best course of action for you."

Dude thinks I'm completely insane. Oh, right . . . I have a spirit that talks to me in my head. Can't exactly prove that to anyone. It's not like any of these adults—except Loreen and maybe Father Massimo—would take me at my word.

We can convince him together, Emily suggests.

How?

I'm here to help you . . .

"Let's go back into the office," he says, holding his arm out to escort me. "I'm very impressed with your perception, Kendall. But I'm still concerned that you're hearing voices and getting headaches and physical traumas." He sits at his desk; I sit in the chair.

"It's just Emily most of the time. Unless it's during a ghost investigation. Then I usually pick up the spirits in the area we're in. Sometimes we get EVPs—you know, electronic voice phenomena—that match what the spirits are saying to me."

"And the headaches?"

I shrug. "The headaches mostly warn me when something's up. Like when I first met Emily. Turns out she's been with me my whole life and I'm just now able to see her again. When I was little, my parents told me I shouldn't have an imaginary friend, and I believed them."

"She's not imaginary then?" he asks, taking more notes.

"No. She's very real."

He wants proof, Emily observes.

Then let's give it to him.

Emily appears near him, directly behind his chair. "Mention law school to him."

I clear my throat. "Umm, Emily says I should talk to you about law school?"

Dr. Kindberg's clearly taken aback. His mouth drops open. "What about law school?"

Smiling at me, Emily says, "He took the LSAT and applied to six law schools. However, he didn't accept any of the offers he got."

"Why didn't you take any of the acceptances you received?" I ask. "You had, like, five of them, didn't you?"

I love when an adult is speechless, especially a professional one like this who my parents are paying top dollar for. I continue to listen to what Emily is sharing with me. It's sort of a sad story about the young Ken Kindberg.

"Holy crap, Dr. Kindberg. Your mom got cancer and so you didn't go to law school? That's the saddest thing ever." I put my hand to my heart, feeling the skittering beat.

"How . . . how do you know that?"

"I don't. But Emily does," I explain. "She says that you nursed your mom through her chemo and radiation treatments for a year before the cancer took her. She . . . she . . . oh my God. She went a bit crazy, didn't she? Poor woman. Almost like Alzheimer's. She was paranoid about everything and talking to herself. Oh, stop, Emily. I'm so sorry your mom died, Dr. Kindberg." The emotional tension in the room rises like a tsunami. It's like the walls are going to cave in and suffocate me from the sorrow and grief coming from him.

I can tell that the man is blown away. Shock is etched all over his face, although he remains calm. "Very impressive, Kendall. Very few people know of my mother's suffering."

"I'm sorry. I wasn't trying to—"

"No, no, nothing to apologize for. It was a difficult time for me, true; you obviously picked up on that. I've been torturing you a bit, so you felt you should do the same."

I jump to my feet. "God, no! I was just saying what Emily told me to say." I look past him to her. "Emily!"

"I wanted to show him that you're—that we're—for real."

"I needed to prove my abilities to you," I say softly.

He nods. "That you did." Dr. Kindberg stands and goes to

the door. "Let's bring your mother back in here to discuss the next step, shall we?"

I stop him with my hand on his arm. This information I don't get from Emily; I sense it myself. "Your mother knows you went to medical school. And that you went into psychiatry to help people like her who couldn't help themselves." I choke back the tears gathering in my throat. "She's very proud of you."

Dr. Kindberg reaches over and rubs my hand. "Thank you for that, Kendall."

He turns and leaves to go get Mom.

Phew! I'm completely worn out.

"Well? How'd she do?" Mom asks, like I've just finished a midterm.

"Mrs. Moorehead, I'm quite impressed with what I've seen from your daughter. Based on our conversations, I believe she does possess some psychic abilities. However, I'd like to schedule a full physical and a review with a neurologist. And I think it would be best for her to have a CT scan to rule out any pressure on the brain."

"Of course, Doctor," Mom says.

Here I thought I'd just proven myself. Great.

Let the poking and prodding begin.

CHAPTER EIGHT

ON MONDAY, BECCA ASIAF JUMPS ME the moment I step foot into the cafeteria for lunch. "You've heard, right?"

"Heard what?"

Celia's next to me and Becca glares hard, then growls, "You didn't tell her?"

"Tell me what?"

"I haven't really, like, had a chance," Celia says defensively.

I look back and forth between the two girls, confused as all get-out. "What's going on here?"

Taylor bounds into the cafeteria, her ponytail swaying like Indiana Jones's whip. "Oh my God, y'all! Courtney's done it this time! I can't believe her."

"Time out on the floor," I say emphatically. "What. Is. Going. On?"

Taylor's eyes get wide as she stares at Celia and Becca. "Y'all didn't tell her yet?"

Grabbing a fistful of her own hair, Celia groans. "What am I, nine-one-one?"

"Four-one-one, you mean." Becca takes charge. "Sit down, Kendall. You gotta hear this."

Jesus in the garden. What now? What more do I have to take, after spending all day Saturday with the psychiatrist and then being in the car with my mother, who didn't believe what he'd told her? That Kendall "does possess some psychic abilities." She hadn't wanted to hear that. She won't be convinced until all reports are in, which entails another visit to Atlanta. Sunday was church, laundry, working on my history paper, and talking to Jason over IM. I haven't really steeled myself for any additional melodrama at Radisson High School, although that's terribly naive of me.

"Can I at least get some food first? I think my blood sugar is in the negative numbers." My stomach groans to back me up.

Becca slides her unopened Diet Coke across the table. "This'll have to do for now. We've got problems."

I can't take any more. "You guys! What's going on?"

Taylor reaches her tanned hand over and lightly scratches me with her carnation pink fingernails. "Kendall. You're not the only psychic in town anymore."

Chuckling, I say, "I know. There's Loreen too."

Becca flattens her lips, ruby red against her pale white skin and jet-black hair. "No, she's talking about that royal bitch Courtney Langdon."

"What? That's a joke."

When all three of my friends just stare at me, I flick open

the soda and down three deep sips, hoping to quench the sudden fiery sensation burning my esophagus. I squelch the inevitable burp and nod at Becca to continue.

She leans her elbows onto the table as if to hide the conversation from others. "I saw her in the bathroom this morning —not throwing up her corn flakes, for once—and she was holding court with a bunch of freshman and sophomore girls. She was tellin' them that she'd read this book over the weekend on opening yourself up, and now she's coming into her own 'psychic awakening.' That anyone can do it; we all possess the ability. We just have to tune in to it and recognize it, like she's done."

"Dear God," I say with a long sigh, knowing exactly what book she's referring to. The book I asked her to read so she'd understand *me* more and not lash out with such hatred. So *I* created this monster, eh?

"Keep going," Taylor says to Becca.

"I'm going, I'm going! So anyway," she continues, "Courtney was saying that she's suddenly getting messages from a spirit guide. A great-grandmother of hers or something or other. And—get this—the messages are coming to her through her Bluetooth."

"Her phone?" I don't freakin' believe this.

Celia snorts derisively. "It's true that cell phones work on a certain frequency and might be able to pick up voices not discernible by the human ear, but it's highly unlikely that a spirit could manipulate the device to place an actual phone call to—"

I lift my hand up. "Hold on, Cel. I need to hear more of this before we start analyzing."

Taylor's face becomes animated. "She was telling this freshman girl all sorts of *détails personnels* about her that this girl swore no one else knew."

"Like what?"

"I don't know," Taylor says. "Like who she has a crush on and stuff like that."

"That doesn't prove anything," Celia chimes in, obviously annoyed by the whole situation. "Anyone who pays attention in the hallways, cafeteria, and parking lot after school can decipher who's zooming who around here."

I spin around, looking for the manipulative little impostor. "Where is she?" My senses tell me to look out the window of the caf into the courtyard. It's where the smokers usually hang out, but right now I see that it's the bully pulpit for Courtney. She's sitting on top of one of the picnic tables, waving her arms and expounding to the crowd that's gathered—cheerleaders, jocks, and those brave enough to wander into her social circle —on her alleged new abilities.

Deep down, in that (genuine) intuitive part of me, I know the girl is full of shit. Full of her own shit, for that matter. But I have no way to prove that she's campaigning for a Daytime Emmy with this new act of hers.

I reach over and grab Becca by the wrist. "Come on. We're going out there."

Celia's in too. "She's making a mockery of your gift and of what we're doing with our investigations."

I can tell Celia's wicked pissed 'cause she's got this frown line between her eyes that's deepening by the minute. She better be careful or she'll have to start using age-defying moisturizers for that. Why am I even thinking such absurd thoughts at this moment? Maybe I'm in shock. Maybe I've astral-projected from my body and am watching this all from afar, unable to absorb the depth of Courtney's loathing of me. I run my hands up and down my body. Nope, I'm still here.

Celia raises an eyebrow at me. "Do I even want to know?"

I shake my head and lead the way outside.

We weave through the impressive crowd that's gathered around the concrete picnic tables. Courtney, wearing a short plaid skirt, white blouse, and a blue sweater tied around her neck, à la Blair from *Gossip Girl* meets naughty Catholic school girl, sits with her knee-socked legs crossed, her eyes closed, and one finger pressed against the silver Bluetooth in her left ear. Mina Moutzourogeorgos, a sophomore, sits in front of her, enthralled.

"I see that you . . . made . . ." Courtney pauses for effect. "An eighty-nine on your Spanish exam."

"I did?" Mina exclaims. "I thought I'd totally failed it and was going to get thrown off SGA."

"Nothing to worry about," Courtney says through her

bleached-white teeth. Then she points at this short black girl with awesome braids down to her waist. "You're worried about your English class, aren't you?"

The girl nods, her mouth open in awe.

"Don't worry, sugar," Courtney says, so syrupy sweet. "Mrs. Flynn has been moody lately. It's because she's—" She stops and listens for a moment. "My spirit guide is telling me that it's because she is refinancing her mortgage and things aren't going well."

The crowd gasps. Even Taylor lets out a little yelp.

"You have to understand she's very concerned about her personal finances right now, but she'll be fine soon, and then your troubles in class will be better," Courtney explains.

"Word," the girl says back.

Courtney's self-aggrandizing smile really is annoying. "Who's next?"

Taylor's pretty face turns beet red, like she's about to explode. Then she does. "Courtney Langdon! You're just a big old phony! *Vous devriez avoir honte!*"

Courtney turns to her. "What did you say?"

I try to stop Taylor, but it's too late.

"Shame . . . shame on you! How can you do this? You're just starved for attention."

"Oh, and like *you're* not starved for attention, Taylor Tillson?"

"What do you mean?" Taylor asks.

Unfazed, Courtney moves her hand to her ear and pauses as

information seems to be given to her. However, I'm not picking up on any kind of spirit energies here at all. *Nada*. Zilch. Zero. Not even a wisp of Emily. Wouldn't I be able to connect with Courtney's spirit guide or sense it if it's here? If it really *is* here? Probably so. Something stinks in rural America, though. I'm seeing a hazy mist around Courtney that confuses me. It's a deep, almost murky pink hue.

"What are you picking up?" Celia asks in a whisper.

"Her aura's mucked up."

"How so?"

I lower my voice. "Loreen's been teaching me this stuff. Anything in the red family relates to a person's physical body. The denser the color, the more friction there is. And this girl's got density out the wazoo."

Celia turns to look but obviously can't see what I'm observing. "I so wish I could do what you do," she says.

"Apparently, so does Courtney." I look again as the pink atmosphere around her shifts, becoming deeper, almost angrier. "I'm seeing a light form of red that means immaturity—"

"Duh."

"—and someone of a dishonest nature."

"Double duh," Celia says. "Was there a picture of Courtney in the book next to that definition?"

I lift my eyebrows in recognition. "This isn't going to end well."

Celia quotes one of my favorite sayings: "I don't have to be psychic to figure *that* out."

While we've been discussing Courtney's aura, Taylor's been engaged in verbal fisticuffs. I need to get her under control. I don't know if she's protecting me or simply lashing out at Courtney for how she treated Jason after he broke up with her. He's protective of his sister, but she's as defensive of him. Must be a twin thing. I don't feel like this is the time for such a confrontation—I mean, I'm holding myself back—but Taylor is hell-bent on contention, literally shaking her fist at Courtney.

"Shame on me?" Courtney asks. "I think it's shame on you, Taylor. Shame on you and all of the dirty little secrets you and your family are keeping from everyone in town."

Taylor freezes in place and I grab her hand. Her pulse drills rapidly underneath her skin, so I squeeze tightly so she knows I'm here for her.

"Wh-wh-what do you mean?" she asks, her bottom lip quivering.

Courtney lasers her eyes at my friend. "Why don't you tell everyone how your mother went crazy and drove your father out of town and now she's seeing a shrink in Atlanta so she doesn't completely lose it?"

Taylor gasps so intensely that I think she's going to pass out cold from the intake of so much air.

Is what Courtney is saying true? I never picked that up. Neither Taylor nor Jason told us about any of this. How in the world does Courtney know it? Can she be for real? Certainly not! After reading one book? It doesn't work like that.

Though . . . judge not, lest you be judged and all of that, right?

Taylor's eyes fill with tears and she turns and rushes off. Becca runs after her, probably to keep from beating hell and four dollars out of Courtney.

"Yeah, that's what I thought," she says with a contemptuous laugh. "Now, who's next?"

I slink away as Courtney continues her "reading" with one of the guys from the wrestling team. Celia's eyes connect with mine and she wrinkles her nose.

"You know how I'm a true believer in the paranormal?" she asks.

I nod wordlessly.

Celia sneers in Courtney's general direction. "This is total horseshit."

We turn to go back into the caf when Courtney shouts out at me, "Hey, Ghost Girl!" She flips her hair away from her face, revealing her Bluetooth. "Guess you're not so special now."

"'Let every eye negotiate for itself,'" I mutter to Celia.

"Yeah, that might be from *Much Ado About Nothing,*" she says, "but this Mean Girl is making much ado about everything. We're going to get to the bottom of this."

I slip away from the girls, debating how to investigate what Courtney's up to, and find a quiet spot in the back of the library so I can gather my thoughts and meditate some. Loreen did a shaman cleansing for me a few weeks back and taught me some good breathing techniques. I need to use them now to focus on Courtney's energies and find a way to battle her without losing my cool.

I picture the air rushing into my lungs and then being expelled as I breathe out. I concentrate on my chest rising and falling, letting my stress and nerves unknot with each inhale and exhale. In my mind, I go to a peaceful, relaxing place. A beach, where my toes can dig into the warm wet sand. A sea bird flies by and squawks. The horn of a departing cruise ship sounds in the distance. The waves break over one another, splashing to the shore in fingers of salty foam.

Yes. This is working. I can feel my pulse slowing, the pressure in my chest easing.

She's using her phone . . . Emily breaks in abruptly.

"Good God!" I say, then clamp my hand over my mouth. "I had the whole relaxation thing going, Emily!"

Mrs. Langstein, the librarian, peeks around a stack of books and places her finger to her lips. I mouth *sorry* and close my eyes again.

Emily . . . I was trying to relax.

I'm trying to help you figure out what Courtney's doing.

I know what she's doing. She's being an ass. She's not psychic at all.

She's not and I know it. Courtney's not pure of heart and she certainly has no appreciation for a gift such as the one I have. All she's doing is making light of my God-given ability for her own entertainment. I twirl my hair around my pinkie and stare at the book cart in front of me. Suddenly, the mist in my brain clears, and I know what I have to do.

She's using her cell phone to get her information.

Exactly . . . , Emily says.

That's it! It's easy enough to prove. All I have to do is view Courtney's call list and see who's calling her and feeding her the information. It's not like spirit guides have caller ID, so it's got to be one of her minions.

I reach for my phone and scroll over to the address book to pull up Celia's information, where I text:

>I no what she's up 2. More l8r!

At my locker, I tug out my physiology textbook and note-pad and rush to lab. Ms. Pritchard has our fetal piglets in place—*ewww, why do I have to do this after lunch*—so I wash my hands in the lab sink, dry them on a paper towel, and then slip on my plastic gloves. Poor little piggy.

I need to do something to separate Courtney from her phone without it being obvious. How to . . . how to . . .

As I'm thinking all sorts of dubious thoughts, Celia texts me:

>Heard CL tell Stephanie she's not feeling well. Sense trip 2 b'room.

Just then, Courtney flounces in and tosses her backpack haphazardly onto the counter. She goes over to talk to Jim Roach, and that's when I get my idea.

>I'm on it.

I pull out the sheet of directions on fetal pig dissection and wait for my lab partner to return. Eventually, she quits flirting and returns to the stool opposite me, where I stare her down with a smile on my face.

"What?"

"Nothing," I say sweetly. "Just ready to get to work."

She flips her hair over her shoulder and reaches for the plastic gloves. "What do we have to do?"

Reading from the sheet, I say, "Today, we're working on the abdominal cavity. We've got to work on and label the large intestines"—I pick at the pig—"oooh, they're like big coils all fused together. And it's right next to the other thing we need to take care of, the small intestines."

If I can believe my eyes, Courtney's usually rosy complexion is starting to turn green. Time for me to administer the final blow. Using my scalpel, I point out, "This must be the small intestines 'cause it's this wicked gnarly mass of coiled tubes here in the bottom of the cavity. The workbook says it's held in place by a tissue called the mesentery. Oh, wow, Courtney, check this out!"

She holds her breath and pinches her nose with her gloved fingers. "What?"

"That mesentery thing looks just like the spaghetti they had in the caf at lunch. Did you eat it?"

With that, Courtney covers her mouth and nose with her

hand and I hear her smother a gag. She stands up hastily, knocking her stool off balance. Then she tugs her Bluetooth off her ear and throws it onto the counter next to her bag.

She says, "Tell Ms. Pritchard I'm gonna be sick" and quickly retraces her steps out the door, no doubt to rid herself of caf's said spaghetti special.

Well, that couldn't have gone more perfectly. I know it's not exactly the classiest thing I've ever done, but the beeyotch had it coming after the way she treated poor Taylor. The only way to exact revenge for—or at least answer—her actions is to find out what's behind her sudden "powers."

The silver shine of her Bluetooth phone beckons to me. I know it's, like, an invasion of privacy and stuff, but it's just sitting there on the black countertop. I grab it and pull it under the table so no one can see what I'm doing. How does this even work? There's no readout, no display, just a button to turn it on. How do you make a stupid phone call on this?

I frantically text Celia of all things techie and impatiently wait for her response.

>That's only a receiver!!! Check her actual cell.

I am so not cut out for the world of intrigue. I feel like all eyes in the room are on me, but in actuality, everyone is busy with the pigs. Luckily for me, Courtney's cell phone is in the side pocket of her book bag. Gritting my teeth, I slip it out and sneak it under the table. Flip. Light. Ahhh . . . I thumb through the sections to find Recent Calls. There are three numbers, so I jot all of them down. One has the ID F. Lewis, which is undoubtedly Courtney's cheering partner Farah. The other two have no names. No worries; Celia can find out later who they belong to.

Just as I put the cell back in its pocket, a very pale Courtney returns to the classroom. Ms. Pritchard checks her status and excuses her for having to leave class so abruptly.

Phew! Maybe I *can* get used to this secret spy stuff!

CHAPTER NINE

IN STUDY HALL THE NEXT DAY, I meet up with Celia, Becca, and Jason.

Oh yeah, the boyfriend. I have so neglected him. He is soooo damn gorgeous, sitting there in a blue button-down that matches his eyes and a pair of black cargo pants. After this Courtney brouhaha is over, he and I are going to need some serious alone time. Together. No ghost huntress team. No EMF detectors. No anybody. Just us.

"So what did you get?" Celia asks me, bringing my mind back to said brouhaha. She reaches her hands forward like a child grabbing at a new toy.

"I think you should maybe pursue a career in the FBI instead of in parapsychology," I suggest and then give the phone numbers to her. She flips open her laptop and boots it up.

"I was right. The Bluetooth is the key to Courtney's abilities," I say.

"I'm on it," Celia says.

Across the table, Becca cracks her knuckles and frowns.

"Why don't you just have me and Dragon let the air out of her tires?"

"Classy, Asiaf," Celia says. "Real classy."

Sitting back, Becca snickers. "I'm into class. It's a brand-new thing for me."

We all laugh until the study hall monitor shushes us.

While Celia's hacking a nearby Internet connection, I fan some textbooks out in front of me, but I can feel Jason's stare on my face. I glance over, and he seems worried.

I thread my fingers through his. He puts his other hand on top of our joined ones and rubs softly. He's so warm and caring . . . I just want to put him in my pocket and take him home. (Oh man, these Southern sayings are already rubbing off on me!)

"Is Taylor okay?" I whisper while still holding on to him. He rests my hand on his upper thigh—*hello!*—and lets out a pent-up sigh.

"No, she's embarrassed like nobody's business and is rip-shit mad at Courtney. So am I."

"Did you tell her that, about your mom . . . you know, being in therapy?"

"No!" he says, too loudly.

Celia puts her index finger to her lips. Becca could care less as she listens to her MP3 player with the headphones on.

"Why didn't you tell me about things at home? I knew some of it, but not all of it."

He laughs, his blue eyes sparkling to life. "Right. 'Hey, Kendall, will you be my girlfriend even though my mom's a nutjob and my dad split and my home life is totally fu—"

"Jason! Don't say that! Like I've got this perfect life? Ghost Girl?"

He rolls those beautiful eyes. "That is *not* your nickname."

"In some circles of RHS, it is," I say sadly. "This isn't about me right now. Is your mom okay?"

His shoulders lift and then fall. "I reckon. I mean, she just sort of lost it one day and totally shut down. Dad couldn't get her to talk to him, and Taylor and I just stayed out of the way. Next thing you knew, Dad left, and Mom was making sure her insurance would cover some pretty serious psychotropic drugs. She's bipolar and was even suicidal for a while."

"Is she okay now?"

"The medicine's working," Jason says.

And here I've been worried about what my mother might put me on when Mrs. Tillson's getting along fine with her chemical dependence.

"What gets me," he says, "is how the hell did Courtney know? Mom's been so paranoid about what people in town would think. That's why she's been going to Atlanta to the doctor. And she's been filling her prescriptions up there instead of at the drugstores here in Radisson." He lifts his free hand to run it through his blond hair. "I've tried so hard to protect her."

"You can't, Jason. *She's* the parent. You can only take care of yourself."

His hand moves over mine, rubbing softly. "And Taylor. And you."

I shake my hair. "You don't have to take care of me."

"Yeah, I do," he says with a half smile and his head cocked to one side. "You're my girlfriend."

I smile too and I swear I feel a blush spread from head to toe. "I like being that."

"Me too." Then he leans over and kisses me fast, before anyone can comment or tell him not to do it.

"I've got it!" Celia sounds out.

"Shhh!" comes from behind us.

I slant down onto the table. "Spill it!"

Celia places her black hair behind her ears and takes out a pen. "Okay, well, you know that Bluetooth is this wireless protocol that utilizes short-range communications technology to facilitate data transfers over short distances from fixed and/or mobile devices, like a BlackBerry or a—"

Becca interrupts. "Jesus, Nichols! Who gives a shit! Get to the point. When can I kick Courtney's ass up around her nose?"

I hold my hand up. "'Be comforted: / Let's make us med'cines of our great revenge, / To cure this deadly grief.'"

"Huh?" Becca asks.

Celia reaches over and high-fives me. "Good one, Moorehead! Ahh . . . *Macbeth,* act four, scene three."

I nod proudly.

"Y'all are weird," Becca says with a smirk. "What's the bottom line, Nichols?"

"Courtney's a big phony."

Jason harrumphs. "You just figured this out now?"

"I knew it!" I did. There's no way she became psychic over-night.

Celia explains. "The calls during the lunch hour when she was putting on her little stage show were from Farah Lewis, Courtney's father's office, and Mina herself."

"Right. I assumed Mina's reading was a gag to get things started," I say. "Why the call from her father's office?"

Jason responds. "Her dad owns Radisson Mortgage Brokers, which is probably where Mrs. Flynn has all of her paperwork. That's how Courtney knew about her mortgage problems."

"That explains it," Becca chimes in. "And the stuff about your mom?"

Celia turns her computer around to show the home page of the Radisson chapter of the Daughters of the American Confederacy. In the front row is Jason and Taylor's mom, and she's sitting next to Georgia Moutzourogeorgos, Mina's mother. "Mina must have heard something that your mother shared in confidence. It all makes sense now." She pauses for a moment. "Actually, if we hadn't reacted on such an emotional level straightaway to all of this—Taylor particularly—we might have been able to use our own female intuition to put the puzzle pieces together and see that Courtney's a fake psychic. This is a desperate plea for help, I think."

"Bullshit," Becca spews. "It's a desperate plea for atten-tion."

An idea hits me. "I think I have a way to show her up."

"How?" Celia asks.

"We plant some information," I say. "Then we'll call her on it. In public."

"Works for me," Jason says. "I'll sell tickets for it."

Celia gives me a thumbs-up. "The only way that could be more brilliant is if I had thought it up."

I turn to Becca. "You in?"

She shrugs. "I suppose so. I still say me and Dragon let the air out of her tires."

I crack up laughing and don't care who hushes me. "Maybe as a last resort."

While Jason is at track practice, he lets me borrow the Jeep (thank God it's an automatic!) to run errands for my mom and to take Becca home after school.

I pull into the driveway of the plain one-story brick house and shut off the ignition. Turning to the Goth girl next to me, I say, "I really appreciate that you stood up for me. And Taylor too."

Becca twirls her diamond stud nose ring. "Courtney's always been a selfish cow, even when we were little. You shouldn't take it personally."

"But I *am* taking it personally because, well . . . it's directed at me!"

"You're just different and new to town and people have taken to you. She can't deal."

"Neither can I," I mumble.

"My dad always says *Illegitimi non carborundum*."

I lay my head on the steering wheel. "Oh God, not you too! How many languages do I have to take to keep up with you, Taylor, and Celia?"

Becca smiles. A beautiful vibrant one, I notice, with straight teeth. The teeth of a former beauty queen and a current Goth princess. "It means 'Don't let the bastards grind you down.' And in this case, Courtney Langdon would be said bastard."

I nod vigorously.

Becca slides out of the Jeep and reaches for her black satchel. "Hey, you wanna come in for a soda?"

I glance at my watch. "I've got to get the Jeep back to Jason after my errands, but maybe for a sec?"

I follow Becca through the carport and up three stairs into her kitchen. It's a modest design. Clean and white with Formica countertops; I can't tell if they're a modern-day nod to the past or if they're the real thing. A small table sits off in the right corner, next to a window overlooking a backyard grown tall with wildflowers, grass, and weeds. An in-ground swimming pool is covered with a royal blue tarp thatched with leaves that have fallen from the nearby pecan tree.

"Take a load off." She drops her stuff in front of the counter, where the telephone is mounted on the wall. "Let's see what we've got."

I take a seat in one of the ladder-back chairs and suddenly get this overwhelming sense of sadness rushing through me, like white-water rapids. My breathing falters and I want to cry rivers of tears for the loss I'm feeling around me. This chair belonged to someone dear. My heart *hurts* like someone is pounding me in the chest. Nothing in my life has felt like this. Well, maybe when I lost Grandma Ethel. What can this be?

Becca tosses a silver can my way. "All we've got is Fresca. Is that cool?"

"Yeah, sure," I manage to eke out.

"I gotta pee, BRB."

Laughing, I say, "I thought being classy was going to be your new thing."

"That wore off." Then she disappears through the den and down a hallway to the left.

I don't know much about Rebecca "Becca" Asiaf other than what I've learned from Celia and Taylor. Most of the info doesn't ring true with the DJ Goth girl I see every day at school. According to my friends, Becca was a regular in local beauty pageants—until last year. Now she sticks to herself when she's not around us, or she hangs with the tough kids like Brent Dragisich and his other crotch-rocket-riding buddies. Ghost hunting for her seems more like a pastime than the calling it is for Celia and me.

I pop the top on the Fresca and take a long sip. It's citrusy and cold, but the ache in my heart is still there. There's a lot of place memory or residual energy here. Not necessarily a spirit present, but a residue of someone's soul and how he or she affected others while here. However, I can feel one memory vividly, as if I lived it myself: It's an old woman with a gray bun at the back of her head. She's shelling peas at the table, right where I'm sitting. I stand up and move around the kitchen, still picking up the strong vibe. My left ear starts to ring like I've been underwater too long. I'm drawn to a closed door next to the television—which looks neither cable ready nor HD capable—and am aware of pure energy radiating from behind here. I know it's closed for a reason, yet I reach forward to twist the knob and then venture in to pinpoint the source of my emotions.

The door creaks open into a dark, musty formal living room with heavy gold drapes pulled closed to keep any light out. I fight the urge to sneeze at the dust gathered up; my tongue tickles the roof of my mouth to prevent it. I gasp as I look around the room. It's one trophy case after another, each shelf filled with crowns, banners, scepters, and awards—some that are nearly five feet tall. Also on the shelves are dust-covered pictures showing a much younger Becca wearing beautiful pageant dresses and posing, singing, or twirling a baton. As a child, she was really gorgeous, even model-like, with her flowing chestnut hair. Her face, skin as porcelain as a fine China doll's, shows happiness, poise, and grace. Class is obviously her "old" thing.

I walk over to one framed photo in particular: it's of the woman I saw in my mind. I pick it up in my hand, and memories —someone else's—rush through me. There's an older lady dressed in her Sunday best standing next to Becca, who's around age thirteen and wearing her Peanut Festival Queen crown. The woman's smile is so bright that her eyes are crinkled shut. Becca has never looked happier.

I have no words to amply describe the sorrow I feel near me. Misery fills my chest in an anvil of pain, heavy and burdensome. Doubts swirl overhead, and I don't know where they're stemming from. A baton lies abandoned in the corner of the room, as does a set of twirling knives and a tattered pair of ballet shoes.

What could have caused this immense grief that flows through this house like it's circulated by an HVAC unit? How did this amazingly gorgeous girl end up dyeing her hair black, piercing her lip and nose—and God knows what else—and turning into a social loner who hangs out with me, Ghost Girl?

Another wave of anguish splashes over me, causing me to grip the closest bookshelf for support.

"Oh, Becca . . ."

Then I hear, "What the hell do you think you're doing in here?"

CHAPTER TEN

"I'M . . . I'M SORRY, Becca."

She glowers at me and takes the photo out of my hands. She slams it back in place on the shelf, rattling some of the ribboned medals that hang loosely around one of the trophies.

Not knowing exactly how to cover up this bumble, I compliment her on all of the plaques and awards. "You should be wicked proud of all these. Why do you keep it all shut up in the dark?"

Becca's top teeth snag her bottom lip. Then she says, "It's really none of your business, Kendall. You shouldn't be in here."

"I said I'm sorry. I was just drawn in."

"How so?"

"There was this intense energy that called to me."

"It called to you, huh? Well, next time, don't answer."

"I didn't mean to offend—"

She hands me Jason's keys, which I left on the counter. "You know, I just remembered I have a lot of studying to do. I'm sure Jason needs his Jeep by now."

I've just been given the teenage equivalent of "Here's your hat, what's your hurry," I suppose. "Sure, I should get going." I nab the opened Fresca from the table and take it with me. "Thanks for the bevvie."

As I'm leaving, Becca stops me. "Look, Kendall. You're cool and we're friends. But there's no ghost investigating here, okay? This is my house and it's off-limits."

"Sure, Becca."

"As long as we're square."

"Whatever you say. See you tomorrow."

I hurry back to Jason's Jeep and back out of the driveway. When I turn to look at the house, I see one of the large, gold drapes in the trophy room fall into place. Becca's hiding something from me. Question is: how do I find out what?

"The bait is on the hook," Becca tells me Wednesday morning.

Celia and I are standing outside the girls' bathroom waiting to set the trap for Courtney. The aforementioned bait is Mina Moutzourogeorgos, who, according to Becca, just entered a stall. I sort of feel bad about what we're doing, but then again, I'm not the one who started this feud. I'm also not the one calling people names or spilling food on them. We're just trying to get Courtney to come clean and stop acting like head bitch in charge.

"Good luck," Celia says to me and then we swing into the ladies'.

I muster up my best acting abilities—I was in a Christmas pageant at church when I was ten, but I only played one of the sheep at the manger, so I don't know if that counts—and then I do my best to start crying.

"Are we alone?"

"I think so," Celia says, really trying to find Mina. "Why?"

"I have a secret. No one can know. Especially Courtney."

"Cross my heart," she says.

"J-J-Jason broke up with me," I say dramatically.

"Why?" Celia chimes in, even though she's bent over, looking under the doors. She gives me an okay sign when she sees Mina's trademark red stilettos lift off the floor. "Y'all are perfect for each other."

"That's what I thought too." I try to project my voice to where Mina's hiding, make sure she hears every word. "But he told me it's Courtney he really loves and he's still all hung up on her. He broke it off with me because he says I'm not so special now that Courtney's psychic too. He wants her back." I add a little breakage in my voice at the end, for effect.

"Oh, Kendall, that's awful," Celia says and then rolls her eyes at me. "It'll be okay."

"No, it won't. How will I hold my head up? You can't tell anyone that I told you. Swear?"

"Sure, whatever." I knock her with my elbow. She's not doing a good enough acting job. "Oh, right. No, I won't tell anyone. I swear on my dog Seamus's life."

I lower my voice to a whisper. "Now you're just overdoing it."

We leave the bathroom and head around the corner to hide behind Mr. Lowry's door and see if Mina got the message. Sure enough, a moment later, Mina emerges from the bathroom with her cell phone to her ear, relaying my convo with Celia.

"Excellent," Celia says and drills her fingertips together. "Now we just have to wait and see what happens."

The lunchroom is all abuzz today. Gossip and rumors are flying this way and that. Man, you gotta love high school and how news gets around. People look at me with gloom in their faces. Yeah, they know. Mina's game of pass-it-on has been, well, passed on. I don't care so much about what random sophomores think; I want to see what Courtney's going to do with this info.

As usual, I grab a tray and slowly move through the lunch line. Mmm . . . roast turkey, dressing, and cranberry sauce. It's only October, but I'm game for a Thanksgiving preview. I pay the cashier and then turn to catch Taylor's eye. She's so good at getting a table for us and spreading out so no one invades our turf.

The music today is a particularly Trance-y groove, with delayed synthesizers and an upbeat, positive, energetic composition. Becca's taught me a bunch about this stuff since I've been here. Songs carry their own energy, I've found, and I'm sure that it's Becca's talent with her DJ equipment that makes her such a great EVP specialist. I really hope I didn't offend her yesterday at her house. Sometimes I just can't control myself. I need to learn how to keep my psychic abilities in check. I don't have to respond to *every* spirit or sensation calling out to me.

"Awesome mix today, Becca."

She slips the headphones off one ear and smiles at me.

"I'm really sorry about yesterday."

Waving me off, she clicks another iPod to her mixing board. "I'm on a music high right now."

"I can tell."

"There's nothing like this. A new DJ I discovered, DJ Adian from South Africa. This shit's layered with three-oh-three bass pulses, Doppler effects, sequencer riffs, and stacks of percussion, and builds up to a climactic tension."

I'm relieved to see she's not harboring any ill will toward me. She's really into this; it's almost like talking to Celia. Not knowing what to say, I smile. "Cool. You should charge for this, you know? You're really good."

Becca lifts her hands in a who-knows gesture. "One day I want to go spin in Europe. We'll see what happens."

"You can do whatever you put your mind to, Becca." As I say this, I realize that she already knows she can do anything. Her racks of trophies, crowns, and awards are a testament to that. But I promised not to go there again.

A knowing silence passes between us, and then Becca returns to her mixing board. "I heard this morning's docudrama was a success."

"Very much."

"I'll come join y'all if any firecrackers start going off," Becca says with a smirk.

With that, I walk through the crowded caf—people's eyes are *all* over me—and I plop down next to Taylor, who's halfway through a raspberry yogurt.

Celia sits opposite me and dives into her turkey and dressing. We eat in silence. Waiting. Watching. Taylor frantically dashes her gaze around the room until I gently kick her under the table. We have to pretend this is just like any other day. Not draw any more attention to ourselves than necessary.

Right on schedule, Courtney enters the caf with Farah and Mina walking behind her, like birds flying in formation. Stephanie Crawford follows along a few paces back, as if she doesn't want to be with them. When she reaches our table, Courtney doubles over and grabs her heart.

"What is it?" Farah asks in a breathy voice.

"Oh, I'm sensing such heartache," Courtney says. "Like someone's in pain." She glances over at me, and it's all I can do not to laugh my ass off at this little performance. Someone should call Mrs. Rachupka, our drama teacher, right away and have her recast the fall play.

"Let her sit," Farah almost orders Celia.

"Take a load off," Celia says.

Courtney sits on the bench and continues to feign her psychic senses. I can see into her thoughts, and she's *laughing* and thinking what a genius she is, pulling this off like she's doing. Suddenly, she reaches her hand over and puts it on my arm, her face full of emotion.

What is this girl on?

"I'm so sorry to hear that Jason broke up with you."

Taylor slams her hands onto the table. Part of our gag. "He what? How dare he!"

Courtney closes her eyes and sways a bit. "My sensitivities are telling me that . . . that . . . he's coming back to me. That he thinks we're meant to be together."

Wow, she should try out for a soap opera.

She goes on a bit more about destiny and her spirit guide directing her, and I just can't hold it in any longer. Especially now that Becca's appeared at the table and looks like she wants to take out Courtney's kneecaps.

I can't help it, and I burst out laughing.

Courtney stares at me with disbelief. "What is so damn funny, Ghost Girl?"

Between gasps, I point and say, "You . . . are!"

And before I can get control of my laughter, Jason sits down with his Mountain Dew and bag of Doritos. "Kendall, are you all right?"

"Jason?" Courtney asks, very confused.

Celia's own giggles harmonize with mine, and next thing I know, Taylor's laughing too. We're all losing it.

"What's going on here? Y'all get some funny brownies from the counter?" Jason asks. "Where's mine? Why wasn't I invited to this party?"

About to fall over, Celia gets out, "You didn't tell him? Oh my God!"

Jason's blue eyes dart from Celia to me, then over to Courtney. "Tell me what?"

"You *did* break up with her, didn't you, Jason?" Courtney asks quite loudly. "You're coming back to me, right?"

Jason looks horrified, like he sucked on a lemon for ten minutes. "Are you kidding me? What planet do you live on, Courtney?" He puts his arm around me. "I'm with Kendall, and you just need to get over it."

"But you broke up!"

He looks at me with a start. "We did? When?"

Becca jumps in. "Yeah? Where'd you hear that? Your psychic intuitions?"

Courtney cranes her neck over at her posse, which has conveniently disappeared. "Oooo, I'm going to get her," she mutters.

"Get who? Your spirit guide?" Celia asks.

"I'm sorry, Courtney," I say. I honestly feel bad for the girl, even if she brought all of this on herself. I still live by the golden rule and I'm not exactly sure we should have done this. I only meant to show her that she can't play these games and needs to grow up. "It was a setup."

"A what?"

"Look, Courtney, you and I both know that you're not psychic. You call me a fake and a crazy person, yet you start acting like you have the same gift I do. It's not something to be mocked or joked about. This is serious business. And you're nothing but a phony. Now, can we bury the friggin' hatchet once and for all?"

Courtney's face turns bright red, and I think her head is going to explode like a Warner Brothers cartoon character's.

A stream of vulgarities and colorful adjectives spew from Courtney, as if she's possessed by pure anger. She points a finger at me and Jason as we sit here.

"You will rue the day you ever crossed me, Ghost Girl. Mark my words."

And with that, she flies out of the cafeteria.

I look around the table and let out a sigh. "I don't know whether to laugh some more or be scared."

"With Courtney?" Jason says. "Be afraid. Be very afraid."

Great.

CHAPTER ELEVEN

TONIGHT IS STEPHANIE CRAWFORD'S Halloween bash at her sick—in a good way—mansion. It might actually be bigger than Celia's Mega-Mart-sponsored palace.

I climb the steps leading up to the porch and press the doorbell, which rings out a breezy, chiming welcome. I half expect a butler to open the door and announce us.

"Come on in!" Miss Evelyn says, a big bowl of Lindt chocolates tucked under her arm. "Don't y'all look adorable?"

I glance down at my getup. I'm wearing a pretty traditional fortuneteller outfit; you know, long, colorful flowy dress, lots of bracelets and rings, and thick makeup. Taylor did this crazy curling-iron job on my hair to give me ringlets all over. Jason winked his approval when he picked me up, so I must have passed the test. He's dressed like Batman, and let me tell what: Christian Bale, eat your heart out. Hotness reigns with Jason Tillson. Taylor looks *très* adorable dressed like a French maid, short skirt and all. Ryan may be misinterpreting her intentions with the attire, 'cause he's eyeing her like she's the star of an adult movie on a late-night cable channel. He's dressed like an ultimate fighter, complete with dried "blood" on his knuckles and chest and a makeup'd black eye. We're a motley crew.

Stephanie bounds down the grand staircase in a Catwoman costume that looks painted on her body. Holy crap! Nothing much left to the imagination there. Then again, being a cheerleader, she has the bod for it and wears it well. "Hey, y'all! You're, like, the first guests."

Ryan mutters to Taylor, "I told you. Totally lame to be the first."

She smacks him with her feather duster. "Kendall has to get set up."

Stephanie grabs both of my hands and spreads them wide. "You look like the real deal."

"It's because I am," I say with a wink.

"Right. *You* are." She drops my hands. "I'm really sorry about all the crap with Courtney. I'd like to say she's really a nice person deep down, but I can't. She's always been like this, and it's what everyone's gotten used to. Sort of a 'that's just Courtney' thing. You know, having to be the center of attention. She can't deal with someone swiping her spotlight."

I shake my head. "I don't want her spotlight."

"Well, you've got it," Stephanie says. "Keep being who you are. She'll get over herself sooner or later."

Sooner, I hope.

Miss Evelyn shows us to the mammoth party room. It must have been a ballroom or something back when the house was built, in the mid-1800s. The hardwood floors shine like they've been freshly buffed, and lining the perimeter there are tables covered with food and Halloween decorations. "Make yourself at home. The caterers have just finished putting out the food. You kids won't go hungry tonight."

"Apparently not," Jason says under his breath.

"A caterer?" I ask Stephanie. "You guys are big-time here."

"That's how we roll here in Radisson."

"Oh, Kendall," Miss Evelyn says. "I've got a table in the corner for you, with a drape around it for some privacy. Will that work?"

"Yes, ma'am." I pat my backpack. "I brought tarot cards, runes, and my pendulum."

"Excellent!"

Jason, Taylor, and Ryan check out the buffet—man, there's, like, a carved roast beef, veggies, rolls, all sorts of canapés and caviar (are you kidding me? for teenagers?)—and while they do that, I organize my reading area. Miss Evelyn comes over a few minutes later with something in her hand.

"I wanted to show you this before the other kids get here." She unfolds a deep purple velvety cloth from around an old book. "This is my family's Bible. It has birth and death records dating back to Ada Parry's time and before."

"Oh, right!" I exclaim. "Your great-great-grandmother that I connected with during your reading at Loreen's. This is really cool." I take the family treasure from her and carefully turn the ancient pages. The book smells of mothballs with a hint of roses.

A small pressed flower falls from the front section and flutters to the floor. "I'm so sorry."

Miss Evelyn picks it up and tucks it into the back of the Bible. "That's okay, dear. That flower has been in there for over twenty years."

"Whoa." As I touch the book, I can literally feel the sizzling energy that Ada Parry left behind. An image of her appears in my mind's eye. Tall, beautiful, and confident. "Ada was quite a modern woman for her time."

Nodding, Miss Evelyn says, "She was known to be head-strong."

"And feisty," I add. Something else too. An air of confusion and sorrow. It's like she fell in love with the wrong person? Not exactly sure what that means, so I keep this little tidbit to myself.

"I also have her diaries," Miss Evelyn says. "You'll have to come see me sometime, and I'll let you read through them. Quite fascinating. It's history preserved."

"That would be awesome," I say.

Stephanie interrupts, tugging me by the sleeve of my costume. "People are starting to show up. You should get ready. Do you want food first?"

"Maybe so."

I follow her around the ballroom, which is decorated to the hilt with black, white, and orange balloons and streamers and all things Halloweeny, like skeletons, pumpkins, and ghosts. We pile a plate with fresh-cut fruit and some veggie sticks, enough to keep me going. "I can't get over how ginormous this place is."

"I know," Stephanie says, snagging a tuna tartare canapé from the nearby tray. "It's been in Mom's family for forever. Dad hated living here, said he always felt unwelcome. Like he was squatting on someone else's property." Her gaze drifts to the distance for a moment, then she snaps back to our convo. "So our relatives used to have all of these exotic balls and events here. I try to keep up the family tradition with my Halloween party. I've been having it since seventh grade. My mom even had her debutante coming-out party here, when she was a teenager. I've fortunately avoided that so far."

I sort of feel like my psychic awakening is *my* coming-out.

I sit down at my designated spot and hope I won't be like a big loser all night, over here in the corner with no one wanting a reading. Stephanie's so superpsyched to have a *real* psychic; however, I'm a little wigged out and nervous about doing tarot readings on my own for the first time—without Loreen nearby, that is.

I'm with you, Kendall, Emily reassures me.

Good ol' Em.

Knowing I can reach out to her for backup warms me; my confidence buds.

Soon the room is jumping. It's like the entire student body of RHS has turned out for this party. And no, I'm not a loser sitting in the corner. I have a ton of people lined up for quick tarot readings. Celia and Clay have arrived—decked out as Sherlock Holmes and Watson—and are hanging out with Jason. Celia waves over at me and gives me a thumbs-up. Becca and Dragon are here as well, but they're dressed in their own Goth attire and leather. Gotta give it to them, not giving a shit what people think.

After about an hour and a half of readings, I seriously need a break. Almost on cue, Jason's there and swoops me into his Batman arms. He pulls me out to the middle of the room to the dance floor and we sway to a Kaskade remix.

"I've missed you," he whispers.

"I missed you too."

I love disappearing into Jason's strong embrace. It makes me feel almost . . . normal. When I'm with him, he's the only thing I'm concentrating on. There are seldom voices or other people's thoughts swirling around, and I'm not seeing—

"Hey, wait a second." I stiffen in Jason's arms and stop moving.

Why would a kid in Georgia dress up like a Union soldier? You know, the whole dirty-Yankees thing and all. Unless . . . is that a genuine Union soldier over in the corner? The outfit is quite realistic, and I don't think the guy is a fellow student; he's got a weathered face, a scraggly close-clipped beard, and he looks older than the rest of us.

"What's wrong, Kendall?" Jason asks with concern in his blue eyes.

"Do you see a kid dressed like a Civil War soldier standing over by the salmon mousse?"

"The salmon what?" he asks.

"Over there. At the table on the end. Some dude dressed as a Union soldier. Don't you see him?"

Jason cranes his neck. "I only see Carmickle over there porking out on the mini-quiches. Which are awesome, by the way."

I swallow the lump in my throat, knowing in my heart of hearts that if Jason can't see the guy, it means only one thing. He's a ghost. And I think I've seen him before.

Over at the refreshment table, which is laden with a veritable smorgasbord, Celia is piling her plate high with goodies.

She crams a dip-covered carrot stick into her mouth and chomps down on it. "The Crawfords really know how to put out a spread."

I touch her arm and get her attention away from the plate of food. "We have company."

"What do you mean?"

"By the back table. A soldier in blue. He's watching me, and I can hear his laughter in my head."

I've definitely heard that laugh before. We've done so many investigations recently that they're all starting to run together, but there's something distinct about this guy . . . and the laughter. I have to get to the bottom of this.

Celia hands me her plate, reaches into the pocket of her coat, and withdraws an EMF meter. "I've been getting some extremely high readings here tonight."

I shake my head at my friend. "*Who* brings an EMF detector to a party?"

She's completely unfazed, as if to say, *Celia Nichols, that's who!*

Even though we're supposed to be chilling out at a fab party, I'm with Celia on this. There's a buzzing in the air that's not emanating from the speakers. The whole house has a hum to it that I sense all the way down to my fingertips.

"Let's take a lap around the room," Celia suggests. We head over to where Clay and Jason are standing talking to a few other guys and excuse ourselves from our dates, saying we'll be right back.

"Are you getting anything, Kendall?" Celia asks once we're in the front parlor.

"I think so." This sensation I'm picking up can only be described as funky. "It's this extremely old feeling. Like I can smell the mustiness. The air is all weighted down around me. Very heavy and dense."

She scans her meter around, watching as the lights blink on and the needle begins registering electromagnetic activity: 2.2, 3.4, 5.5. "We're definitely getting paranormal activity," she confirms.

I lay my hand on a nearby bureau with a vase of fresh flowers on the top. The furniture nearly murmurs with place memory, flashing images of others who have come before me through this room and left their energetic mark. "Some serious shit went down in this house many years ago, but I can't quite put my finger on it yet."

"Should I get Taylor and Becca?" Celia asks.

"No." I stop her with my hand on her arm. "Let's not interrupt their fun."

Out of the corner of my eye, I see that guy who's dressed like a Union soldier. "There he is!"

"Who? Where?" Celia yells after me.

It's too late, though, because I take off down the hallway after him. Only, by the time I get down the corridor, there's no one there. I know for a fact that it's definitely a spirit who hasn't passed into the light. I know it in every fiber of my being.

"It was a soldier," I say to Celia.

"What did he look like?"

"Umm . . . a soldier."

"Duh, I mean specifically. Age, rank, serial number."

"I didn't get a good peek at his face."

Celia points her meter down the hall, continuing to get readings. "If you can see him close up, then you can describe him to me later and I can try and sketch him out."

"Smart thinking," I say.

I follow the curve of the house, passing a large dining room that a lot of my fellow partygoers have overflowed into. The next room is a library area and a cut-through to the kitchen. I freeze in my tracks at the sudden intense pressure I'm feeling, like I've landed after a long flight and my ears haven't popped properly. My temples pound fiercely, and the noise inside my head is equivalent to being strapped under an Amtrak locomotive. There's churning and twisting, and then I feel myself being pushed. Not physically, but mentally. Someone is trying to get me out of the way. Or get my mind. My soul. What is going on?

Celia picks up that something is totally wrong. "Kendall! Kendall!"

I stare at her with what must be glassy eyes. I'm entranced by the force inside me that's telling me to make way. "Oh no, you don't!" I eke out.

"Those aren't your eyes, Kendall. Where have you gone? Talk to me!" Celia screams.

The music from the party plays loudly overhead, filling the entire house. No one can hear either of us as we battle this unknown entity. Hot tears sting the corners of my eyes, and I squeeze them shut, concentrating as hard as I can to stay grounded and in my body. It's as if my ribs are expanding from the pressure within. My lungs fill to capacity, making even the slightest breath seem like it takes an act of Congress to accomplish. Hot liquid rushes through my veins, searing me from the inside, as the impact of mentally fighting off this assault begins to take a toll on me. My muscles cramp and my bones crackle in a knuckle-popping-fest of the ages. Whatever this is, it's big and strong and thinks it can bully me.

"S-s-something is trying t-t-to get *inside* me."

Flicking the meter my way, Celia gasps as the needle flies off the charts. She grabs my hand and says, "You don't know how to channel a spirit, Kendall. Don't do it. You've got to do everything you can to kick this guy out."

I muster up my mental strength, seeing myself as a Herculean woman of some sort, a Greek goddess come down from Olympus to defeat the bad guy; Wonder Woman in her stars and stripes and bulletproof bracelets and lasso of truth (man, what I wouldn't give for one of those). I'm all of these things, and yet I'm just me trying to stave off this aggression. I begin to say the Lord's Prayer, nearly begging the Holy Father for assistance against this spirit, whose intentions are quite clear. He tells me everything. He wants to be seen and heard and "make her pay." I don't know who "her" is, but I won't let him use me as a weapon against anyone. Red flashes before my eyes. Gold sparks tinge the air, like Fourth of July sparklers. Except there's no celebration here. Just my will to survive and stake a claim to what is rightfully mine. There's nothing but ill will and malice attached to him, and I'll be damned—literally—if I'm going to let such a ghost inside of me. I scream bloody murder in my brain, hoping to jar this bastard loose.

And finally I lose it. All the fire and rage I've pent up comes spilling out over my lips. "Piss off, ghost! I'm not a Holiday Inn!"

Unexpectedly, a warming sensation coats me with comfort and clarity; it's a near peacefulness so serene that I almost think this menace *has* pushed me out of my body and I've gone to that happy place in the sky.

But no . . .

I'm with you, Kendall. I won't let him hurt you . . .

Emily! Help me!

Focus on your breathing, Emily whispers.

It's like her arms are wrapped around me, loving and protecting me. A vortex of wind spirals around me. The roots of my hair stand at attention, and there's a relief of sorts that washes over me. Almost as quickly as it started—which was probably about five minutes ago in real time—my struggle for control of my body, soul, and sanity is over, and I break free with a *whooooosh* of energy that nearly lightning-bolts out the top of my head.

In desperate relief, I fall to the floor in a heap.

"Holy crap, Kendall! Are you okay?" Celia asks as she helps me up.

"Yeah. I'm gonna be fine." I try to catch my breath. "That was nasty! I-I-I've never felt anything like that ever before. Where did he come from?"

"No clue," she says. "Too bad we didn't have any camera equipment with us."

I rub my head. "Not exactly the time to bring the ghost bag along, you know?" I swallow against the aridness of my throat, choking on my memories of what just happened. "I need something to drink."

"Let's go back and find the guys," she suggests.

I grab her arm. "Don't tell Jason what we were up to. You know, we're supposed to be having fun and not investigating. He'll feel slighted, like it's not enough for me to just be with him."

"Clay kinda feels that way too."

We link pinkies and then break loose, silently swearing allegiance and loyalty to each other—how fifth grade of us.

As we walk back into the crowded ballroom and find our Batman and Watson, I hear Emily in my head whispering a warning.

Beware of tomfoolery . . .

"By whom?"

"What?" Celia asks.

"Sorry, Emily was talking to me." I have no earthly clue what that's supposed to mean. I'll file it away in the back of my mind.

"Where have y'all been?" Clay asks, reaching for Celia's hand.

Celia covers. "Oh, you know. Bathroom. Girl chat."

"Are you sure you weren't ghost hunting?" Jason asks, flattening his lips.

Something he doesn't really understand is that investigating hauntings is sort of like being a doctor: you're on call all the time. Ghosts don't take vacations or sick days. But even though there's a creepy-ass spirit here who just tried to set up shop inside of me, that doesn't mean I can't enjoy dancing with my boyfriend. As long as I keep my eyes wide open for when that spirit decides to show himself again.

Jason pulls me onto the dance floor to slow groove to some Mariah Carey number. That's when I hear it. Plain as day. That same sinister laugh that I heard mocking me at Mrs. Lockhart's house. I'd never forget *that* sound.

It's the ghost from Mrs. Lockhart's carriage house.

And this time, he's here to play.

Chapter Twelve

"I'm not limboing," Jason says firmly.

I tug him into the middle of the ballroom, urging him to get into the horrible limbo rock Stephanie and Roachie have going using a Swiffer Sweeper as the bar. "Come on!"

Jason resists. "Do I look like I limbo?"

I do my best batting of the eyelashes—which I can do since I've got these fake ones on—and then ask, "Not even for me?"

"I run track, Kendall."

"Fine. Be that way," I say with a laugh. I'm really trying to get back in the spirit (no pun intended) of the party and not let that Union ghost get to me. I join in the limbo line behind Taylor (who needs to be careful about how low she goes in that French maid's costume), but I can't help but think about that baleful laugh that still reverbs in my head.

The DJ's playing Flo Rida's "Shawty Got Low" for everyone to limbo along with. I don't have on any Apple Bottoms jeans or boots with the fur, but I do feel like the whole room is looking at me. I'm too ungraceful to be attempting this. Just as I'm about to bend backwards to try to get under the two-foot-high Swiffer, Celia rushes up to me, waving her Sherlock Holmes pipe in the air.

"Kendall! You've got to come with me."

Relieved that I don't have to go through with getting "low, low, low, low, low, low, low," I let Celia pull me aside.

"She's at it again."

"Who?"

"Courtney."

Taylor rushes up. "Where is she? I haven't seen her all night."

"Well, she's here," Celia says. "And this time, she's not effing around with stupid ploys like a spirit guide in her Bluetooth. This time, she's crossing the line. Majorly."

Is this the tomfoolery Emily warned me about? A long sigh escapes from my lungs, and I feel the air scorching on its way out.

"Courtney's in the library with a bunch of people." When Celia pauses, I'm afraid of what will come next. Her mouth flattens. "She's getting ready to conduct a séance."

Immediately, Emily appears before me, full-bodied, holding her hands up and waving them. They're raised in a warning, and she's telling me telepathically that the séance can't take place. Something beyond horrible is going to happen. Emily knows it. I know it.

Shoving between Celia and Taylor, I scream, "I've got to stop her!"

———

Celia and Taylor must have grabbed Becca from somewhere, because it's all four of us who burst unceremoniously into the darkened library. There, Courtney sits on the floor in her princess costume—how appropriate—surrounded by her usual flock of followers as well as a lot of kids that I don't know. Probably a dozen of them. Twelve idiots who don't know what the hell they're getting themselves into. Courtney sits at the top of the circle, and a plethora of candles surrounds the group, casting an eerie golden haze over the room. Her eyes are closed and she's humming while everyone around her holds hands . . . and watches.

"She's certainly got a flair for the dramatic," Celia whispers to me.

I'm in too much shock and awe to say anything. My tongue seems to be the size of a Kaminsky Park kielbasa, and there's nothing I can do to voice my concern. It's like something's holding me back, controlling my ability to speak.

Courtney stops humming and opens her eyes. "If there are any spirits in this room or in this house, I invite you to please step into this circle and communicate through me."

Next to Courtney, Mina holds her hand tightly, looking scared shitless. Sean Carmickle sits on Courtney's other side, riveted by her every word, like this is some sort of special-edition game on Wii and he's going to score big.

A chilling breeze spins tornado-like through the room, caus-ing an ache deep down to my bones. Are others experiencing this? I don't think so. There are entities present here that I can't identify. None that I can see, but I can sense them all around me. Spirits of the deceased. Visitors from the past. Dark shadows waiting in the wings to step forward and make their presence known, playing with the living, almost for their own entertainment. More street ghosts who've bebopped in to get some attention from this stupid, stupid girl who is opening the floodgates to something she knows nothing about. I've read about things like this, calling to the spirits without knowing what conjuring them up will be like. Spirits are lonely and want attention—very much like Courtney—but you never know if they will want to punish the living for bringing them through. That's why if you don't know what the hell you're doing, you never mess with Ouija boards or séances that open up portals to the other side. I mean, *I* would never attempt a séance without Loreen's guidance.

You must stop her, Kendall, Emily pleads.

I'm trying!

I tug Celia by her sleeve and nudge her forward. "Come on."

She, along with Becca and Taylor, follow me as I step over the circle of joined hands and stand in the middle. We're definitely busting up these shenanigans.

"Courtney, you have no idea what you're doing. You've got to stop at once." I know I'm begging, but I don't care. "Stop pretending before someone—particularly *you*—gets hurt!"

Courtney closes her eyes again, and a menacing cackle

emerges from her. "Kendall Moorehead is jealous of my new powers and the fact that she's not the only one in school anymore who can contact the other side."

All eyes shift to me as if echoing Courtney's sentiment. This isn't about me though! It's about seriously doing what my mother has accused me of—dabbling in the dark arts.

"I don't have an ounce of envy. Trust me. What you're doing is wrong. Dangerous, even."

Tell her what I'm saying, Emily says in my head.

I obey without hesitation. "You have to be prepared when contacting the other side. You have to know who you're reaching out to and what you're doing and what you could possibly be up against. There's a certain amount of protection and blessing and prayer you do ahead of time so no one gets hurt. Did you do any of that, Courtney?"

She cracks one eye open and stares at me. For a moment, I think I've gotten through to her.

Finish . . .

I fist my hand and shake it at her. "You have to be prepared for whatever spirit—confrontational, lonely, mischievous, angry—you might encounter. You're putting yourself and everyone else in this room in danger with your frivolous behavior. All for what?"

Courtney screams at the top of her lungs, bringing all eyes to her now. "Get out of my circle, Ghost Girl. I'll show you how it's supposed to be done."

There's a thick wall of energy moving through the room,

something negative and angry surrounding my fellow students. Why can't people understand the danger Courtney is dragging them into? This isn't a game. But it is to all of them. Simply another fun thing to scare everyone on a Halloween night.

Jason and Clay enter the room; Jason reaches out for me. I take his hand as I step back from the séance circle, defeated. The air inside my lungs feels heavy, and I find it hard to lift my feet from the floor to walk toward him.

"Are you okay? I heard Courtney yelling."

"No, I'm not all right," I manage to say. "She's making a mistake, Jason, and she won't listen to reason."

He pulls me against his chest and kisses me on the forehead. "You have to let her mess up on her own."

"It's more than that," I say into his Batman suit. "Emily told me to warn her. She's luring evil in."

Jason's chest rumbles with his laughter. "I think it's a little late for a warning."

I look up at him. "I'm serious."

"So am I." He turns us toward the door. "Let's go. Hell with her and her games. Quit giving her the attention she's craving. It's a party. We're supposed to be here having fun."

Oh, except it's anything but.

Walking is a chore. It's like I'm slogging through wet sand on the beach. I'm helpless to stop any of this, although I know there's something ominous lurking in the shadows. I'm 100 percent sure of it.

Behind me, Courtney continues to call out to the spirits.

"What is she doing now?" I turn and see our hostess, Stephanie, standing next to me, staring ahead. "Is she conducting a séance?"

I nod.

Stephanie leans over and whispers to me, "Mom says we really do have spirits in this house. Courtney knows that too, 'cause she's spent the night over here before."

"The spirit of Ada Parry?" I ask.

"I don't know. Maybe. Maybe others," she says. "Mom once had this medium try to contact spirits here in the house. She wouldn't let me sit in on it, so I don't know what-all happened other than the lady left the house in tears."

Before I can do or say anything, I see a shadow person move behind Courtney. The silhouette of a male is quite clear to me, and I wonder if anyone else can see it. Like a super-slow-mo replay during a sports game, the shadow morphs into a clear figure: The small billed cap. The tattered blue uniform. The buttons on his coat, which remain shiny despite the wear and tear. Boots clotted with the red Georgia clay. And then his face appears in more detail. Irate, gloomy, eyes pinned on Courtney as she sways and chants and opens herself up.

I know this man. He's the one from my vision during Evelyn Crawford's reading. The same man who was speaking to Evelyn's ancestor Ada Parry. The same one whose ominous laugh knocked me off my game when I was searching out Delaney Lockhart at the carriage house next door. He lurks on this property. He's connected here.

The soldier locks his hateful eyes on me and then snickers underneath his bushy mustache. The sound of his laughter echoes through my head again, causing needle pricks of pain to shoot up and down my spine. I'm helpless to move or speak or warn. All I can do is stand stock-still and watch as he glances down at Courtney in full faux-séance mode, nearly licking his chops.

Unbeknownst to her, he turns his back and then appears to sit on her lap; slowly, he disappears completely into her body.

She sits up with a jerking jolt. The soldier laughs. Only this time, the sound originates from Courtney's mouth.

With that, I scream like a banshee.

CHAPTER THIRTEEN

THIS TIME, I KNOW Courtney's not acting.

And everyone knows that I'm not playing around.

She begins to thrash about on the floor, like someone's spilled hot coffee all over her. Both Mina and Sean try to let go of her hands, but Courtney's clinging on for dear life.

"Someone get my mom!" Stephanie screams out.

The music has stopped and people are swarming the room. Taylor pushes her way to where I'm standing with my hand over my mouth. Jason holds me tightly, waiting to see what he should do next.

"Call Loreen," I say to Taylor. Then I add, "And Father Massimo! We can't handle this alone. Wake them up if you have to!"

"I'm on it," Taylor says, whipping her cell phone out from her cleavage.

I don't even want to know.

I lift my skirt and literally crawl back into the circle. I kneel in front of Courtney with Celia at my side.

"What happened to her?" Celia asks.

"Something went into her."

"You saw it?"

"I saw *him*. We've got to talk her through this until help gets here."

"What if she's faking?"

"She's not this time, Cel."

I certainly don't know what to do for her. I'm not exactly qualified to do an exorcism or whatever is needed. God, what have I gotten into with all of this? How did it get this out of hand? I just wanted to use my psychic gift to help troubled and trapped spirits move on and to bring peace to the living. I never intended to have to intervene in a possession. Especially for the one person in this world who's making my life hell.

Courtney's eyes flutter open. "I'm famished. I haven't eaten in weeks on my way here."

"What?" Celia asks with her eyebrow lifted.

"Someone get her some food," I yell over my shoulder. I want to reach out and shake Courtney back to reality, but my intuition tells me not to do anything. "Can you hear me?"

"Yes, I hear you," she says. Her voice is deep and distant. Certainly not her typical high-pitched cheerleading tone. "Where is the rest of the unit? Why aren't they here?"

A guy laughs from behind me. "Dude, she's gone totally spaz."

"This is awesome!" another exclaims.

"We're here," I assure Courtney. "We're trying to help."

With the strength of almost three men, she shoves me in the chest hard, knocking me backward with a hard *thwwwaaack!* Ouch! That hurt!

"Who said I needed your help? You're the one who tried to stop me. When I was down by the river that time and when I was looking for supplies next door. You meddled."

My psychic headache taps at my cranium and it's then I realize that the Union soldier is speaking through her and it's not Courtney at all. Where has she gone? What has he done to her? I see her, scared and shaking somewhere in the corner of her own mind. I've got to get him out of her. Now!

Looking around, I see everyone is still holding hands, dazed by the happenings around them.

"Let go!" I beg. Words collide in my throat and I find it hard to put a complete sentence together fast enough. "Your hands. Drop them."

Everyone remarkably does as I say, and the energy in the room shifts abruptly.

The soldier screeches, "Damn you!"

Some guy from the basketball team passes Stephanie a fork and a plate of mashed potatoes and roast beef. Stephanie holds it out to Courtney. "Here's the food you wanted."

Courtney reaches out and begins scooping the food into her mouth, not even bothering to chew before she swallows. The fluffy white mixture smears all over her face, and gravy trickles down the front of her costume; she finishes and begins to lick the plate clean, like a starving dog.

I stare up at Celia, who shrugs in return. I wish I could tell everyone in the room what's going on, but it would only make them think I'm completely nuts, beans, and crackers.

"Do you want more?" Stephanie asks. Courtney tosses the plate at her and it breaks into ten pieces on the hardwood floor. "Crap! That's Wedgwood. My mom's gonna shit a brick."

"I think we have bigger problems," I say to Stephanie.

In front of me, Courtney begins to cry; mascara cascades down her porcelain cheeks, mixing with the remnants of food and totally ruining the perfect-little-princess effect she's been going for. A whimper escapes from her chest and I believe it's Courtney trying to break through.

"Come back to us," I instruct, hoping I'm doing the right thing.

The soldier is still present. His breath touches my neck. The stench of his life permeates my nostrils. His creepy mocking tone fills my head, bringing a deep-seated pain to my inner ear.

When Courtney peers at me, I see that her eyes aren't the normal gray color. Instead, they're dark and dilated and belong to the soldier inside. His laughter continues to knife away at my skull and I hear him whisper, "She invited me in."

"But she didn't understand what she was doing!"

Everyone in the room snaps around to look at me shout out to no one.

"Oh God, oh God," Courtney quivers out in her own voice. "Someone help me!"

Then the soldier takes over again. "I'm not going any-where."

I want to take Courtney's hands, but Emily is suddenly fuss-ing at me.

Never touch anyone who might be possessed by a spirit.

Not knowing what else to do, I start praying for her. Hard. The hardest I've ever prayed in my life. I ask God to take this spirit from her and make him leave her alone. I mean, Courtney's a holy terror to me and has been treating me like dog shit since I stepped foot onto the RHS campus, but not even she deserves to be controlled by a 150-year-old ghost who apparently has an ax to grind.

A hand moves to my shoulder and squeezes. I know right away that it's not Jason but Celia. Calming, yet concerned. "Is there anything I can do to help, Kendall?"

"I don't know, Cel."

In my head, I ask the spirit his name.

Wouldn't you like to know?

Yes, I would.

Courtney lunges forward at me and wraps an iron grip around my wrists. Jason moves in to stand up for me and re-strain her, but she begins kicking her feet. Believe me, no one wants to get stabbed with those three-inch stilettos she's wield-ing. Next thing I know, I'm in a semi—wrestling match with

Courtney and the Union soldier. I can't help but touch her now since she's trying to scratch my eyes out with her fresh manicure. It's not her at all though. The soldier is controlling her moves—although something tells me that inside Courtney, she's not doing much to fight him. Damn, he/she is strong.

"Cool, girl fight!" some guy shouts out.

"My money's on the chick from Chicago."

"Tillson, get in there and help your woman," another says.

There's laughter and cheering. These kids are sick. Or they think this is an act.

"What are you kids doing? Stop that!"

Evelyn Crawford moves in and tries to pull Courtney off of me. "I know it's Halloween, but there's no reason to act like hooligans."

"Mom, it's not Kendall's fault. Courtney's gone wack," Stephanie tries to explain. "She was doing this séance and then everything went crazy."

"A séance? In this house?" Miss Evelyn is not pleased.

Just then Taylor rushes in with Loreen in tow. Loreen's hair is all mussed and disheveled, like she just got out of bed. I wish I could appreciate the humor of her T-shirt, which reads "Jesus Is a Capricorn," but now is not the time.

"Did Taylor tell you what's going on?" I ask immediately.

Loreen nods. "Evelyn, these kids didn't know what they were doing. Let me help."

"Of course, Loreen." And Miss Evelyn stands aside.

Loreen brings out a small spray bottle from her purse—

more than likely her magical blend of holy water and sage—and pulls me away from Courtney.

"There's a Union soldier in her," I whisper. "She's possessed."

"She's oppressed."

"What?" Semantics . . . really? Now?

"I'll explain later," Loreen tells me and begins showering Courtney as she says the prayer to Saint Michael.

As if touched by molten lava, Courtney begins to twitch and squirm against the holy water, and then she collapses. Loreen continues to pray over her. I mean, Courtney's a bitch and all, but I don't want anything to happen to her just because she was trying to show me up.

While Courtney lies on the floor panting, I see the spirit of the Union soldier rise from her and stand tall, brushing at his uniform.

That was fun. I'll have to try it again.

"Like hell you will!" I say to him—and everyone.

He tips his hat to me and then is gone.

In the background, kids begin clapping, hooting, and hollering.

Sean Carmickle carefully shifts on his bum leg and says, "Man, that was better than last year when Josh Waters puked up green beans all over the place. You sure put on a helluva floorshow, Stephanie!"

The room erupts with laughter and more applause.

I know this show's not over. Not by a long shot.

———

"Here, sweetie, have some water," Miss Evelyn says to Courtney in the front parlor, away from everyone. Courtney seems completely out of it. "I couldn't reach your parents on their cells, so you'll spend the night here with us. We'll get you cleaned up and you can borrow some of Stephanie's pajamas."

Courtney takes the water and drinks it down, nodding obediently.

I can't believe she'd want to stay in this house after what happened. Not me, man. I'd get the hell out of here as fast as my feet—or Jason's Jeep—could carry me.

Over in the doorway, Loreen curls her index finger at me. "May I speak with you, Kendall?"

"Thanks for coming so quickly," I say, able to breathe easy for the first time in an hour. "I wasn't sure what to do."

Loreen's not amused though. "I can't believe you've allowed things to go this far in your feud with that girl."

My mouth drops open. "I had nothing to do with it, I swear. I was dancing and having a good time when I was told she had this séance going in the other room. Emily told me I had to stop her, and I did."

Her face softens. "Well, then . . . I'm sorry."

Father Massimo comes into the room and goes to Miss Evelyn. They whisper with their heads bent together for a moment and then he checks on Courtney. She's more tired than anything else and doesn't seem to remember exactly what happened.

Crossing the room, Father Mass asks if I'm okay.

"Yeah. It was a little hairy there for a minute when I nearly got put in a headlock, but I managed. Emily told me I couldn't let Courtney continue because something bad was going to happen."

"Spirit possession?" he asks.

"Oppression," Loreen corrects. "It's when a spirit uses its powers in a cruel or unjust way, weighing down a human's body or mind for the spirit's own enjoyment or purpose."

"Do you normally sound like a dictionary?" Father Mass asks.

Loreen just levels her stare at him and almost dares him to doubt her.

"In any event," Father Mass says, turning away, "the young girl lost control of her own mind, body, and spirit."

"She invited it in," I say, although the adults seem to be more interested in duking it out between themselves.

"The girl has been trying to one-up Kendall by pretending to be psychic," Loreen explains to him. "I think the situation is more dire because there is now an entity involved who's using this girl as a tool for his enjoyment."

Father Mass's dark eyes settle on Loreen's face with curiosity. "And you are?"

Without faltering, she holds out her right hand. "Loreen Woods. I'm Kendall's mentor. And *you* are?"

Since he's wearing a black sweatshirt and jeans, it's hard to tell he's part of the clergy.

He takes her hand and shakes it politely. "I'm Father Massimo Castellano, from the Episcopal church."

Loreen seems slightly offended. "You brought your priest here too?" she asks me.

I have to literally choke back the snarky urge to say, *I need a young priest and an old priest,* à la *The Exorcist.* Not exactly the right time.

"I needed all the help I could get."

He continues, his eyes slicing up and down her. "Ahh . . . so you're Loreen. I've heard a lot about you." Did he just check her out? I mean, I suppose she's cute in an older person way in her jeans and T-shirt, but now's not exactly the time for the adults to be playing Match.com. I need them to focus.

"All good, I hope," she says, now with a hint of a smile.

Oh. My. God. Are they flirting with each other? I have to stop this.

"Look, Courtney was an idiot. She brought this on herself by pretending she's got these supernatural powers. It's all an act to show me up and get attention." I shove my hands into my hair, messing up the lovely do Taylor styled for me. "I frickin' hate this. It's asinine. I don't know how to get her to quit competing with me over something I'm still trying to understand myself. Everyone here at the party thinks this was some sort of play we put on sheerly to entertain them for Halloween. This is serious shit though." I pause and cover my mouth. "Sorry, Father. Serious stuff, I meant."

He smiles at me. "No worries, Kendall. The word *shit* is in the Bible."

Loreen pulls me into a side hug. "Tell me what happened."

I relate the whole thing with the street ghost and what he said to me. He's doing this for fun and sport. He's got a chip on his shoulder the size of Stone Mountain, Georgia. I don't know exactly why, but it's there.

"Good, Kendall. You're really strengthening your gift. The time will come when you'll be able to help this soldier cross," Loreen says. "I believe that. And I believe in you."

Clearing his throat, Father Mass crosses his arms over his muscular chest and says, "Loreen, don't you think you need to be more responsible in your guidance of Kendall?"

She stabs her fists to her hips. "I guide her just fine, thank you. I always tell her to be smart and to protect herself through prayer, meditation, and holy water before she goes on a ghost investigation."

He furrows his brow. "This wasn't an investigation, though."

"What do you suggest she do, *Father?* Bathe in holy water every day in the event that she runs into a situation she can't handle? She's still a teenager trying to get through school and the social scene. It's hard enough on her as it is."

"Which I realize," he says. "It's a good thing that her faith is so strong and she has support from you, me, and her family."

"Exactly," Loreen says, seemingly proud that he recognizes her as a positive influence in my life.

Jason comes up behind me and wraps his arm around my waist. We're joined by Taylor and Ryan, Celia and Clay, and Becca and Dragon. Dragon's gotten a good kick out of all of this, but I also think he's a little buzzed off the flask inside his leather jacket he's been nipping from.

"So, everything okay now?" Celia asks.

"That's one way to stop a party," Jason teases.

"I'm fine," I say, although I am pooped by my contact with the soldier.

"Well, Stephanie, why don't you take Courtney upstairs and get her settled," Miss Evelyn says.

"Aren't you going to call the girl's parents?" Loreen asks.

"I already tried. They're out for the evening," Miss Evelyn notes. "I left them a voice mail saying Courtney's staying here."

"As if they'll care," Courtney mutters. I don't think anyone but me actually picks up on it.

"I guess my work here is done," Father Mass says. He ruffles my hair. "Next time, don't wait so long to call for help. I'm here anytime, Kendall."

"Me too," Loreen adds.

"I did the best I could, considering the situation."

Jason snuggles me to him. "You did perfectly fine, Kendall."

We watch as Stephanie escorts Courtney up the staircase to her room. Miss Evelyn claps her hands to get the attention of the onlookers in the adjoining rooms. "I'm sorry, everyone, but the party's over. Thanks for coming."

I stand gripping Jason's hand, getting strength from his touch, while I watch fellow students file out of the house. Over by the base of the grand staircase in the foyer, I see the Union soldier standing there, leaning against the banister with his ankles crossed. He's whittling something with a knife and smiling like a Cheshire cat.

Stephanie's party might be over, but this spirit's festivities have just begun.

CHAPTER FOURTEEN

AFTER HOLY EUCHARIST on Sunday morning, I borrow Mom's car, pick up Celia at the back of my driveway, and then head over to Stephanie's house. Miss Evelyn answers the door wearing a cheery yellow dress that contrasts with the leaves outside that have begun to change color and fall to the ground.

"Hello, girls," she says politely.

"Hey, Miss Evelyn," Celia says. "We thought we'd come check on Courtney."

I inwardly groan, knowing I'm the last person Courtney wants to see the "morning after."

Stephanie appears from behind her mother, her hair pulled to the left in a side ponytail. "Hey, y'all. Courtney blew out this morning with barely a word to me or Mom."

I frown. "What did her parents say?"

"They didn't seem fazed or worried at all," Stephanie reports. "Her mom brushed it off as her just trying to be the center of attention at the party."

Miss Evelyn waves us into the house. "Have y'all eaten lunch yet?"

"No, ma'am," Celia says.

"We're just about to sit down. Come join us."

After all the weirdness that happened here last night, I'm too tired to decline. I simply follow quietly down the hallway to the airy white kitchen in the back of the house, wondering if everything I saw last night was merely part of a dream. But no, something did try to push me out of my body, and something definitely knocked Courtney out of hers.

The kitchen is roomy and bright, big enough for a banquet. Cold baked chicken, potato salad, deviled eggs, and three-bean salad sit out on the table—quite a feast for just a mother and daughter. Miss Evelyn goes to get plates and silverware for us, and Celia, Stephanie, and I each take a seat.

"If you ask me the truth," Stephanie starts, "I think Courtney was faking it last night. She's always loved being a drama queen. I mean, if she was really attacked by some ghost or whatever, wouldn't she have been more shaken up? I would have peed my pants!"

Celia shrugs. "Different people react different ways to contact with entities. It also depends on how she'd opened up her mind to allow the spirit to use her."

"Yeah, whatever," Stephanie says with a smirk. She passes me the chicken. I hold on to it as I wait for my plate. "She was snoring in her sleep last night, which tells me she wasn't bothered by too much."

Celia snickers. "Wait'll every guy at RHS finds out she snores."

I scowl at my friend. "You wouldn't."

"Nah."

A flowery plate is placed in front of me. "Now eat up, girls. We have tons of food left over because of last night's early exodus," Miss Evelyn says.

Celia piles the chow on her plate like she hasn't eaten in a week—I don't know where she puts it in that skinny body of hers—and I stab a small chicken breast with my fork. I usually love good old-fashioned deviled eggs, but for some reason the smell is not appealing right now. I'm anything but hungry. Nausea coats my stomach, the sour response to a feeling of ill will. Is it residual energy left from last night's activities? I turn my head, seeking out the entity I encountered at the party, but he's not here at all. Something else hangs in the air.

While Miss Evelyn, Stephanie, and Celia chatter on, I zone out, glancing around the kitchen. The walls are pristine, and every pot and pan hangs neatly from an overhead rack. The windows sparkle with the midday sun, and the smell of fresh lemon is in the air. It's all window-dressing though. The warmth and glow of this room is a façade, masking the true pain captured in the walls and furniture. I've read in some of Loreen's books that houses have lives of their own. That they keep the energies of those who have lived within them. In my head, I see images of all sorts of people who have used this room, zooming up to reflections of Miss Evelyn and a tall dark-haired man with Stephanie's eyes. Mr. Crawford. I feel her parents' anger at each other. The tenseness of their relationship. The accusations and acid words over money, extramarital affairs, and long working hours. I see Stephanie—only a few years younger—run away from the kitchen up to her room, seeking refuge while her parents fussed, feuded, and bickered over the tiniest little thing, words slashed about between two people who were supposed to love each other until death parted them. That would never happen though, as the State of Georgia saw to their official separation two years ago.

Miss Evelyn reaches out to me, knocking me out of my vision. "Can I get you anything, Kendall? Perhaps some iced tea?"

"Y-y-yes, ma'am. That would be nice."

She rises from the table and disappears deep back in the steel-applianced kitchen. I breathe a sigh of relief and appreciation over the fact that my parents are still together. So many kids come from broken homes. I mean, I know I'm going through this whole awakening thing that Mom doesn't get, but at least both she and Dad—and Kaitlin, when she's not being a brat—are there supporting me, for the most part.

I take a bite of chicken and chew quickly. "So, Steph, where does your dad live now?" Geesh, I hope that's not too personal.

She doesn't seem bothered at all. "He moved to Nashville before the divorce was final. I spend Christmas and summers with him, which is pretty cool since Vanderbilt University is one of my college choices."

"That's cool," I say. "I'm glad you get to spend time with him."

"Me too." She pokes at her potato salad and then says, "I really miss having him around all the time. Their fights just got to be too much and he . . . left."

"It happens," Celia says sadly. "People are mean to each other for some very odd reasons."

A sheen of tears appears in Stephanie's eyes, and her bottom lip begins to quiver. "Kendall, I'm, like, so sorry for how shitty Courtney and everyone's been to you. Farah, Mina, and Megan are actually nice girls, and if they weren't under Courtney's influence, they'd like you. I know they would." She wipes her hand under her eyes.

Miss Evelyn places a glass of iced tea in front of Celia and one in front of me. "Now, sweetie, you don't always have to do what the popular kids tell you to do."

Stephanie rolls her eyes. "Right, Mom. And there was no such thing as peer pressure back in your time of the Stone Age."

"Of course there was. I'm only saying that you and Kendall can be friends, and you and Courtney can be friends. It'll all work out. You're all getting older and wiser, and the games of childhood will fall off by the wayside."

Celia snorts, but then covers it with a deep sip of her tea.

"I promise to try and get Courtney to mellow out," Stephanie says. "You know, since she's sort of ridden this as far as she can now."

"I appreciate that," I say, even though, deep down inside, I know Courtney Langdon and I will never be anything in the vicinity of the neighborhood of BFFs.

And *I'm* the one in therapy.

Speaking of therapy, I soldier through almost a week of evil glares from Courtney across the lab table and our poor pickled pig and make it to Thursday, when Mom takes me out of school early for another visit to Atlanta and Dr. Kindberg's office. And more tests.

Perched in his large armchair (I won't do the couch!), I tell him all about Stephanie's party and how the Union soldier tried to take me over. He sits quietly in his chair, tapping a pen against his lip and listening.

"So did anyone else witness this?" he asks.

"My friend Celia. She was with me as I forced the ghost out of my head."

"I've heard of this," the doctor says. "It takes a very strong person to withstand a body thief's attempt like that. And from what you tell me, this spirit is belligerent and crafty."

Finally, an adult other than Loreen who takes my claims seriously. Of course, he may just be humoring me before he jabs me with a needle full of Demerol.

He continues though. "The tests we've done so far on you, Kendall, show an incredible mental strength. Your IQ is 152, and your school records indicate no learning disabilities arising from your gift." He flips back in my chart a couple of pages and then narrows his eyes at me. "Having dealt with children in your similar circumstances, shall we say, I believe we've ruled out all of the mental obstacles that could be in the way of solving this mystery. I am inclined to believe that you do have the abilities you claim. However, being a medical professional, I feel it's my duty to explore all physical options as well."

I swallow hard. "Right. The CT scan you scheduled today."

"Exactly." Dr. Kindberg sits forward. "Look, Kendall, we've got to explore every avenue before we let you go. If you are psychic, you'll need to make a decision about how you want to live the rest of your life. There are counselors trained to help children with abilities like yours. Also, there are camps throughout the United States that specialize in psychic kids, helping them understand their gifts and honing their talents."

"What are the other avenues?"

"Ignoring your abilities. Going on with your life in a regular manner. There are medications we can prescribe that might possibly curb the visions and headaches, but you will also have to make a concerted effort to bury your gift."

I think of the parable in the Bible about someone taking a talent and turning it into many and someone else who buried his and always regretted it. I don't want to *not* do what I'm apparently destined to do. Wouldn't that be scoffing at what's been given to me?

"I want to keep helping people," I say. "My ghost-hunting group has already done a lot of good for folks. I've crossed several spirits into the light; we helped find a missing person; and we even debunked six or seven episodes of what homeowners thought were hauntings but which turned out to be things like bad wiring in the basement or leaky pipes or their teenager smoking in the attic."

He smiles at me. "It sounds like you've already made up your mind then."

With great confidence, I agree. "Yeah, Doc. I have."

"Good, Kendall. Let's get you over to the hospital for those tests so you can get on with your calling."

"Thanks for believing in me, Dr. Kindberg."

He winks. "That's what I'm here for."

"Are you okay, Mom?" I ask in the waiting room of the St. Joseph's radiology department. Mom fiddles with the crinkled pages of a two-year-old *Good Housekeeping,* which is a red flag for me that something's bothering her.

"I'm fine," she says softly.

"You're not fine. You're worried about me. You don't have to."

Her eyes darken. "I . . . but . . . how—"

I give her a wide smile. "I'm psychic, Mom."

"So you tell me." Her eyes drop to the magazine again.

I reach over and snag the hand closest to me and hold on tightly. "I know we've talked about this before and I understand that it's, like, your duty as a mom to worry about me twenty-four/seven. I'm okay. I promise."

She shakes her head. "I keep telling myself that. It's just so hard for me to reconcile the beliefs and teachings of a lifetime, from my parents and priests and the church, with your ability to communicate with the dead. It goes against my religion, and I'm struggling with that."

"I know. Even Father Massimo is trying to help us get through this."

"He is, Kendall. I appreciate his spiritual guidance. What scares me the most is knowing that I can't protect you if you're out there trying to contact the dead through all sorts of means that I find to be against the Holy Scriptures."

I do get where she's coming from. I pull my purse up next to me and rummage through the mess of pens, packs of gum, and loose change to find the sheet of paper my priest gave me on Sunday. I pass it over to Mom.

"Check this out. Father Mass did this. There are Bible verses that refer to what I'm going through. So maybe I *am* doing what God intended for me."

Mom reads the paper. "Matthew chapter fourteen, verse twenty-six: the disciples see Jesus as a ghost."

"Right! So if Jesus was a ghost, maybe they are real?"

She pulls her lips tight. "I just don't know, Kendall."

"Keep reading. There's the one in First Corinthians that talks about how the Bible is largely based on spiritualism with God. Then in Psalm Ninety-one and Luke, chapter four, verse ten, there are references to angel and spirit guides." I point at the last notation on Father Mass's list. "In John, chapter sixteen, verses twelve through twenty-three, Jesus talks of future truths that will be revealed to the world through mediums. Like me! Don't you see?"

Mom's eyes are filled with dewy tears, and I feel like a major shit for making her cry . . . again. She's just trying to protect me. But I want her to see that I *am* protected. That I was chosen to have this gift.

"I appreciate that you have all of this research, Kendall. It means a lot to me," Mom says, squeezing my hand. "We'll see what the CT scan shows. You know I only want to keep you safe and never let anything hurt you."

"I get that, Mom. But I'm growing up. I can't wear a bicycle helmet forever. Loreen says that the only way we mature physically, mentally, and spiritually is experiencing the good *with* the bad. That it makes us well-rounded and sympathetic. I want to be like that."

Mom's voice raises some in the waiting room. "It's my job to protect you from anything that could hurt you."

"Some things," I assure her, "I have to learn for myself."

A nurse steps through the double doors opposite where we're sitting. "Kendall Moorehead?"

"That's me," I say, standing.

"Do you want me to come with you?" Mom asks. "I have experience with CT scans and I can talk you through it."

Now's the time to cut the cord a smidgety-bit. "I can do it, Mom. I'll be fine."

Mom kisses the top of our joined hands and smiles up at me.

I follow the nurse around the corner to the left and down a long hallway, where she shows me a changing room and a stack of neatly folded hospital gowns.

"Everything off that has any metal in it, including your bra."

As I change into the terribly unfashionable garb, I'm reminded of when I was a little girl and Mom used to bring scrubs and gowns home from the hospital for me to play with. I loved pretending I was a nurse just like Mom. I thought I was special because no one else had clothes from the hospital like I did. Now, as I look down at the mauve and cornflower crisscrossed design, I feel like a sick freak.

My BlackBerry beeps at me from inside my purse. I withdraw it from the leather case and smile when I see the instant message from Jason:

>Who luvs ya?

Moving my thumbs like I'm thumb-wrestling, I type back:

>U do! I hear u!

Shortly after, I get:

>Good luck w/everything.

>Thinking of u!

Time to get this over with. Knowing Jason's with me in spirit boosts my confidence. I stash the BlackBerry in my purse and grab my clothes. Outside the dressing room, a nurse takes my personal things and locks them in a cabinet for me. I return to the small waiting room and wait.

Fifteen minutes later, I hear, "Hey, Kendall, I'm Patricia. I'll be taking you through your test. Come over here and I'll start an IV so we can put the contrast substance in. Then we'll get you into the room for your test."

I wince when the sharp needle pokes me in the crease of my arm. I've never been a fan of needles, although Mom makes us get flu shots every year. Patricia finishes securing the IV and taping it onto my arm so it won't move.

"Is this test going to hurt?" I ask, barely recognizing the childlike voice. Sure, Mom explained the whole procedure to me in the car, but she's all blinded by the protective-mother thing, so I need to hear the word straight up.

"Well, there's a lot of lying still, which some people don't particularly like," Patricia says. "And you can get a hot-flash sensation when the contrast material is injected. It can also give you a little metallic taste in your mouth, but other than that, the test is pretty cut-and-dried."

I let out a long breath. "Let's hope so."

Patricia leads me down the hallway farther and through a set of swinging doors. "Are you claustrophobic?"

I hadn't really thought about it until I fix my stare on the machine in front of me. The scanner part is this monstrous—okay, not really, but to me it seems that way—machine with a tunnel-like area burrowed out in the center. A sliding table sits in the hole, and I can see that the X-ray equipment is inside the rotating middle. It's straight from *Deep Space Nine* and I'm starting to feel like the captured alien they're experimenting on.

It's okay, Kendall . . . , Emily whispers in my head.

I steady my breathing and try not to freak out too much. It's no big deal. It's a camera. And a moving table. And it's gonna swirl around me with bells, lights, and whistles and peer into my insides.

Patricia pats the table. "Climb on up here, Kendall, and get comfy."

I do as I'm told, careful not to flash my undies to the technician behind the lead wall in the other room.

"So, my mom's a nurse," I say as I get situated, "and she says a CT scan is like slicing up a loaf of bread and then putting it back together to look at the images."

Chuckling, Patricia fluffs the pillow behind my head. "That's an interesting way to put it. She's right though. The scan will run with several sets of electronic X-ray detectors spinning around. The table you're on will slide through the scanner so the X-ray can follow a spiral path that works with the computer software in the other room to create the cross-sectional images."

Did Celia Nichols just enter the room?

"All you have to do is remember to breathe and not to move, Kendall." Patricia pats the pillow a final time and then moves to strap my legs down to the table. Flat on my back, I stare up at the industrial ceiling tiles. I center my energies on my breathing and try to relax, lulling myself into a meditative state until this is over.

"Okay, sweetie, here we go."

As the table begins moving into the tunnel, I do my best to

ignore the thoughts creeping through my mind. I take myself somewhere else. I'm in a beautiful field of flowers. The wind is blowing, and the sun shines down brightly. I'm wearing a long flowy dress that drifts in the breeze as I run through the meadow. Peace and calm surround me. Nips of honeysuckle and juniper fill the air as I touch my fingertips to the blades of tall grass.

For a moment, I'm oblivious to the humming and drumming of the scanner as it inspects my brain for abnormalities. But then the machine jerks somewhat, knocking me out of my happy place.

A voice over the intercom says, "Sorry, Kendall. That happens sometimes. Are you okay?"

"Fine," I manage to eke out.

Okay, now I'm not tranquil at all. I'm lying in a frickin' metal tube that's shooting radiation into me. My heartbeat accelerates to breakneck speed, and my mind starts playing games. What if they've found something? What if they're zeroing in on a massive tumor pushing against my temporal lobe? What if I'm sporting a rare case of a disease they've never seen before and don't know how to treat? They work miracles with drugs and lasers today though, don't they? I could be the poster child for a new experimental procedure that saves lives and brain function. Would I have to have more radiation and chemotherapy? Would my hair end up in a pile on the floor? Oh God, it's bad enough being the new kid in school who claims to be psychic—now I'm bald too? I wouldn't expect Jason to date the bald chick. How uncool. But he already dates the psychic girl. He's not that superficial, so why am I painting him with that brush in my panicked state?

Questions, questions, questions. And I'm not the one to provide answers.

I need to just calm down and wait this out.

Suddenly, I'm not alone in the tunnel. A tender blanket of warmth covers me from my head to my toes, love so strong that it propels itself through my veins, powering my confidence and tranquillity. A delicate hand covers mine as it lies perfectly still on the table.

Emily.

She's here with me, holding me the best and only way she can. I literally *feel* her surrounding me in a soft bubble of shielding white light.

You're going to be fine . . . , she comforts.

I understand completely and try to gulp down the anxiety clogged in my throat.

The CT clicks and spins around me, moving just as the nurse had told me it would. Instead of focusing on the negative of what *might* be, I concentrate on the images now flashing through my head of the people who have come before me on this table. There's John Sullivan from north of the city . . . a town called Acworth. He had an accident with his motorboat on Lake Gwinnett. There's also a woman named Lucille Something-or-other who was diagnosed with a malignant brain tumor—eek!—but was treated successfully with surgery and chemo. Little Timmy Dennis, a boy from Minnesota who was visiting his grandparents in Buckhead. He rode his bike without a helmet and had some nasty hemorrhaging from a spill. Hundreds of others. Some nameless. Some faceless. All with a story.

And then there's me.

What will the test show?

A perfectly healthy, normal girl . . . , Emily reassures me.

Somehow, I know she's right. I just do. There's nothing wrong with me. *This* is normal for me. I am who I am (excuse the Popeye reference) and can be what I am because that's the way it's supposed to be. I'll keep working with Emily and Loreen and Celia, Taylor, and Becca.

This is what I was destined to do.

Yes, you are, Kendall . . .

CHAPTER FIFTEEN

"I'M DONE," I announce to Mom in the front waiting room.

The television blares out the latest episode of *Oprah* and whatever disease-of-the-day topic they're discussing. Wouldn't I make a great guest for her? I am a Chicago native, after all.

Mom gathers her things and comes over to hug me. "I've been thinking about you in there on that table and how scared you must be. I haven't been very understanding or open-minded through all of this, Kendall. I've been so convinced that there was something physically wrong with you that I didn't want to accept the possibility that you *actually* are psychic."

Wow, was there a preview of "Psychic Kids—How to Handle Them" on the next *Maury*?

"And you know that would be so much easier to handle than a physical malady," she adds.

"Dur," I say with a laugh. "That's what I've been trying to tell you!"

"We'll get through this together, sweetheart. I know we will. Faith and family love and support. That's what matters the most."

I reach out for her hand. "I know, Mom."

"You are special, Kendall. My own precious gift from God. You'll never know how precious." She kisses me on the forehead and then hugs me again.

"How would you classify Kaitlin? She's more like a curse than a gift." I crack myself up.

Mom swipes at me and laughs. A good long one, like I haven't heard from her in a couple of months. "Let's go to the cafeteria and get a chocolate milk shake. I hear they're the best anywhere. They use real gooey chocolate fudge."

"Sounds decadent . . . and perfect."

Ten minutes later, I find out she's absolutely right. This is *the best* milk shake evah. Made even more special because I'm sharing it with my mom.

"Just as I expected," Dr. Kindberg tells us in his office three hours later. "The CT scan came back clean as a whistle."

"Wasn't that fast?" Mom asks.

"I knew you were anxious, Sarah," he says. "What can I say? I pulled some strings."

"Thanks, Doc!" I chime in. "So, no brain tumor or other funk in my head?"

"Funk-free," he says with a straight face. "Your blood work looks fine. White blood count is normal. A slightly high blood pressure, but I'll attribute that to the 'white-coat syndrome' of being at the hospital around doctors and all the stress you've been under with these tests."

"So, I'm okay?"

"You're a perfectly healthy sixteen-year-old girl."

"Almost seventeen," I add. With a snicker.

Mom folds her hands over her purse. "What about the special tests you did, Dr. Kindberg?"

"Ah, yes. Kendall scored a seventy-nine percent on the objects test we did and an eighty-one percent on the scene images. Very high indeed. Some of the highest I've seen in a while." He runs his hand over his chin, deep in thought. "My professional diagnosis is that Kendall is exactly what she claims to be: a budding psychic. I am happy to work her into my regular rotation for therapy visits, just to keep up with her progress, but I don't feel that it's necessary."

Did my heart just stop beating? Did he just say I'm not a freakazoid?

Mom licks her lips; tension is emanating from her as she's trying to be more understanding. I can read it all over her, as if the words were printed on her cheeks.

"You don't?" she asks.

"I only offer therapy as a way to help Kendall with any questions or issues she has along the way. However, it seems she already has a support group in place with her ghost-hunting team, this fellow psychic Loreen Woods, and your priest. I would say that you and your husband, as well as Kendall's sister and friends, continue to treat her as a normal person . . . only one with some very special abilities. You, Sarah, need to be more open-minded and just listen to Kendall and what she's experiencing at all times. It's very important that she knows she can come to you and doesn't have to hide anything from you."

I squint over at Mom as she struggles through this; her face is flushed and pale at the same time.

"I-I-I'm trying. I want to be happy for her, Dr. Kindberg, I do. I'm just so worried about her being scared and how I can help her through that." Mom's voice breaks on the last word.

I slip my hand in hers. "I'm not scared of the spirits, Mom. I promise." Okay, that Union soldier guy skeeves me out a lot, but it's just because I haven't gotten a handle on what his glitch is yet. "If anything upsets me, I promise to tell you. You can read all of my case files and look at our Ghost Huntress website. You will know exactly what we're doing."

Her eyes dance over my face. "I'd like that. I'd like to be involved as much as I can without hindering you in any way."

"If you'll trust me with Loreen, like you've been doing, then she can help me hone my abilities. After all, she's already gone through this and wants to make things easier for me."

Mom swallows hard but then nods her head. "All right, Kendall. Whatever is best for you."

"I've got your blessing?"

"Yes, sweetheart. Just be careful."

As she and I hug tightly, I peer over her shoulder at Dr. Kindberg. He winks and smiles at me.

Everything's going to be fine. Just like I knew.

Mom dabs her eyes with her knuckle. We finish up with Dr.

Kindberg and agree to check in with him regularly or whenever needed, and then we head out.

In the elevator, Mom smiles and clutches my hand, swinging it back and forth in the space between us like we used to
do when I was a little girl and we'd walk along the shore of
Lake Michigan. This is a great Mom moment. You know . . .
one you'll remember in the years to come and feel the special
love and connection with the woman who gave you life.

"Do we have to go straight back to Radisson?" I ask.

"No. Why?"

I shift weight from one leg to the other. "Maybe we can go
to dinner or something. The two of us. I can tell you all about
our cases and the things I do during an investigation."

"I'll go one better than that." She whips out her cell phone
and speed-dials a number. "David, it's me. Yes, dear. Everything's
okay. All of Kendall's tests came back normal. I'll tell you more
later. Right now, Kendall and I are going to have some girl
time. If it's okay with you, we're going to stay here and shop
and see the city—"

"Ooo, let's go to the Georgia Aquarium!"

Mom waves at me and continues. "I'm going to use some
of your Starwood Points and check us into the Westin in
Buckhead. How's that? Okay, dear. We love you too.

"How does that sound?" she asks with a vibrant smile.

"Like total perfection."

And it is. The next day, Mom and I shop together, have an
amazing dinner at the Buckhead Diner, get pampered with a

massage, manis, and pedis, and I get to see Nandi, the ginormous manta ray at the aquarium.

During all of this, Emily silently disappears into the background to give Mom and me room. But not before she whispers:

You're lucky to have Sarah Moorehead in your life . . .

Tell me something I don't know.

"I missed you."

"I missed you too," I say to Jason Saturday night at the football game. Mom and I got home from the ATL just in time for
him to pick me up. I'm wearing my new Lip Service Teacher
Hit Me with a Ruler plaid jacket and a black asymmetrical
skirt that totally rocks. "Wait until you see all my new clothes.
I got this sick Abbey Dawn by Avril Lavigne T-shirt and a Kill
City striped hoodie. Oh, and we went to A and F for—"

"Kendall, don'tcha think this is a conversation more suited
for Taylor?"

I laugh in spite of myself. I've never been a fashion bug, but
I'll admit that shopping with Mom was amazing fun and I got
carried away with all of the stores at our fingertips.

"You're right, Jason. Sorry!"

"No need." He chuckles and snuggles next to me on the
bleacher seat. "I bet you'll look hot in all of 'em."

I blush clear down to my Ed Hardy "Love Kills Slowly" slip-
on shoes. What? I'm not addicted to designer clothes. I'm not!

"Jaaaason."

"I'm your boyfriend. I'm allowed to tell you you're hot."

"I think you're hot too," I confess, blushing even harder.

Celia and Clay return from the concession stand with sodas and popcorn. She clears her throat at our bout of PDA and then sits next to me.

Jason lets out a holler as the football team runs onto the field. Taylor squeals when she sees Ryan. She has her camera and her video recorder with her tonight so she can capture his feats on the field. "Come on, beat Hillside like they're rented mules!" she screams.

I laugh so hard that I almost choke. "Why do people want to beat rented mules? Are they different from regular mules?"

"You're so literal-minded sometimes, Kendall," Jason says.

"Sorry, it's the Midwesterner in me."

We watch our team run Hillside up one side of the field and down the other. Halftime comes and goes with the band and a dance routine. We all make silly faces and huggy poses for Taylor's video. It's so much fun to have a gang to hang out with like this. I actually feel normal.

That is, until toward the end of the game, when I begin to sense spirit energy around us. I can feel it weaving among the people, as if it's seeking out someone in particular.

Jason interrupts my thoughts by knocking me on the arm and then pointing down at the cheerleaders. "Courtney looks like she's doing a striptease at the fifty-yard line."

I sit up. "Seriously?"

"Yeah, man. I don't know what kind of Kool-Aid she's been drinking. Check her out."

The team has just gotten a first down, and the cheerleaders are going crazy. Taylor moves toward the fence to get a better camera shot of Ryan. When several people in the crowd start mumbling and laughing, I see her spin the camera around on Courtney.

"*What* is she doing?" Clay asks.

I glance down at her. Instead of leading the cheer of "First and ten, do it again, go, go, go," she's looking down at her body, and—no, she did'unt!—she's feeling herself up! She's rubbing her own boobs like she's never felt them before.

"This is totally rental porn," I hear from some guy behind me.

And it just gets better. Next thing we know, she goes over to her bag and pulls out chewing tobacco. She begins to chaw away on it, spitting on the ground.

"Did she just grab herself between the legs like she's . . . adjusting herself?" Celia asks with shock on her face.

Jason seems embarrassed for her. "It's like she's playing pocket hockey."

"Oh my God." She's lost her mind. I smack Jason on the leg. "Stop watching her!"

"Kendall, *everyone* is watching her."

It's true. I peer out onto the field, and even the safety for Hillside is so distracted by the sideline show that he totally misses Ryan when he sprints by him and into the end zone.

While the crowd erupts into cheers, I watch as Courtney takes her sweater off. Thank heavens the cheerleader sponsor is out on the field with a letter jacket and covers her up. What in the world would possess Courtney to do that? Then I stop my own thoughts at the word *possess*. My skin itches. Something's not right in suburbia.

"Kendall, are you all right?" Jason asks.

"We've got to gather the team and look at the video that Taylor's shooting."

He groans. "Not another investigation. Come on, Kendall."

"We have to, Jase."

The ghost huntresses have work to do.

CHAPTER SIXTEEN

"ROLL IT BACK, TAYLOR," I say Sunday afternoon, glued to the television set. We're all at Casa Nichols, spread out in Celia's room watching the video from the football game last night. Even Seamus, her bulldog, seems engrossed. "Watch what she does right there."

Sure enough, Courtney Langdon grabs her crotch in front of the several hundred people who have turned out to see RHS play Hillside.

"Why is she doing that?" Taylor asks. "Bless her heart."

Celia turns her eyes on Taylor. "Bless her nothing. She's a bitch."

Taylor's mouth falls open. "She's still a person, and she's making a fool out of herself."

I watch closer as Courtney keeps scanning around her, like she's seeing something in her peripheral vision. Then you can see her pompoms moving next to her; her head jerks quickly to see what's going on. She's definitely aware that something is around her.

Celia leans forward. "This is the best part. Watch this."

Riveted, we all stare glassy-eyed as Courtney throws down her pompoms and lets out what can only be described as a war cry and charges the field. Coaches nearby drop their clipboards as they dash off after the wayward cheerleader.

My mouth drops open. "What the hell?"

Taylor points. "*Absolument incroyable!* Absolutely unbelievable!"

This was the most bizarre occurrence of the night. As the players are shaking hands after the game, Courtney barrels into the crowd and completely tackles one of the visiting team's players. She starts pounding him with both of her fists until one of the RHS guys pulls her off him, her legs still flailing about.

"Holy shit. She's gone," Celia notes.

"Is that your professional opinion?"

"She's off the chain. What's happened to her? Is she possessed?"

I think for a mo' and then say, "Not according to Loreen. Spin that back, Taylor." After the tape resets to where Courtney's looking around her like something's there, I explain. "See how she seems to be spotting something out of the corner of her eye? Well, that's more of a sign of an oppression than an actual possession. If she were possessed, she wouldn't be so aware of what's going on around her. Here, she's sensing something's not right and may even be seeing the spirit in her peripherals."

"I don't get it," Taylor says.

"Well, Loreen tells me there's a fine line between spirit oppression and possession . . . being that possession is nine-tenths of the law." I try to laugh, but the joke falls flat. "I mean, if she were possessed, she wouldn't really have any control of her body at all. Thing is, we see her cheering one minute like there's nothing wrong and then, all of a sudden, she's aware of a shift in energy around her and she starts acting like a weirdo. Here, where she's touching herself, it's like it's not her at all. There's a faraway look in her eyes, like she's taken a step back and let someone else take control."

"You ask me," Jason says, "the girl has lost her facilities. Gone-zo!"

I shift my gaze between Taylor and Celia. "How did she explain this to everyone? To the coaches, her cheerleader sponsor . . . her parents? Does anyone know?"

Taylor waves her hand in the air dismissively. "I talked to Stephanie this morning, and she said that Courtney claimed that time of the month and blamed it on popping too much Pamprin."

"And people bought it?"

Celia scowls. "What else are folks going to believe? That Courtney Langdon is so threatened by you that she invited an evil spirit to dock inside of her?"

"I see what you mean."

All this while, Becca has had her headphones on, listening

to the sound from the video on her laptop. "Hey, y'all, check this out. There are EVPs here."

"You can hear them through all of the stadium noise?" Jason asks.

Becca says, "Yeah, the spirits appear to be manipulating the energy created by the crowd's buzz. Listen to this."

We transfer the DVD to Celia's monstrous computer and turn on the speakers. We all circle around Celia as she clicks where Becca tells her to. There's definitely a garbled sound when Courtney's rushing the field. Then again, it's a football game, so there's going to be a lot of background noise.

"This sound is different than your standard crowd noise," Becca says. "Lemme sit, Nichols."

Celia shoves out of the chair so Becca can sit. She clicks on the video, copying and pasting here and there and doing all sorts of computery things that I just don't get. She opens the editing software, pastes a portion in, then amplifies, cleans up the background noise, and takes out the distortions. Man, look at her go! She hits Play and Rewind several times, listening intently, until she's pleased with the results.

Becca says, "I think I got it this time. Listen. There are two EVPs here."

She cues up the first one.

"Reeeeeeeeeeeebels ev'rywhere."

"Rebels everywhere?" Taylor repeats.

Jason snaps his head up. "Hillside High is the Rebels. I don't get why you would get an EVP about the football game."

I think I do.

"It has more to do with the Civil War, I think," Celia says. "What about you, Kendall?"

I gulp down the dry lump that's formed in my esophagus. "I'd like to hear the other one."

"You got it, chief," Becca says, fast-forwarding to where we see Courtney up close. "Here we go." Becca hits Play.

You can hear the camera rattling as Taylor rushes to catch up with Courtney while she's being escorted away. She asks Courtney if she's okay, and then the EVP.

"Geeeeeet . . . me out . . . of . . . daaahkness . . ."

"Again, please," Celia asks.

"Geeeeeet . . . me out . . . of . . . daaahkness . . ."

Celia looks to me. "'Get me out of the darkness'?"

"That's what it sounds like to me," I confirm. The EVP is clear as day.

"Man, that's one helluva class A EVP, don't you think?" Becca says proudly.

"It's proof that something paranormal is going on with Courtney," Taylor says. "The girl is totally *not* in her right mind. The question is, What's doing it?"

"No, Taylor," I say. "That's not it at all. The question is, Will Courtney let us help her?"

"We won!"

Monday afternoon, Kaitlin bursts through the back door into the kitchen and drops her lacrosse gear next to the refrigerator while she digs out a Vitaminwater. Celia and I look up from our homework to take in my sister's appearance. Her blue, white, and yellow uniform is covered in grass stains and red Georgia dirt. A tuft of grass is caked on her right shoulder. Her left knee is scraped up, and her ponytail has seen better days.

"God, you're a mess. What does the other team look like?" I joke.

"We kicked their ass!" Kaitlin proclaims.

"Watch the mouth, kiddo." I don't remember being allowed to say *ass* when I was thirteen. I probably shouldn't even say it now, come to think of it.

"Why? Are you going to tell Mom?"

"Tell me what?" Mom asks as she walks into the kitchen laden with grocery bags from Super BI-LO. She holds some out toward me. "Here, Kendall." I jump up.

"Can I help, Miss Sarah?" Celia asks.

Mom relinquishes several bags to both Celia and me. "Thanks, girls."

The clock reads only 4:30. "You're home early," I say.

"Needed to get something for dinner. I think all we have in the fridge is butter, Diet Coke, and three-day-old baked chicken." She turns to Kaitlin. "And what are you going to tell me? That you've been wallowing in a pigsty?"

Kaitlin snorts Vitaminwater out her nose. "No! Umm, nothing other than we won today. You should have seen me. I was awesome! Totally kicked—" She stops and connects her gaze with mine. "—Butt. Totally kicked butt."

Good save, brat.

"That's wonderful, sweetie." Mom picks the grass off of my sister's shoulder and tsk-tsks at her.

"Strip out of those nasty clothes and go take a shower, Kaitin," I tell her.

"Duh, I was just going to." She sticks her tongue out at me, and I roll my eyes.

"What was that all about?" Mom asks. She takes a big hunk of meat out of the bag and places it on the counter.

"Kaitlin said a wirty dord."

We hear the shower start upstairs and Mom sighs. "I guess that's inevitable. I can't keep my girls little forever." She continues pulling out carrots, potatoes, celery, and onions. Mmm . . . she's making Yankee pot roast, one of my faves. No one cooks like my mom. Celia knows this 'cause she has to suffer through re-heatable meals that their housekeeper, Alice, makes in advance for the busy family that never eats together. I guess that's why Cel's so damn skinny.

She and I help unload the groceries and then finish up our homework. I'm so tired of this pig-dissection project with Courtney. Fortunately, we only have another week and then we're done. Courtney was zombielike in class today, and I had to do pretty much all of the work to remove the pig's heart. Like . . . *ick.*

Mom flits around the kitchen getting the pot roast going; the air is filled with the tang of seared meat and simmering vegetables. It's truly a comforting smell.

"Are you girls working on a case?" Mom asks from the other side of the kitchen.

Celia sits up. "You mean like a ghost investigation?"

Mom stops wiping the counter. "Well . . . yes. I'm interested to learn what it is that you do. I'm trying to be more open-minded and accepting of my psychic daughter."

A warm rush of pride slides through me. I pull out the kitchen chair between Celia and me and invite Mom to sit down. Celia has a couple of files from closed-out cases that we're going to discuss. We're deciding what evidence we can put on our website. However, there's one file marked Active, which Mom zeros in on. I can read it in her mind as well as her eyes.

I clear my throat. "We're helping a fellow student who's been seeing a spirit. He's sort of . . . messing with her."

Mom raises an eyebrow. "How so?"

Celia laughs. "He makes her act out and do things that only a guy would do. It's actually quite fascinating."

With a gasp, Mom says, "Isn't that dangerous? It could be something demonic."

I scowl across the table at my friend. Mom's trying to participate in my life, and I don't want to scare her off immediately with talk of spirit possession and whatnot. I think Celia gets the message.

Waving my hand, I say, "No, no, don't worry about this. We can show you something a *lot* more interesting. It's this new thing that Celia and I started doing."

Mom seems slightly relieved. "Whatever you want to show me."

"Let's do the spirit-art thing," I say, almost bouncing in my seat.

Celia pulls a sketchpad from her book bag, along with a tray of pencils. She sharpens a couple and lays them next to the blank sheet of paper and a gigantic pink eraser. "Ready when you are, chief."

I inhale a deep breath. "Okay, you see, Cel here is wicked good at drawing. So what I do is describe the spirit that I see in my head or however they show themselves to me. It's like getting a police-artist sketch. Then we can show it to the family or whoever to see what the connection is to the deceased."

With a nod of her head, Mom seems intrigued. "I'd very much like to see you two do this."

"Excellent!"

Celia frowns. "Who do you want to draw though, Kendall?"

"Oh, I've got it! Let's draw Emily!"

"Who's Emily?" Mom asks.

"The ghost that lives here in the house." When I witness Mom's cheeks pale, I reassure her. "She's nice, Mom. Don't worry. Pretty too. You'll like her."

Her hand slips up to grip her neck like she's trying to force herself to breathe . . . to accept. "I'm not too sure, Kendall."

"It'll be cool. Let's do it."

I close my eyes and center my breathing, slowing it, almost.

I block out the sound of Kaitlin moving around on the upper floor and the pot roast bubbling away on the stove. The sole focus of my attention is Emily. I've seen her so many times, it's like conjuring up an old friend in my memory. However, she helps out by appearing for me, right next to Celia.

Trying not to freak out Mom any more, I speak to Emily in my head.

Thanks, Emily!

"I don't know if that's such a good idea, Kendall."

Why not?

"Your mother is very skeptical. I don't want her to send me away."

Don't be silly, Emily. No one's sending you away until you're ready to go.

I begin describing my spirit friend. "She has long dark hair and soft green eyes, not too far apart. Her nose is slender, as is her face. And she's really pale."

Celia glances at me over her notepad. "She's a ghost, Kendall. Of course she's pale."

That gets a laugh out of Mom.

Over the next fifteen minutes, I describe Emily from memory and by how she appears to me now at the kitchen table. I decide to have Celia give her a pretty smile instead of the glower she's tossing at me.

What?

"I just don't like this, Kendall."

I need the practice, Emily.

"I wish your friend wouldn't practice on me."

You're just being silly.

"Almost done," Celia says. I love watching her draw. She's like a five-year-old with a crayon in her hand for the first time. Her tongue hangs out of her mouth and circles her lips, as if she's sketching with it as well as the pencil. Her eyes are focused on her task, and then a smile breaks out over her face. As she flips the notepad around, she says, "Ta-da!"

"Awesome! You drew her perfectly!" I exclaim.

My joy is short-lived though; Mom sucks in an enormous gulp of air and nearly falls out of her seat.

"Mom! Are you okay?"

"Miss Sarah?"

"Wh-wh-where did you see that woman?" she asks through short breaths.

"What do you mean? This is Emily. The ghost here in our house."

Mom's eyes tear up, and her face reddens. "That's impossible."

"What is it, Miss Sarah? You look like you've seen . . . well, a ghost."

Mom regains her balance, stands, and pushes the chair back to the table. She turns and heads to the fridge, where she grabs a bottle of water. I watch the liquid disappear in three, four huge gulps. Mom is shaking and is afraid to tell me something.

Fear radiates off her in a halo of light. Her aura is a shocking muddy blue to my eyes. Quickly, I dig my aura-meaning reference out of my bag and flip to the right section. The color I'm seeing means fear of the future, fear of self-expression, fear of facing or speaking the truth.

What truth? My mom's no liar. Maybe I'm just wigging her out with all of this. Yet I swear I saw recognition in her eyes when Celia showed her the drawing of Emily.

I silently cross the room and touch Mom in the middle of her back. She jumps three feet in the air, like she's been zapped with a Taser. "Mom? Are you okay?"

Her back is still turned, but I sense her calming herself and compressing her unease into a neat pocket somewhere deep inside her stomach. "I'm fine, dear. Just overwhelmed to actually *see* this ghost you say is in our house."

Celia brings the drawing to us. "She's not frightening though, Miss Sarah. Look how pretty she is. So young. I wish she'd tell Kendall how she died."

Mom swallows. "You don't know?"

"No, I don't. Emily won't tell me anything. Says she's just here to guide me, that's all. But it's a mystery I'd love to solve." Emily's still standing next to the kitchen table, not pleased with me at all. Her eyes reflect a gloominess that I'm sorry I brought on. Maybe she thinks Mom and Dad will force her to leave me now. "Emily's just a little older than I am and she'd never do anything to hurt me. It's like having a big sister, almost."

Mom begins to choke, and lifts the plastic bottle to finish off the water that's left in it.

The ends of my fingers tingle where I'm connected to Mom, and I'm wondering if she's hiding something from me. That fear of facing the truth that her aura is radiating; she couldn't . . .

"Do you know her, Mom?"

She spins toward me, horror painted on her face. "What? I don't see spirits like you do!"

"No, I mean, did you *know* her when she was alive?"

"I don't know what you're talking about, Kendall." She rushes around the butcher block in the middle of the kitchen to tend to the pot roast on the stove. The rich savory aroma no longer appeals to me; instead, it makes me feel a little nauseated. Deep in my heart of hearts, I know my mother is lying to me. The woman who taught me the Ten Commandments. The one who punishes me when I'm caught in a fib. She's ducking the truth on this, and I want to know why.

"You *do* recognize her." I grab the notepad from Celia. "Look at her again, Mom. Who is she? I need to know!"

She pushes the sketch away. "Kendall, enough of this." Her breathing is ragged, but then, she composes herself. "I simply thought she looked like this woman I saw on *Inside Edition* the other afternoon. A woman who was wanted for the murder of her boyfriend in Buffalo."

"Since when do you watch *Inside Edition*?"

"Oh, you know, I was cleaning and the TV was on. I just remember seeing a drawing like that. It's really no big deal. I'm still not altogether crazy about the idea of someone else living with us, watching us eat and sleep and bathe."

Emily giggles in my head. At least she's not still mad at me.

"Emily doesn't watch us bathe."

Mom hugs me and kisses the top of my head. "That's what I get for watching those awful TV shows. I'm sorry I reacted negatively. You have a great talent, Celia. I think the two of you make a wonderful team."

I grit my teeth together and grind them a bit. "So, you don't think that Emily's some black-widow killer or what have you?"

Mom stirs the vegetables. "No, certainly not."

However, the muddy blue aura still surrounds her. What does my mother have to hide? What isn't she telling me, and how does her seeing Emily fit into all of this?

"Celia, why don't you stay for supper?" Mom asks. "There's going to be plenty of food."

Somewhat rattled by the whole scene, Celia finally perks up. "Sure thing, Miss Sarah. Beats another night of Alice's cooking."

"You girls run along and wash up while I get this finished."

As we head up the staircase to my room, Emily stops me on the fourth step.

I'm so sorry about that, Em. Mom's trying to understand me.

"You don't have to apologize, Kendall."

I will get to the bottom of who you are.

"Please don't, Kendall. Let me just be your friend and guide you like I'm supposed to do."

I'm pretty stern though. *When this case with Courtney's over, we'll talk.*

And with that, Emily fades away.

Chapter Seventeen

Emily wasn't around this morning when I woke up, although Sonoma the Bear had been moved from my rocking chair to my bed in the middle of the night. I guess she's giving me some distance after the whole freak-out with Mom; I've hardly seen her this whole week.

Saturday, I help Mom out in the yard, planting some bushes around the back fence. I never knew her to have such a green thumb, but she seems motivated to be the Happy Homemaker today. Plus, it's good spending time with Mom as just her daughter, not the kid she's worried about.

Mom and Dad have a dinner date with another couple, so Jason comes over to watch movies with me and hang out. Kaitlin's got Penny Carmickle sleeping over, and I'm allegedly chaperoning. All I want to do, though, is lock them in her room, turn off the lights, and make out with Jason.

He seems annoyed with me. Has he seen the drawing of Emily too? As one of my favorite movies of all time, *French Kiss,* plays on the DVR, I try to snuggle into the nook of Jason's arm.

"Can't we watch *Iron Man*?"

"I thought you wanted to watch something romantic," I say with a frown.

"No, Kendall, I said I wanted romantic time with you."

I spread my hands wide. "What do you call this?"

He rolls his eyes skyward. "I call it baby-sitting."

"Yeah, sorry about that. It was the only way Mom and Dad would let us be alone in the house."

He harrumphs. "Don't they trust you?"

I laugh at him and pick at the zipper of his hoodie. "I don't think they trust *you*."

Jason sighs hard and removes his arm from around me. "Jesus, Kendall. How many people's permissions do I have to get to be with you?"

I sit up, and my mouth drops open. "No one's. I mean, what are you talking about?"

He stands and nearly trips on the sneakers he discarded when he got here an hour ago with pizza, soda, and a smile. "Between not having classes together at school and you always being with my sister, Celia, and Becca, and all of your ghost hunting, and this obsession with what Courtney's going through—"

"Hey! Now, wait a minute. I—"

"And now your parents not trusting us to be together and you having to baby-sit. Not to mention your imaginary friend who's constantly around. It gives me the creeps knowing she's always watching us." He spins back to me, his blue eyes ablaze.

"When do *I* rate some of your time, Kendall? I'm your boy-friend."

"I know, Jason! I'm so sorry. There's just so much going on, you know that."

"That's the sad thing, Kendall. I do know it. You know how long it's been since we just hung out, you and me?"

"We're hanging out now."

"With your little sis and her friend upstairs."

"We went bowling," I say meekly.

He throws his hands up. "Yeah, with Taylor and Ryan and Celia and Dragon and—"

"I know—"

"And it turned into a ghost investigation."

My chest hurts over his words. Not 'cause he's being mean, but because he's right. I don't make him cookies or leave him love notes or fix up for him like I should. I look down at my ratty jeans and Bobby Hull Chicago Blackhawks hockey jersey that I love so much. Would it have killed me to put on a little eye shadow and blush and foof up my hair and wear one of those new outfits from my Atlanta shopping spree?

"Jason, I'm sooooooo sorry."

I walk up to him and wrap my arms around his firm waist. He's hesitant, but he finally gives in and hugs me back. "It's hard being with you, Kendall."

"Why?" I ask, muffled against his chest.

"Because I'm never just alone with *you*."

Pulling away a little bit, I stare dreamily into his amazing eyes that had me from the get-go. "We're alone now," I say with a tease in my voice.

He smiles. "Sort of."

Feeling bold, I lift up on my tiptoes and place my lips on Jason's. At first, he's a little stiff and distant, then he cuddles me into his arms, nearly raising me off my feet as he deepens the kiss. Ahhh . . . there we go. That's much better.

We work our way over to the couch in the flickering light of the television. Images of Meg Ryan and Kevin Kline traipsing through the French countryside fade into the distance and all I concentrate on is the feel of Jason's mouth on mine and his taut, athletic body lying next to me as we make out on the couch.

I love kissing. It's so personal. And so giving. There's nothing like it. I think I was born to do nothing but kiss this boy. His lips are soft and full, and he certainly knows what he's doing. I don't want to think about all the practice he's had before me—especially not the hours spent with Courtney Langdon. I hope he thinks I'm as good a kisser as she was. God, I shouldn't think of things like that. Jason must think I'm a good kisser too 'cause he does this little moany-groan thing when our tongues touch. It's like the best dessert I've ever had without the guilt of thousands of evil calories.

Jason's hands get a little bold, roaming across my stomach and into the waistband of my jeans. I wiggle a little bit to resist. However, I'm also enjoying his warm touch as his fingers grip my stomach and bunch up my shirt. I unzip his hoodie and push it off his arms. I want to be closer to him. I can feel his body heat through the thin Atlanta Braves T-shirt he's wearing. He moves in again to nip at my lips and continue our soul-bonding kiss.

Everything's going just fine until his hands move lower on my belly, dangerously close to the snap of my jeans. Then— pop!—the first button fly is loose. I'm exhilarated! I'm scared shitless! I don't know if I'm ready to take this to the next level with Jason. Certainly not with my little sister and her best friend upstairs. We've only been dating a couple of months af- ter all, and we haven't really had a lot of quality time together. But I am enjoying the sensations rippling through me. Things I've never felt before.

Right now, I'm not a psychic, a sensitive, or a ghost hunt- ress. I'm just Kendall, Jason's girlfriend.

Maybe one more button, but I won't let it go any further.

Then Jason reels back. "Ouch!"

My eyes jerk open. "What?"

"Shit, Kendall! Why'd you pull my hair?"

"I didn't." Did I? I mean, my fingers were woven into his soft tresses at one point, though I don't remember tugging on them. In fact, I know I didn't.

His eyes are dark as he peers down at me. He looks per- turbed.

"I would have stopped. All you had to do was say so," he says, releasing a pent-up sigh.

"I swear, I didn't pull your hair. One of my hands was on

your back and the other was . . . well, it was sort of on your butt." The heat of my blush raises my temperature to a feverish degree.

Jason sits up and reaches to the floor for his hoodie. Suddenly, he falls off the couch and hits the hardwood floor with a resounding boom.

"Damn it! Why'd you go and do that?"

I scramble up and rebutton my jeans. Diving for the nearest light, I turn it on and look around to see if Kaitlin's in here mucking with us. "I swear I didn't do anything, Jason. Maybe you just slid off."

He stuffs his arms into his zip-up and huffs at me. "I got *kicked* off the couch and you know it! What's the deal, Kendall? I thought we were having a good time."

"We were!"

I'm perplexed about why this is happening. We were making out and getting in to each other, and it's like my parents walked in and caught us in the act of—

Suddenly, it's very clear to me.

Emily.

"Emily! You're intruding."

He was taking advantage of you, Kendall.

"Oh my God! It's not taking advantage when I'm going along with it. You know, the whole takes-two-to-tango thing?" And baby, we were tangoing.

Jason runs his hands through his mussed hair. "I don't believe this. You're talking to your ghost, aren't you?"

"Emily pulled your hair and kicked you, Jason. Not me. She's really protective of me."

"Are you kidding?" he asks derisively. "You don't need protection from me. I love you!"

"I love you, too. Emily, leave us alone, please!"

The boy wanted to have his way with you.

"So what?" Not that I was gonna go all the way or anything.

Don't make the same mistake I made.

"What mistake was that?"

"I'm not a mistake," Jason says.

"I wasn't talking to you."

Jason jams his feet into his sneakers, not even bothering to untie them first. "Great. Now you're talking to her instead of me, or whoever. I can't do this, Kendall. Either you're with me or you're with your ghost friends."

"Jason, please. I'm finally getting some clues on who Emily is and trying to—"

"I don't want to hear it, Kendall." He snatches the keys to his Jeep off the top of our piano, which is by the front door. "Call me when you have time for me, okay?"

"Jason, don't leave!"

Too late. I'm staring at his back, and then the door slams shut.

If I weren't so pissed off, I'd cry.

Emily, I swear to God . . .

Don't do that, Kendall. I was just protecting you.

"Look, ghost! I already have a mother. I don't need another guardian."

I have to watch out for you, Kendall . . .

"Umm, no, you don't. I didn't ask for you to be in my life and I didn't request that you run my boyfriend off. Thanks for ruining my night."

Please don't be that way. I only did what I thought was right. Boys get carried away and girls are too emotional to stop them . . .

I grab my hair, wanting to jerk every strand out of my head from frustration. "Ugh! Why don't you find someone else to haunt, Emily."

With that, I storm up the stairs, bang the door to my room shut . . . and I do cry.

Sunday morning, I have a heartache hangover. I tried calling Jason last night, but it went straight to voice mail. Fine. I needed to get some sleep anyway, which I did. Emily didn't bother me and I didn't even wake up when Mom and Dad got home.

My dreams were racked with images of ghosts and spirits and all of the conflicts in my life. Jason was there in the distance, standing apart, as Celia, Taylor, Becca, and I investigated an old abandoned warehouse. Courtney was there, channeling the spirit of every ghost who'd ever been in this building. She was crying out to me, begging for help, asking that I do everything in my power to free her. I awakened with a jolt, knowing

I have to exorcise this chick from my life. Only then can I make things right with Jason.

I dress and head over with my family to Christ the Redeemer Holy Episcopal Church for some solace.

Ahhh, church . . . the last refuge of a scoundrel.

When the service is over, I tell my parents I'll walk home and to go ahead without me. I linger in the vestibule of the church as all of the other parishioners compliment Father Massimo on his sermon. Something about Peter and the Church and I don't know because I was so kerfuffled over thinking about how to help Courtney. Courtney, Courtney, Courtney—she has taken over my life! Ghost hunting has taken over my life. Jason's right. Ugh!

Still, I can't get past the unavoidable fact that Courtney was stupid enough to open herself up to something that is now imposing its will on her. No matter what Jason or anyone thinks, it *is* my duty as a psychic medium to try to wrestle the thing away from her.

I cram down the sting of Jason's walking out on me last night and keep my eyes on the task at hand, getting the best advice that I can.

"How'd you like today's sermon, Kendall?" Father Mass asks when the last few people head out of the church.

"It was great, one of your best." Man, I'm lying to a priest in church. *Now* who's evil? "Can I talk to you?"

"I don't know. Can you?" he says with a smirk.

Great. Even my priest is a smart-ass. "May I?"

He lifts his vestment off of his shoulders and nods his head back toward the church. "You know I'm always here for you."

I follow him up to the altar, where he gathers the remains of today's Communion and puts them away. He kisses his vestments and hangs them carefully in a cabinet behind the choir loft.

I strike out with the burning question. "Can I ask you about exorcisms?"

His handsome face is scrunched into a pained look when he turns to me. "Now, why would you need to know anything about that?"

"I thought I'd read somewhere that the Episcopal Church has a ceremony for it."

Father Mass removes his robe slowly and hangs it in the closet also. Then he lets out a long sigh. "The *Book of Occasional Services* does indeed talk about exorcisms and provisions that can be made for them. However, there aren't any definitive rites or rituals to be followed."

"But you know how to do one, right?"

He squints. "I might. I'm not allowed to though."

"Why not?"

"Because there are rules within the church, Kendall. I can't perform an exorcism without the permission of the bishop. He has to bring in psychiatrists and physicians to examine the person in question and approve of a cleansing of the possessed."

I hold my index finger up. "Aha. What if it's not a possession but an oppression?"

"Semantics, Kendall."

I sit in one of the choir chairs. "Loreen says if a spirit is oppressing you, he or she is influencing your actions and behaviors without actually inhabiting your body or possessing you."

He harrumphs. "Loreen again, huh? She sure has a lot to say about everything."

"Loreen's given me tons of good advice. That's why I'm here talking to you. I e-mailed her about what's going on, and she said I needed to get guidance from you."

His mood lightens. "Very well, then. Why don't you tell me exactly what's happening?"

Father Mass sits next to me, and I tell him what's been going on with Courtney since the incident at the Halloween party escalated like it did.

"Oh, that girl. I tried contacting her family afterward. Only, no response."

"Yeah, her."

And like that, his disposition darkens again. "Look, Kendall. If that girl is possessed, we're looking at some nasty business that you and your friends should *not* get involved in."

"We haven't done anything yet, Father, I promise. But Courtney's messed up and needs help."

He places a finger beneath my chin. "Under no circumstances are you ghost huntresses to attempt an exorcism on your own. Don't fool with that!"

Defending my group, I say, "We don't think it's something demonic; we think it's this Union soldier we've encountered over and over again who just generally seems pissed off at everything." Ooops. "Sorry about that, Father."

"That's okay. 'Piss' is in the Bible." He pauses a moment. "Kendall, you've got a good head on your shoulders, and you've been taking advice very well. If you need me to intervene and talk to Courtney, I'll do it. But she has to know what's going on first. It has to be her decision."

"I know. That's the tricky part."

"Well, you'll think of something," he says with a devilish smile.

"Loreen said she'd help too."

Father Mass chuckles as he stands up. "It doesn't hurt to have all of your bases covered."

"Thanks, Father. I'll keep you posted."

As I head out of the church, he calls to me. "Kendall. If Courtney truly let a spirit inside her or is allowing it to manipulate her, only *she* can dispel it."

A moan involuntarily escapes me. "That's what I was afraid of."

The next day at school, my BlackBerry *bbbbrrrrrrringggs,* signaling a text message. From Celia.

>More Courtney oddities.

>Dish

Two seconds later—

>Chk e-mail

Sure enough, there's detailed information from Celia.

From: TechGeekGirl@mail.com
To: kendall.moorehead@chicago.net
Subject: Langdon Case

Overheard Mr. Preston, the band director, talking to the school nurse, known forward as Witness 1 and Witness 2. Seems C. Langdon was in the band room this morning sitting on a table, playing a brass instrument, thought to be a cornet perhaps. Witness 1 says C. Langdon doesn't actually play a trumpet or cornet that he's aware of. Witness 1 says C. Langdon was playing a "soulful rendition of 'Amazing Grace' and was crying as she was playing." Witness 2 reports that C. Langdon was brought to the office where she complained of having a stomachache. Tums were dispensed and C. Langdon returned to class.

Celia

She is *such* a dork. But I appreciate the information all the same.

I observe Courtney across the cafeteria. The girl has two trays in front of her and she is shoveling in food as if she hasn't seen a decent meal in months. (Which, considering her daily gastrointestinal pyrotechnics, is probably the case.) This is so not like her well-documented near-bulimic self. My God, there's so much food: Rice and beans. French fries. A cheese-burger with the works. Chocolate cake. Mac 'n' cheese. Carbs, carbs, carbs. There is no way in holy hell that I'm going any-where near the girls' bathroom after lunch for what's sure to be a puke-fest for the ages.

Later on, in physiology, I'm busy working on our piglet while Courtney stares down at it as if she's hypnotized. And she very well may be.

"Courtney?" I prompt softly. "You okay?"

She hunches her shoulders and then begins scratching un-der her left armpit. Ewww!

"Damn lice," she mutters in a dark voice. "I've done every-thing I can to get rid of them."

My mouth gapes as I scrutinize her actions. Others around us turn to look.

I lower my voice. "Courtney, are you telling me you have lice?"

She starts pawing through her long blond hair. "With all of this, the bugs are liable to take root for years. Colonel told all of us to wash good with the lye."

Senses on overload, I'm picking up images of the Union soldier who entered her body at the Halloween party. He's in an encampment, sitting around a fire with other men. He's preoccupied and distracted. He's worried about getting dysen-tery. The image shifts and disappears as quickly as it came.

Courtney interrupts by saying, "So many of my friends have died from dysentery."

"Really? Like who?"

Picking at the pig with a scalpel, she says, "Mills, Doyle, Clark, and Dolan. Hell, Dolan was just a baby—only nineteen. Didn't deserve to die like that. Had a girl back home. He wrote to her all the time and carried her picture with him. No one ever wrote to me."

This isn't Courtney at all. Sure, physically it's her, but she's not alone in her body. The soldier from the party is with her now! He was the one making her act all weird at the football game. And here he is, right beside me.

Boldly, I take her hand and squeeze hard.

"Courtney. Are you in there?"

The soldier's ominous laugh echoes not only in my head but throughout the science lab. Pain like a steak knife slicing through a piece of meat spreads from one temple to the other. My right eye begins to twitch, and the hand I'm holding pulsates underneath my fingers like the blood is nearly at a boiling point.

"Who are you?" I ask.

No response.

I move closer, leaning to whisper in her ear. "Courtney, is there any way you can reach out to me? Anything. I'll help you. I swear I will, no matter what."

The soldier jerks her hand away, knocking it onto the corner of the lab table and breaking one of her perfect nails.

"What's your name?" I ask.

"I know your game," she growls through clenched teeth. "I know all about you."

While Courtney moves to "adjust" herself with one hand, she nabs a pencil with the other. She tries to write something, but it seems the soldier inside won't allow her to do this. Instead, she reaches for her cell phone, which I doubt the soldier would have the first freakin' clue about. She furiously moves her right hand over the buttons and then turns the phone to face me.

The soldier cackles again in my head, intensifying my pain and the eye twitch.

I slide the phone toward me and hold my breath.

>PLZ SAVE ME!

Courtney is in there. She heard me. And she wants my help.

"I'm on it."

Chapter Eighteen

Just as I'm about to fall asleep in my history class—discussion of the Restoration, Reformation, Renaissance, or some other historical *r* word—my phone vibrates in my pocket. My heart soars when I see it's a text message from Jason.

>it's me.

>hey me.

>what up?

>tryin 2 stay awake.

>me 2.

This is the first time we've talked since he stormed out the other night. I don't know whether he's still ticked off at me or what. I attempt to break the ice as Mrs. Hixon blathers on about Martin Luther and the Peace at Westphalia in 16-some-thing-or-other.

>so . . . ?

>I'm sorry I wuz a dick.

>U wrn't a dick.

Yeah, he really was, but I get it.

>Yes I wuz.

>I understand. Em was out of line.

>So wuz I I'm sorry.

>u said that. ☺

>mean it.

>love u, mean it.

>ur adorable.

>no, u r.

>;) c u soon.

The bell rings, signaling the end of the day, and I stash my BlackBerry in my purse. Jason and I have definitely begun *our* restoration. Could we *be* any cuter?

On Thursday, I sigh as I look at the folder that Celia has compiled on my archenemy . . . and our new client: File GH-0023— Courtney Langdon.

"Great," I mutter.

"Was Courtney in school today?" Celia asks from her computer.

Taylor sets her Nikon D40 camera (a new toy she got off eBay) on the floor and pipes up. "She called in sick the last couple of days. Stephanie and Farah told me she was completely embarrassed about what-all she's been doing in public and has been hiding out in her room feigning some incapacitation."

Yeah, I've been on my own with the pig dissection, which is fine with me. A person can only take so many gnarly looks in a day.

"Whatever," Becca says. "She deserves what she gets. The bitch toyed with the spirits and bagged on what we're doing. She asked for this."

Sadly, Becca's right. However, it's our duty as ghost huntresses to help anyone who reaches out to us. Even Courtney Langdon.

"That's why we've gathered the team." I stand up in front of the girls and smooth out the wrinkles in my jeans. Jason and Clay—de facto members of the team—are absent right now, doing whatever it is that boys do after school on a Thursday, while we establish a game plan for dealing with the Union soldier who's playing marionette with one of the most popular girls in school. "Celia, you wanna tell us what you've been able to dig up?"

She swivels in the leather chair and plants her Reeboks firmly on the carpet in front of her. "So, I've done some research on the Crawford house."

"Why?" Taylor asks with a bit of a pout. "Shouldn't we be looking at Courtney's instead?"

"No," Celia explains, "this entity seems to be tied to the Crawford house. That's why he felt comfortable enough to bust in on our investigation in the carriage house with Stephanie's grandfather, and then later to attend a party and step into one of the guests."

"Who just so happened to have invited him in," Becca interjects.

Celia rolls her neck for a moment. "Annnyway. According

to the registrar of deeds, the house has been in Miss Evelyn's family dating back to the early 1800s. In the Radisson library, I found some old lithographs of Union soldiers encamped in the area during Sherman's March to the Sea. Throughout Georgia, troops were left behind to police the locals and secure whatever properties they could. One of the places where Union soldiers camped out was right on Crow Lane." She pulls a large map off her desk and spreads it on the floor, pointing to the location of the property where Evelyn and Stephanie Crawford live.

"So because of the ginormous yard, the Yankees made it their home?" Taylor asks, poring over the map. "I hope no one got raped or pillaged."

"It wasn't the Middle Ages," Becca says with a smirk.

"Yeah, but that shit happened," Celia says.

"Those poor people," Taylor says and adds another good pout. Often I wonder who the real empath is here. That girl feels everyone's pain.

Taylor shifts on the floor and stretches out her legs. I hear the *click* and *ping* as she scrolls through her digital images. I know without looking that they're the pictures she took the night of Stephanie's party.

I crawl across the room on my hands and knees to perch next to Taylor and gaze over her shoulder. Typical party pics of people making silly faces and all smashed together in group hugs and stuff. There are a lot of goofy ones of all of us in our costumes. My heart instantly picks up speed when I see Jason in his tight Batman attire.

Taylor straightens. "Ooo . . . is that a soldier?" She points at a pic of Celia, me, and Becca all sticking out our tongues at the camera. "See. Look."

Sure enough, in the background, there's a man in a navy blue uniform circa the Civil War era. My instincts tell me it's the same soldier I was dealing with that night, even though I can only see him from behind. I can literally smell the musty wool of his uniform and sense the dirt clogged under his fingernails from weeks—months, even—on the battlefield. The stench of iron-y blood and sweat and tears and lives lost in a war of brother versus brother.

"Is this dude following us around?" Becca asks, obviously referring to the Lockhart case.

"It's possible. Anything's possible." I pause for a moment and tune in to all of the vibrations creeping through my body. The pinch of the psychic headache. The tremble of my hands and legs. The immense sorrow filling my heart. The symptoms permeate my entire being. "We've got to get back to the Crawford house, set up our equipment, and really begin to dig around there. It's the only way we can help Courtney."

Celia reaches for her cell. "I'll call Stephanie right now."

"We need reinforcements on this one," I say.

"I'm on it."

A while later, three visitors arrive at Celia's house: Stephanie, Loreen, and Father Mass. Steph plops down onto the living room sectional and lets out a long sigh. The last two are confused as to why the other is there. I can read it in both of their eyes as they move into the Nicholses' house and take seats opposite each other.

Animosity swirls in the air between them. Eyes cut across the room, touching on each other. I wish they could just be friends, since I trust them both with my life.

"Thanks for coming, you guys," I say, breaking the tension in the room.

Loreen shifts her gaze to me and smiles. "Anything you need, Kendall." I try not to giggle at the latest T-shirt she's wearing. It reads, "If You're Telekinetic, Raise My Hands."

"Are y'all really going to go ghost busting in my house?" Stephanie asks.

"We don't bust," Celia says, a bit irritated. "That's for the movies. We'll investigate the instances of paranormal activity by interviewing you and your mother, and we'll do all we can to rid Courtney of the entity that seems to be occupying her."

Father Massimo puts up his hands. "Now, look, I don't want you girls trying to do an exorcism. Kendall, we've already talked about this."

I shoot back, "I promised you that *we* wouldn't. That's why you and Loreen are here. Between the two of you—your age, experience, wisdom—we can work together to help Courtney. First, we've got to know what we're up against."

Loreen tosses a smug glance Father Castellano's way. "If

we're dealing with an oppression, we just have to convince the girl to muster her strength and throw the bum out. I'm willing to work with you if you're willing to work with me."

"I shouldn't be involved in this."

"But you are," I say.

He sighs. "Tell me your plan."

"First we'll investigate Stephanie's house and try to flush this guy out and see what his deal is," I explain.

"What do I do?" Stephanie asks with a concerned look.

Celia swivels from side to side in her chair. "We'll need full access to your house and any historical documents you or your mom have about the time when the Union soldiers were encamped in your yard."

"Sure, sure . . ."

"Your mom told me that she had diaries from Ada Parry—that's Evelyn's great-great-grandmother," I say to Loreen and Father Mass. "If we can read through those, perhaps we can piece together a narrative and see where this ghost might fit in."

"You've got it," Stephanie says. "My house has creeped me out my whole life, so maybe this'll help cleanse it too."

"We'll do our best," Loreen assures her.

"Okay, Celia, fill them in on what we've got so far."

After Celia details everything we know to date, Father Mass frowns.

"I don't know about this whole oppression thing. I think we're dealing with something more serious. Perhaps demonic."

"Kendall would know if she was dealing with something demonic," Loreen says sharply.

"I don't think it's—" I begin. However, the adults talk around me, not hearing what I'm saying.

Loreen seems exasperated at Father Massimo. "You're being a stick-in-the-mud."

"And you're taking this too lightly," he responds. "If you want me involved, I'll need to bring the bishop in on this and get his permission for a formal exorcism."

Loreen scoffs at him. "Under your rules and regulations, that'll take weeks. This girl doesn't have weeks."

"I know that!"

I try to mediate. "You guys—"

Continuing, Loreen insists, "Courtney's in the driver's seat with this and she has to get rid of the spirit herself."

I notice that the more these two argue, the closer they get. Their auras are practically on fire with desire and passion, whether for the topic or for . . . each other? Seriously? *That's* what I'm picking up? Honest to Pete, if that's the case, why don't they just do it and get it over with? Sheesh!

"Can't you do this for her?" Loreen shouts.

"You want me to lose my job?" Father Mass says back sternly.

Loreen pushes her strawberry blond curls out of her face. "I didn't know they could fire priests."

"I can lose my parish."

"Guys! Please!" I say, waving my arms. "I appreciate both of your suggestions and we'll take everything into account. As long as I know you're both onboard, that's what matters. We've got a lot of research to do before our next step. Courtney reached out to me, but will the soldier allow her near us? That remains to be seen. We'll see what we can do." I glance at Loreen. "With your help, of course."

Her eyes light up. "Whatever you need. Right, Father?"

He stares her down with his dark eyes and I can see his hesitation melt somewhat.

"You don't have to do anything that the bishop wouldn't approve of," she says. "Just *be there* for Kendall. Can you do that?"

"Then it's settled," I say. "Loreen, Father Mass, we'll set up Saturday night for an investigation. We want you both with us. Ten, okay?"

"Absolutely," she says.

Father Mass is still noncommittal. "I can't promise anything, Kendall. I have to operate under the rules of the church."

"You have to do what you have to do, Father. So do I."

"I'll pray for you all," he notes.

Celia stands up. "Then we go back to the Crawford house and start figuring this out."

Yep. We'll get to the bottom of this. My Spidey senses tell me so!

———

On Friday night, at the Crawfords' Miss Evelyn sets down an antique chest that she's pulled out of the attic. Dust floats out in gentle puffs as she heaves the lid off to delve into the contents.

"I haven't opened this in years." She plunders through delicate silk materials that appear as thin as butterfly wings and removes a jewelry box, a pack of letters, and several deep red journals with crinkled old pages. "I read Ada's diaries when I was in my teens, but I couldn't tell you for the life of me what's in them. The only thing I recall is feeling like I was reading a romance novel."

"Great," Becca says with a sneer. I knock her in the side with my elbow.

Miss Evelyn hands the three diaries over to me. I promptly turn to Becca and plunk them in her arms. "I think you and Taylor should read over these while Celia and I try to get a sketch of the soldier."

"Whatever you gals need," Miss Evelyn says. "Stephanie, you help them however they want."

"Yes, Mom."

The front-door bell chimes, and next thing I know, Jason and Clay walk in.

Jason kisses me quickly on my temple and slips his arm around my waist. "What do you need me to do?"

"Yeah, put me to work," Clay says with a wink to Celia.

She blushes slightly at the obvious PDA.

"Jason, you can help Taylor and Becca read the diaries. The quicker we can get a handle on Ada Parry's background and whatever angst she put in her journals, the sooner we can piece this together."

Celia hands an EMF detector to Clay and sets him off to explore the Crawford house and draw a map of the layout, highlighting the areas of high electrical energy coming from fixtures and plugs. The Tillsons and Becca spread out on the couch in the living room and get to work reading. Tomorrow night's the ghost hunt, so tonight—Friday—we're doing some preliminary research, trying to find out as much as we can about Ada Parry and what happened in this house so long ago.

"You ready for me?" I ask Celia.

Picking up a small fishing-tackle box and a large drawing pad, she asks me, "Where you wanna do this?"

"Let's go back into the ballroom where we got the pictures of the guy and where I first saw him clearly."

The ballroom seems so empty compared with its festive appearance at the Halloween party. On the back wall is a century-old crushed-velvet settee. I lower myself to it, feeling the aged springs creak under my weight. Celia sprawls on the floor in front of me and opens the tablet. She nabs a few pencils and is ready to get down to business.

Over the next fifteen minutes, I describe the soldier to the best of my ability. She's sketching away furiously, with her tongue wiggling out of her mouth. She probably isn't even aware that she's concentrating so hard on the drawing.

"No, closer together," I say, pointing to the outline of the eyes that she's drawn. "And his mustache isn't that bushy."

"Back off, Moorehead," she says with a laugh. "I'm still creating."

A few minutes later and Celia flips the pad my way. "Voilà!"

"Un-freaking-believable," I say with a gasp. "You nailed him."

She smiles up at me from the floor.

Stephanie enters the room with two Diet Cokes for us. She freezes in her tracks when she see Celia's latest masterpiece. The sodas nearly slip from her hands. "Holy shit! That's him!" She gives us the sodas.

"Who him?" I ask.

Pointing, Stephanie says, "The guy. I've seen him in our backyard and over at my grandparents' house." She shakes the memory out of her head. "I always thought I was dreaming or hallucinating. It was a few years back, when Dad still lived here. I saw this dude outside and he was laughing. Mom and Dad were having one of their famous fights and I'd left the house to give them some room. That guy was there. He was, I swear."

I move in to hold her hand and comfort her. "I believe you, Steph."

"But . . . but . . . but he's a *ghost*? I saw a ghost? That is beyond freaky."

I scrunch up my face. *Welcome to my world.*

"He's obviously connected to you, your family, and your house."

She begins to shake in my grip. "Don't worry, Steph. We're here and we're going to help."

We've got to get through those diaries and find out what on God's green earth is going on here.

CHAPTER NINETEEN

"ANYONE WANT ANYTHING from the kitchen?" Celia asks.

I stifle a yawn with the back of my hand. "I'll have another Diet Coke."

Taylor looks up from the diary she's reading and shifts her eyes to the clock. "It's way past one, Kendall. You'll never get any sleep with that much caffeine in your system."

"Like I ever really sleep anymore."

You need your sleep, Kendall . . .

I bolt up, startled by Emily's appearance in my thoughts.

Where have you been?

Trying not to get in your way . . .

But I need your help with this ghost, I nearly beg inside my mind.

You're doing just fine. Your friends are all the help you need right now . . .

"But—"

Emily's gone though, just as quickly as she popped in.

"Check this out," Becca says. She moves the pile of papers

Celia printed out from Stephanie's computer and comes over to where Taylor and I are sprawled on the rug. "There's this passage here in Ada's diary that mentions spending a lot of time with a Union soldier named Major Nathan Fair, from Columbus, Ohio. She says he was kind to her, 'not like the rest of those beasts.' Wonder if that's our guy?" She clutches the sketch Celia did, as if she's trying to see if the drawing matches what she's been reading about.

"I didn't realize people from Ohio were in Sherman's ranks," I say.

Celia sticks a pen behind her right ear. "Sure. By that time, a lot of the corps and divisions were scattered and devastated due to loss of life and armies splitting to go in different directions. After Sherman left Atlanta, he divided his army into two wings that went separate ways to the sea. I think one of them headed to Macon, while the other moved toward Savannah and Augusta. They flanked each other by about twenty or so miles, never getting too far apart, in case they needed to pull back together for any leftover Confederate resistance."

"And that's when they did all of the raping and pillaging?" Taylor asks.

I shake my head. "It couldn't have been that bad, since Ada Parry wrote about it in her diaries so calmly, like Miss Evelyn said."

"Sherman and his guys were real dicks," Celia assures us. "They ravaged farms and livestock and God knows what else.

I mean, it horrified Southerners. All that time, they'd thought they were safe in their own homes, but there comes Sherman and his band, and soon people were hungry, had very few belongings, and were generally demoralized in every way. You saw *Gone With the Wind*. Seldom did the Union troops show sympathy for the towns and farms they raided, so it's an anomaly that Ada would write about any of the soldiers in any kind of a romantic manner."

A pent-up sigh escapes from my lips. "Wars are just the stupidest things ever. Started by men because of pride and power and prestige. And who gets hurt? Women, children, animals, and soldiers who had to fight for what they thought was right."

"Yeah, if women were in charge, things would be different." Taylor raises her fist high and cries out. "*Alimenter aux femmes! Power to women!*"

I know I started the topic, but the pain from so many Civil War soldiers—from both sides—permeates the very land and air here in Radisson. The jillions of tombstones in the Radisson cemetery from that time are a testament to the death toll in the town. Citizens, strangers, slaves, and Indians. Death wasn't discriminatory. "I don't mean to put a damper on your twenty-first-century suffragette movement, but we need to concentrate on the diaries," I say. "Can we get back to this Major Fair character?"

"Sure," Becca says. She carefully flips a couple of pages back in one of Ada's journals and reads out loud:

"'Today Major Fair brought me an egg. I haven't had one in weeks. The soldiers have taken all of our chickens and either eaten them or cooped them up to take when they leave. *If they leave*. The egg was a special gift and an answer to my prayers to God. I believe Major Fair took pity on my soul because a few days earlier he had found me praying in what was left of my mother's treasured rose garden. I was crying to the Heavenly Father, asking his mercy and deliverance from this fate we were experiencing. Major Fair approached me with his hat in his hand and extended a tattered and yellowed handkerchief. The gesture was appreciated, even if it was from a Yankee.'

"Then three days later, there's another entry," Becca tells us.

"'Major Fair brought me vegetables today, along with two roasted chicken legs. One carrot, one potato, one radish, and one beet. I used the ingredients to make a soup for Father, who is still feeble and weak from the scarlet fever that spread through the county. Major Fair understands that my concern for Father and my younger sister is greater than that for my own well-being. I simply want these Yankees off my family's land so we can start anew.'"

Jason clomps into the room holding a diary. "Are y'all talking about the Union soldier Ada had a crush on?"

"A crush?" I ask, somewhat taken aback. "What have *you* been reading?"

"Yeah," Jason says, thumbing through the journal. "She took walks with him and he brought her flowers and courted her like a proper gentleman, even though it was a weirded-out sitch."

"You can say that again," Celia chimes in.

"Go on," Taylor prompts her brother.

"Well, Ada gushes on for a ton of pages about poetry they talked about and music and how she always wanted to travel to Vienna, Austria. He told her about Columbus, Ohio, where he was from, and how the people weren't any different than Georgians. The people of Columbus were just as affected by the war."

As an aside, Celia says, "Did you know that ninety percent of the bullets used in the Civil War—and the railroad ties of the time—came from the factories in Ohio? The North's industrial strength allowed it—"

I stop her with my hand. "Celia. Not now. History class is Monday."

She blows her bangs out of her eyes. "But it's all part of the puzzle, Kendall. The more we understand about these people and what they experienced, the more we'll be able to talk to this soldier on his own level and convince him to leave Courtney alone, once and for all."

My heart pings as I remember that I also need to help this ghost cross into the light. Into peace. "You're right, Cel."

"What else did you read, Jason?" Taylor asks.

He scratches his blond head. "I know I'm just a guy and stuff, but I swear Ada was bat-shit crazy over this Fair person, even though he was the enemy and occupying her land. He treated her like a lady and protected her from the other horny men in the unit."

Becca snickers. "You just said *horny* and *unit* in the same sentence."

Jason smacks at her with the old diary and the two of them laugh. Celia dives over to retrieve the precious historic book.

"Jesus, Tillson! That thing's like a hundred and fifty years old! Careful!"

"Sorry!"

These diaries allude to a special relationship between Ada Parry and Major Nathan Fair, but was there more? I reach up and take the journal from Celia and clutch it to my heart. The metal buckle on the outside of the book radiates energy that tickles the ends of my fingers. Is this Ada's vigor coming through to me, like when I held Evelyn Crawford's keys?

"Ada, if you're here, please talk to me," I whisper.

Nothing. No psychic vibrations. No headache. No tingles.

"Ada? I'd really love to connect with you."

"We have a lot of questions," Celia pipes up, trying to help.

Still, the airwaves are silent.

I grip the book tighter, like that's going to help. "Please?"

She's long passed, Kendall . . .

So are you.

It's different . . .

How so?

Ada Parry has crossed over and is at peace.

And you're not. My shoulders sag forward. I can't even help Emily. How am I supposed to help Fair?

I breathe in the musty tang of the old pages, trapped in time and filled with flowing memories of a society long gone. I can't fathom what it must have been like for Ada Parry—only eighteen years old—when the Union soldiers marched into her town and took over her home. Her mother gone and her father sick, Ada was the only barrier protecting her eleven-year-old sister, according to her missives. It was a total tectonic shift to her entire world. Gone were the afternoon picnics on the lush green lawns. No longer did their ballroom ring with sweet string melodies for fine ladies and gentlemen to reel along with. Those days of wine and roses were gone, replaced with hardships, lack of food, and immense poverty. Still, I clearly see Ada, her clothes dirty and torn, her hair falling from its usually neat bun, forging ahead through all of this. She stands tall against Sherman's men, keeping her family first and her own needs second.

Until . . .

It's so lucid to me, almost as if I'm sleepwalking through her life. No, that's not a good way to put it. It's more like flashed images. Frame-by-frame instances. The overall plot of her life's tale spun out for me. The message is clear. In a world gone mad around her, Ada Parry found love. Not just any love, but the love of her life. The kind that poets write about and pop singers croon about. A deep, powerful adoration based on mutual respect and intense attraction.

"Ada Parry was in love with Nathan Fair."

Jason's eyes pop and he stares at me. "Damn, Kendall. You are good. I'd just gotten to that part in the diary."

Taylor holds up a bundle of letters that's held together with a faded pink ribbon. "That might explain these. Love letters."

"They're from Fair to Ada, aren't they?" I don't even wait for her answer because the flowing words of unadulterated devotion scroll across my mind like I'm reading them myself.

"My Southern beauty who's been touched by the sun to shine on my dreary day and make it bright with the light of your heart's glow."

Wow. Fair knew how to woo.

Taylor carefully rummages through the letters, scan-reading as fast as she can. At times, she places her hand to her heart. At others, her blue eyes fill with tears.

"What is it?" Celia asks.

One droplet escapes down Taylor's cheek, and she quickly swipes it away. I can see that she's thinking of the love her own parents once shared. Seeing the love of Fair and Ada on the page before her is conjuring up the melancholy she tries so hard to keep below the surface.

"This is poetry to the one he loved," she says with a sniff.

Jason's true thoughts are betrayed when I see him roll his eyes at his sister from across the room.

"He professes his love and affection for her in such a beautiful way. Star-crossed lovers. Enemies in their time. Yet they found a way to be together."

I need details. "Can you sum up what you've read?"

Taylor nods and then shuffles through the precious memories in her hand. "Major Fair was in Radisson for two months while the brigade gathered supplies and made decisions as to the next course of action. He was with the part of the army that was portioned off to go to Savannah. He didn't want to go—begged his commanding officer to let him stay—but soon he was off. There's a letter here from Savannah and another from Augusta."

I take over, using my psychic senses, because everything is suddenly crystal clear. Like a light has illuminated the pathway before me. All I can do is follow and relay what's being told to me. "I see him. It's the soldier I've run into. He matches the drawing Cel did. He's the one who constantly laughs in my head. The one who's toying with Courtney. The one who was so totally butt-crazy in love with Ada. Now, he's . . . well, he's very bitter about everything."

How does a romantic near-poet like Major Nathan Fair become so cynical and vindictive? What happened to him while he was in Savannah and Augusta? "It's obvious that he's angry at having to leave her, but—" I rub my temples, trying to get the terminology correct, but none of the phrases of Ada and Fair's era work here. "There's no way around it. He's rip-shit that he never heard from her." I grip my chest as the searing heat intensifies and spreads throughout my lungs like blistering air, stifling my breathing. "Why did she give up on him? Why didn't she answer him? Was she even alive? Had something happened to her? He's crazy-mad with doubt and the insatiable need to get back here to Radisson, despite orders from his commanding officers to stay with his unit."

I slice my eyes over to Jason, then Becca, then Taylor. "Did he come back here?"

Taylor shakes her head. "Ada's diaries just sort of trail off. There's no ending, per se, that I can see."

Celia glances about. "Do we have them all?"

Becca shakes her head. "That was all Stephanie's mom gave us."

Unexpectedly, my visions shift, like dark gray thunderclouds covering the brilliant blue sky. The information seems jumbled and garbled and I can't see clearly what happened to Fair or Ada anymore. *Come on, Emily . . . help me out, please.*

Silence reigns in my brain, which is free of any hints or clues from anyone.

"When did you die, Major Fair? On your way back to Ada?"

I steer my gaze over to Celia. She gives me her trademark shrug. "We've hit an informational brick wall."

I raise my voice. "Come on, Fair! Talk to me!"

Nothing but the sound of the fall wind dancing with the dried leaves outside on the lawn.

Celia groans. "We'll just have to see what we get out of the spirits tomorrow night at Stephanie's house. We *will* get to the bottom of this."

Another Saturday night at the Crawford house. Only this time, there's no party.

"Are we going to do another séance?" Stephanie asks.

"No." I'm not doing anything of the sort. I'm neither experienced enough nor prepared for that. "We're doing this the old-fashioned way. We're going to talk it out with the spirit . . . if he'll listen to me."

"Ahhh, the UN of the paranormal world, eh?" Stephanie says with a laugh.

"You could say that."

And again, it's another Saturday night in Radisson and I'm doing an investigation. However, Jason understands this time, because he sees the severity of the case and how it's touched us all. He knows it's something we all have to do.

I have my work cut out for me tonight, since I need to make Nathan see that what he's doing to Courtney is wrong. This has to end.

Celia walks up to me, wearing jeans, a long-sleeved black T-shirt, and her ghost-hunting vest. An EMF meter and a temperature gauge hang off her belt, making her look like a paranormal gunslinger. "Base camp is set up and we're good to go. We have cameras in the front parlor, the library where Courtney had the séance, and the ballroom."

"Sounds like it's time to go dark," I say. "Becca, is the place wired?"

"Like a CIA tap job!" She blows a huge bubble with her gum and then pops it. Chewing quickly, she says, "Digital recorders in the rooms, as well as a couple of handhelds to try to get some EVPs."

"I've got night-vision cameras in the rooms," Taylor says, "a mini-DVD, and my standard Sony camera. Clay's going to take digital pics for me so I can concentrate on the video."

Clay stands tall and gives Taylor a proper salute.

"What do I do?" Jason asks.

My first thought is, *Hug me,* to stop the slight tremors rolling through me. But it's not the time to see him as my boyfriend. He's a teammate right now, albeit the skeptical one. That's good though, because it keeps us honest and questioning our findings.

I hold Stephanie's cell phone out to him. "We need you to get Courtney here."

His blue eyes blaze. "Why me?"

Celia steps up. "Because Fair's just waiting for Kendall or me to approach Courtney for help so he can block us. He knows we're on to him. If you call, you can appeal to Courtney on her girlie level, and Fair will allow her to come see you because it's something he won't be able to resist." She casts a sidelong glance at me. "Ummm, well, that's at least what we're hoping will happen."

Jason lifts his shoulders to protest, then drops them. "Whatever. I just don't want her—or *whatever* you think is in her—to make a move on me. Not cool!"

"Just make the call, please."

He smiles and dials.

Jason puts the phone on speaker, and I hear Courtney knock something over at the sound of his voice.

"Come over to Stephanie's," he says to her.

"Why there?"

He swallows deeply, his Adam's apple bobbing up and down. "'Cause Kendall won't think to find me over here. She's in Atlanta with her mom anyway, and Stephanie's having some people over to watch movies. It'll be . . . like old times." He sneers at the memory, and my heart swells with total love for him. He's the best boyfriend ever.

Clicking off the phone, Jason says, "She bit."

Evelyn enters and clears her throat. "You have more help," she says.

Loreen walks in with a backpack slung over her shoulder. Her T-shirt reads, "The More I Know the Living, the Less I Fear the Dead." True dat, sistah.

Then I gasp when I see who she's brought.

Father Massimo steps out from behind her, wearing his priest attire and his vestments.

"Did you get the bishop's permission?" I ask through my dry lips.

His smile is heavenly bright. "I decided that you needed me, Kendall."

Loreen smacks him hard on the arm.

"Ouch! What?"

Indignantly, she says, "*You* decided? Like hell you did." Her sentence is punctuated with a girlish laugh.

"Okay, okay. Loreen stopped by and basically told me— well, it had to do with me growing a certain male part that she felt I was missing."

We all laugh, and I go to hug my priest for being here to support me.

"I'm here when you need me. All you have to do is look my way." He tousles my hair for good measure.

"Then let's get this show on the road."

Loreen passes around a vial of holy water and we all say the prayer to Saint Michael in unison—even Jason. Father Mass stays quiet, knowing this is our show until he feels the need to step in. And with that, we're ready to go.

Little does Courtney Langdon know that waiting for her will be a ghost-hunting team, a parent, a psychic, and an Episcopal priest, all ready to free her of the evil that haunts her.

Well, maybe not *all* of her evil.

We can only do so much.

Courtney arrives fifteen minutes later. I witness a hint of confusion on her pale lips as she steps into the ballroom where we're all gathered.

"I thought you said Kendall was in Atlanta."

Jason winces. "Sorry, I lied."

He takes her hand and escorts her into the middle of the room. Somehow, this contact doesn't bother me at all. Through her weary gray eyes, I see a scared girl.

"Why am I here then?"

Jason bends down to whisper to her and I hear him say, "We're going to help you."

Fair swiftly takes over. His own sinister scowl morphs onto

her face, making him completely recognizable to the discerning eye.

"He's here," Loreen whispers from behind me.

"I know."

Courtney works up a good spit and propels it onto Miss Evelyn's expensive Chinese rug. "Wha'd'ya want?"

Stephanie grimaces and moves forward at the action, but Taylor holds her back.

"We'd like to talk to you, Major," I say as calmly as possible, even though I pretty much want to throw up Mom's famed chicken and rice casserole. "We haven't been formally introduced, even though we've run into each other a lot. I'm Kendall Moorehead."

"I know who you are."

"Yes, sir," I say, trying to be polite to him in spite of his hostility. "These are my friends."

Courtney's face seems aged and weathered. "How do you know me?"

"I've read all about you, Major. Major Nathan Fair from Columbus, Ohio, assigned to the Seventeenth Corps of General Sherman's army. We're here to help you, Major."

"You're not here to do anything of the sort," Courtney growls in a deep voice. Then she coughs and sputters out, "Help me!" in her own cheerleader falsetto. She falls to her knees and begins to cry.

Father Mass doesn't hesitate. He steps forward and holds out a cross. "God of gods and Lord of lords, Creator of the fiery ranks, and Fashioner of the fleshless powers, the Artisan of heavenly things and those under the heavens, whom no man has seen, nor is able to see, whom all creation fears: Into the dark depths of hell you hurled the commander who had become proud, and who, because of his disobedient service, was cast down from the height to earth, as well as the angels that fell away with him, all having become evil demons. Grant that this my exorcism being performed in your awesome name be terrible to the master of evil and to all his minions who had fallen with him from the height of brightness. Drive him into banishment, commanding him to depart hence, so that no harm might be worked against your sealed image. And as you have commanded, let those who are sealed receive the strength to tread upon serpents and scorpions, and upon all power of the enemy. For manifested, hymned, and glorified with fear, by everything that has breath is your most holy name: of the Father, and of the Son, and of the Holy Spirit, now and ever and into ages of ages. Amen."

"Amen," we all repeat. Wow—he *did* come prepared.

This prayer only serves to anger Fair even more; Courtney begins pounding her fists on the carpet. "You don't understand! You'll never understand!"

I drop to my knees as well. "Then *make* me understand!"

I toss holy water around Courtney until she starts screaming. The piercing sound stabs at my chest, breaking my heart in two. Is this Courtney yelling out in pain, or Fair unleashing his rage?

I try to comfort the girl who dislikes me so. "Courtney, can you hear me? You've got to help me help you."

Totally ignoring me, Courtney/Fair knock me backward as she gets up and paces around the room like a caged animal. Jason's lips flatten and his eyes darken. Now's not the time for him to get all alpha male on my ass. Sometimes dealing with spirits can be a little rough. I'm okay.

I put my hand to his chest, feeling his uneven breathing underneath my fingers. "It wasn't Courtney. It was Fair."

"Either way, I'll rip his throat out."

"He's dead," I note.

"That's right. So I'll have to hit him harder."

Ahh, my alpha wolf. *Très* cute.

Meanwhile, Courtney's screaming continues at decibel levels that would make a dog's ears bleed. Loreen can't take it anymore; she crosses the room and puts herself in Courtney's/Fair's face.

"Get out of the girl, you monster, and enter me," she nearly commands. "She's not strong enough. I am. You can speak through me and we'll do whatever we can to assist you."

The laugh—that nasty dark one—reverbs off the walls of the near-empty ballroom. Courtney's lips lift in the corners and she says in a deep growl, "You aren't strong enough for me, Loreen Woods."

Loreen and I make eye contact. Behind us, Father Mass is still reading from the *Book of Occasional Services*. Something's got to get through to this ghost.

A soft hand is on my shoulder, and I look up to see Loreen's concerned expression. Her eyes plead with me. "You've got to talk to him, Kendall. Make Fair listen."

"I don't know what to say."

"Just try," Loreen says. "You're the one he approached first. If anyone can convince him to move on, it's you."

I wheel around in time to see massive tears gushing out of Courtney's eyes. No longer do I see the cocky bitch who terrorized me with pomegranate applesauce or the cheerleader who mockingly called me Ghost Girl. I see the good inside Courtney that's crying out for help. I concentrate on her soul and the peace it's seeking. As I try to connect with her on a spiritual level, her face becomes blurred in my sight. Her image shifts into that of a man in a blue uniform. Tall, too thin, and terribly hurt and confused. He steps forward, away from Courtney, but not totally out of her, and she slumps to the floor.

"What do you want, girlie?"

I'm standing face to face with Major Nathan Fair.

And, boy, is he pissed.

CHAPTER TWENTY

"WHAT HAPPENED, MAJOR?"

"Can you see him, Kendall?" Taylor asks softly.

I nod. So does Loreen. I don't know if she can see him as plainly as I can, but I know she senses his presence.

Nathan Fair growls in my direction. He's taller than I am, but the hazards and wear of war have made him hunch over slightly. He seems dirty and sad and . . . lost. Does he even know he's dead? That the war was finished a century and a half ago? How do you convey that to a spirit stuck in time?

"What do you mean, what happened?" he snarls beneath his mustache. "*War's* been happening, child! Death and starvation and weeklong marches. Pestilence and dysentery and blood and dismemberment. Men killing men without a thought about what the other may have left behind. Armies rising and falling. Women with no husbands returning. Babies with no fathers. Losing years of youthful days and love in your life."

Fury emanates from him toward me, and I feel each surge of his wrath hit me like a radioactive wave. I've encountered several spirits these past couple of months and none has had this amount of resentment and negative energy.

I close my eyes and try to breathe out love and understanding to him. "What can we do to ease this anger inside you? The turmoil that you've been taking out on Courtney."

He glances over his shoulder at where she sits, huddled on the ground, whimpering.

"She opened herself up to me."

"I understand that," I say, trying to be diplomatic. "But oppressing her like you've been doing isn't right. She's just a teenager and you're making her act the fool in front of the whole school."

"That was her choice."

"She didn't know any better," I plead. "She was jealous of me for a really stupid reason."

"I saw an opening and I took it."

Loreen steps up next to me. "Ask him about Ada."

Fair lurches forward, suddenly on my left, then my right, then straight on. "What *about* Ada? What do you know? Nothing!"

I take one of those long yoga breaths Mom's always telling about and I center my energies so I can focus solely on Nathan Fair. I've got to remain calm—and not freakin' pee my pants like I pretty much want to do. "We—my friends and I—we read Ada's diaries. They just . . . end . . . as if you . . . just ended."

Furiously, Fair pulls his cap off and throws it to the ground. "Oh? Is that what her diary implies? Does it also say that Ada didn't wait for me?"

"Huh?"

His voice roars like the engine of a 747 whooshing away from Chicago's O'Hare. "She got married!"

I spin to face Becca and Jason. "Ada got married?"

Jason shakes his head. "I didn't read that."

"Neither did I," Becca adds.

Miss Evelyn speaks up. "Why, yes, she married. I could have told you that. The family Bible has her name as Ada Parry Kenney."

"Kenney!" Fair screams out so powerfully that I jump.

"That struck a nerve," I say as my pulse strums under my skin. "Who is Kenney, Major Fair? Did you know him?"

Becca moves her digital voice recorder in the direction of where I'm speaking. I hope she gets some of this! Taylor's taking pictures left and right. I have to ignore their investigative work and give my full attention to the spirit before me and the electrifying connection flowing between the two of us.

"Yes, I knew the bastard. His rank was colonel, but his status was weasel."

Now we're getting somewhere. "Was Kenney in your unit?"

"Aye. Colonel James Kenney from Connecticut," Major Fair explains as he strokes his beard. "At one time, I considered him a friend—before I left Radisson, that is."

While they're working, the rest of my team is on pins and needles listening to the one-sided conversation. I fill them in the best I can. I soften my voice and meet Fair's eyes with mine. "See my friend over here? That's Stephanie. She's Ada's great-great-great-granddaughter."

"Lovely child," he comments after a moment.

"What did he say?" asks Stephanie.

"He said you're pretty."

Her face reddens. "Oh. Thanks."

I face him again. "Tell me about Ada, Major. We all want to know."

This request seems to soothe him some. He takes three paces to the left and stares out of the lace-curtained window like he's reliving a precious memory. "Ada was a strong woman on the outside, but I saw into her soul, to the fragile and frightened girl. It was wartime. What do women know of war?"

I decide not to tell him that our armed forces have been letting women in since the mid-1960s and women are now going to war just like men. Not information he necessarily needs to know.

"But you were there for her. You showed her great kindness," I tell him.

"I tried." Fair's eyes are distant as he remembers the woman he loved. "Her hair was so thick and soft. Delicate ladylike hands that could dance over the piano keyboard with such care. Those hands became rough as she constantly waited on us and worked to grow any food she could in the garden for her father and sister."

I smile at him. "She mentions in her diary that you brought vegetables to her."

"That I did."

I hate to rile him up when he seems unruffled right now. However, I've got to piece this puzzle together and get Fair to move along. "Sir? Without getting too upset, can you please tell me about this Kenney guy?"

Loreen puts her hand on my arm. "The energy in the room just shifted. I feel something dark and brooding again."

"I heard a growl," Becca says.

Celia agrees. "Was that someone's stomach?"

No one fesses up.

I watch Fair fist his hands at his sides, the knuckles losing all color.

"Kenney was my friend. We fought side by side. We drank whiskey together. We celebrated the fall of Atlanta together. And we both ended up here in Radisson. Kenney knew I was in love with Ada. Hell, everyone knew. I couldn't keep it to myself. The morning that I was instructed to head east to Savannah, well, it damn near broke my heart. Hers too. She wanted to come with me. Of course, that was impossible. Kenney promised me he'd watch out for Ada until I returned. He watched out for her, all right," he says through his clenched teeth, seething.

I relay this to my team. Taylor sniffles at the sadness of the tale. Celia steps forward. "How long was he in Savannah?"

Fair hears her. "I had no sense of time without Ada. It was days, weeks, months—who knows? I wrote her constantly. Every night, in fact."

"Did you hear back from her?" I ask, careful where I'm treading.

"No. My heart was broken, thinking something had happened to her because I was gone. I trusted my fellow soldiers, but they're only men in a desperate time. I feared for her sanctity and her virtue although Kenney assured me he'd watch out for her. Had something become of him that he could no longer protect my Ada?"

My chest aches at the colossal pressure and loss of love Nathan Fair is experiencing. It's hard even to catch a good strong breath for fear the searing air won't properly fill my lungs. This is such total sadness. There really isn't a bigger word for it. Like a death . . . sorrow, misery, grief . . . any of these words will do.

Loreen moves her hand over her chest and doubles over with a groan. Next thing I know, Father Mass is at her side. Her face is contorted in pain and tears stream from her eyes.

"I've never felt such despair," she says between quick breaths.

"Loreen, what can I do to help?" Father Mass asks.

She doesn't answer; she grabs his hand and holds on tightly. "It'll pass. He knows I'm stronger than Kendall and he's testing me. Testing all of us."

"Come on, Major. Leave Loreen alone!" I shout out. "We're here to get to the bottom of everything."

At that, Loreen's knees collapse and she falls into Father Massimo's arms. She continues to hold his hand as her breathing returns to normal. "He showed me everything," she manages to get out. "He went crazy with worry for Ada, to the point that he went AWOL from the army."

"Holy crap," Celia exclaims.

I notice Loreen lean into Father Mass and put her head on his chest. He shushes into her hair, pushing it away from her face. She continues though. "H-h-he stole a fellow officer's horse and rode for a week to Radisson with hardly any food or water. By the time he got here, he was completely mad. H-h-he saw that Ada was married . . . to Kenney. Fair took his pistol and was going to shoot Kenney, but it backfired in Fair's face and killed him instantly."

I slink away, my own knees wobbly, and sit on a nearby chair to collect myself. The team is taking in this information as Loreen regains her composure. Fair has faded away, but he's not gone. I still sense his essence plainly. I guess we all need a break.

Taylor reaches into the hip pocket of her jeans and pulls out a small pack of Kleenex. She dabs her eyes with one and then passes them to Becca.

"Are you kidding me?" Becca shakes her off and puts the headphones on. "I don't know what exactly the two of you were talking to, but the recording software is picking up shit left and right. We've probably got a ton of EVPs on here."

I will my erratic heartbeat to calm the hell down. "That's good."

Celia's face is buried in her computer screen; the light blue glow highlights her features. "The whole time you were talking to him, the barometric pressure was slowly dropping, as was the room temperature."

"It's freezing in here," a quiet and removed Stephanie whispers.

"Yeah, I feel it too," Jason adds. I can see chill bumps on his bare arms, and I know that Fair isn't far away.

I steady myself for the next wave of information and interaction. "Major? Nathan?"

Nothing.

I stare down at my feet as a swell of roiling emotion coats me in a cloak of unhappiness. I suppress the urge to cry like a baby, tamp down the hot tears that threaten behind my eyes. "You can't stay here, Major. You have to move on."

Through all of this, Courtney sits perfectly still, staring as the events unfold around her. She's quietly bawling too. Red splotches cover her pretty face, and her eyes are absolutely bloodshot. Her breathing is shallow and staggered. Is this her, or is it Fair? I can't tell anymore.

I am sure about one thing, a fact that stands at the forefront of my thoughts, though who put it there, I don't know. What I do know is that Major Nathan Fair is still stuck around the Crawford manor here on Crow Lane because he took his own life.

He has a century and a half of unfinished business that he must understand before he can be at peace. "You can't keep doing this. You can't stay around anymore. This isn't right for the people who live in this house. It's not fair to torture people because your life fell apart and you killed yourself."

"It wasn't like that," he roars.

I don't back down though. "You've got to move on, Major. Leave. Courtney. Alone."

He appears behind her and strokes her hair. "I can't do that. She invited me in. And she reminds me so much of my Ada. So young. So lost. She needs me."

I tell the team, "He says he's staying with Courtney because she reminds him of Ada."

"That explains a lot," Celia notes.

I take a step in Fair's direction. "I really must insist that you leave Courtney alone. She doesn't want you around anymore. She asked for our help."

"No, she didn't. She's just like Ada. She needs punishing. Ada has to pay for not staying loyal to me and our love. I've been waiting for so long for someone to invite me in." His voice isn't growling now; rather, it's quite melancholy, as if he doesn't actually want to hurt Ada at all.

Loreen must hear him again because she says, "The girl isn't Ada and she no longer wants you around."

Miss Evelyn bursts into the room and hands something to Becca. "I couldn't stand watching what y'all were doing so I went up in the attic to see if there was anything else I could find. This was wedged between two old trunks."

"What is it?" Taylor asks.

"It's another one of Ada's journals," Becca explains.

Celia rushes to Becca. "Let's see." She carefully thumbs through the pages. "This one's from the time after Major Fair left."

The major slides away from Courtney and makes his way to the other side of the room. I follow his every motion while Becca and Taylor speed-read the diary.

Taylor gasps at one particular entry and puts her hand to her throat. "Oh, bless her heart. She was told that Major Fair died on the way to Savannah!"

He growls, "What?"

"Give me a minute," Becca says. She's a horrendously fast reader, so we can get to the bottom of this sooner rather than later.

"I need water," I say to Jason.

"I'm on it."

Ten minutes later, Becca lets out a huge sigh. "Okay, so here's the deal. Ada Parry married James Kenney because he said Fair had wanted it that way if anything happened to him. Kenney told Ada that Fair died, and also intercepted every letter that was sent to her. She was completely miserable in her marriage with him after she found out the truth."

I'm somehow relieved to hear this. To know that the special love that Ada and Nathan shared wasn't just a fleeting thing.

Becca continues. Fair is directly behind her, listening keenly. "She was convinced that Nathan was dead, so life meant nothing to her anymore. After she agreed to marry Kenney, for safety's sake more than anything, she heard him bragging to one of his fellow soldiers one night that he had only married her for her family's land and to 'one-up that bastard Fair.'"

"I'll kill him with my bare hands," Fair snarls.

"Um, he's already dead," I say. "Anything else, Becca?"

"Yeah . . . and he ain't gonna like this."

From the expression on his face, she's right. "Go ahead."

"Kenney was the one who signed the order for Fair to be sent to Savannah, away from Ada."

With that, every door in the house slams shut and I hear Fair howl to the rafters.

CHAPTER TWENTY-ONE

GLASS SHATTERS in the front hallway.

"That's my mother's gilded mirror she bought in New Orleans," Miss Evelyn shouts.

More crashing. This time it's plates falling from the kitchen cabinets. I can see it like I'm in the room watching. Drawers fly open and the chairs are tossed backward.

"Stop it!" Stephanie screams. "You're destroying everything!"

Fair is in my face, so much so that I can almost detect his cold breath on my neck, chilling me to the bone. "Kenney did this! I want my revenge on them both!"

Instinctively, I reach out for him, only to meet vast emptiness. "It's past the time for revenge," I beg.

Father Mass takes two steps toward us. "Vengeance doesn't belong to us, old friend. It belongs to the Lord."

Becca shoves the diary into my hand. "Read it to him."

Without hesitation, I glance down at the page Becca picked out and in desperation read:

"'There is no love in my marriage. I never should have

married a man I had no feelings for. It seemed the best thing to do at the time. I had to save the farm. I had to save Father. I had to protect myself, and James had seemed so kind to begin with. My heart bleeds for the joy I felt in Nathan's arms. Why, oh why, was he sent away from me?'"

Fair's wrath ebbs momentarily as he's caught up in Ada's words.

"Then there's another entry.

"'Never a day or a moment goes by when I don't think of what life would be like had Nathan Fair lived and returned to me. I cry myself to sleep every night with this strange man beside me. I weep in the mornings for what could have been. I shy away from all I have known, destined to live a life without warmth and true affection.'

"Don't you see, Major. She loved *you*."

"But she married *him*. She believed his lies. She didn't trust in our love. She betrayed me!" Again, his voice roars up to the ceiling, punctuated with acidic anger.

Loreen speaks up. "I've sensed the overwhelming sadness ever since the first time I walked into this house, and now we know what it is, Kendall. No one who lives here will ever truly be happy because of the resentment with which Fair oppresses this building."

My hands shake, not from psychic sensitivity, but from nerves. "What can I do? I'm at a loss."

"We have to get him to leave the girl alone."

An image shifts in my mind's eye, and I see Ada, young and

beautiful, calling out to Nathan, her hand extended for him to take. Then it hits me!

"That's it!"

"What?" Celia asks.

I lower my voice so only Loreen and Celia can hear. "The onus is on Courtney. I've got to get through to her, piss her off even, just get her to throw the bum out like the squatter he is."

Celia looks at me like I'm crazy. "Can you do that?"

I say, "I have absolutely no freakin' clue, but I'm sure as hell gonna try!"

I walk over to where Courtney is sitting on the floor, her arms wrapped around her knees as she rocks back and forth. Her tear-streaked face is pale, and her eyelashes are clumped together. I smile at her, hoping she sees me for the friend I'm trying to be. Taking her hand, I squeeze tightly. She grips back.

"Courtney, can you hear me?"

She blinks several times.

"I know I'm not your favorite person, but you've got to listen to me. I want you to push him out with all of your might. Muster up all of your feelings and emotions—and hatred and anger at me, if you need to—and tell this ghost that he's no longer welcome. That you want control of your mind, body, and soul. I'm here to help, but you've got to do it."

She nods slightly, enough of an acknowledgment that I know she's going to try.

Father Mass kneels next to her, mumbling Scripture. Surely that can't hurt.

A moment later, Courtney's face turns scarlet red. She struggles and fights, writhing on the floor. "That's it, Courtney. You're strong. You're a cheerleader. You can do this!"

Father Mass tosses holy water and blesses her. "In the name of the Father, the Son, and the Holy Ghost. I beseech you to leave this child of God and be on your way. Pray with me, Courtney."

She mutters the Lord's Prayer under her breath the best she can with tears still gushing out. She collapses onto the floor, kicking her feet. Jason moves to help her and puts her sweat-covered head in his lap.

A tortured shriek escapes from her chest, as if she's cheering for the most important sports event of her life. *"Leaaaaave meeeeee!"*

Taylor, Becca, Celia, and Stephanie stand wide-eyed, locked in place. I too don't move and resist the urge to do anything other than pray.

Courtney's body sags in Jason's arms, and she tries to speak. "I-I-I need a garbage can."

"Quick!" Jason states.

Stephanie grabs a decorative brass pail that sits by the door and hurls it to Jason. Next thing we know, Courtney retches into the bucket, dry heaves that have her sobbing even more. Then, all is quiet.

Loreen holds her hands out. "He's left her."

"You think?"

"Yeah," Courtney whimpers. "He's out of me."

Father Mass dips his thumb into the holy water and makes the sign of the cross on Courtney's forehead while whispering something.

A feeble smile crosses her face. "I'm, like, Southern Baptist. Will that still work on me?"

"God is interdenominational," my priest says.

"Is the soldier gone?" Taylor asks. She looks around the room and then back at her camera. "I don't know if anything will show on the video, but I got every bit of it recorded."

"Good work," Celia and I say in unison.

I hate to be the bearer of bad news. "I don't think he's gone though."

The snicker inside my head that turns to soft weeping confirms that Major Fair is still around. Out of Courtney, but not at peace.

"Nathan? Where are you?"

"Trapped. Destined to be in this purgatory forever."

My heart races in my chest. "Not if you don't want to be. This hell is of your own making because you took your own life."

"The gun backfired."

"But you intended to kill Kenney," I say.

"I'd killed hundreds before. You can't say that's what's keeping me here."

I plead with my eyes to Father Massimo.

"Tell him to pray for God's mercy."

There isn't a need for me to repeat anything because Nathan closes his eyes, and his lips begin to move. Then he falls to his knees with his hands clamped together in front of him.

"God forgive me! Ada, forgive me! I just want to go to heaven and be with her."

My heart surely breaks into millions of tiny pieces over the sincerity in his voice. Will he be rewarded with entry into eternity, where he'll hopefully find Ada?

"Do you see the light?" It's got to be there.

"Not yet . . ."

But I see a light. Holy crap! What the—

Loreen nudges me. "Are you seeing what I'm seeing?"

"That's not what I think it is, is it?" I ask with a tremble in my voice.

"No, it's not *that* light. But it's something loving and . . . special."

I can almost hear a host of heavenly angels singing out softly as this light spreads and encompasses Nathan Fair where he's kneeling in prayer. Warmth surrounds me, yet every hair on my body seems as if it's standing on end.

"Taylor, I don't know if you're getting this, but keep that infrared video on that spot right there."

She trains her camera in the right direction and hits Record.

Out of the glowing light, a luminescent figure of a young woman takes shape. She's dressed impeccably in a pale green silk dress with lace and velvet trimming. White gloves adorn her small hands, and a proud hat sits upon a chignon of chestnut brown hair. This woman has her shining eyes on one person only. Major Nathan Fair.

Before I can form any words, Loreen whispers, "It's Ada."

Fair sees her too, and his tears flow even more freely in the face of her beauty.

"But how?" I ask. "She hasn't been haunting this house. She's been at peace."

Loreen's smile is vibrant, and a layer of fresh tears covers her eyes. "There's so much energy here tonight from all of us. Ada was able to break through her higher level to come help her love cross into the light. We've managed to reunite them in death. Now they can be together forever."

"*What* is going on?" Celia begs. "Tell us—this is insane just standing here while y'all can watch everything."

I do my best to narrate, knowing my chosen words will fall short of the miracle before me. It's beyond beautiful. More amazing than anything I've witnessed during my awakening. I watch as Major Fair goes toward Ada. Love radiates from both of them in soft red and pink waves. The two of them have been separated for a lifetime, yet they'll now have peace together forever.

"They're taking each other's hands," I choke out. "It's . . . it's . . . it's like being at a wedding. The whiteness. The brightness. Ada's so gorgeous. And Fair is smiling so proudly. Like a man in love. Like a man seeing for the first time." My heart's totally going to burst into ten thousand pieces at the emotions clogging my throat and chest.

"There's so much love in this room now," Loreen says. "It was meant to be this way. This ethereal reunion. A forever match."

Fair wraps Ada in his arms and kisses her. They break apart, and he turns to me. He tips his soldier's hat and winks. Ada and Nathan shuffle off into the mist and light, and then disappear.

Loreen and I grab each other for support and sheer exhaustion after what we've just viewed. It's something I will always treasure, especially because we shared the moment. Father Mass comes up behind us and wraps his arms around the two of us. Right then and there, I envision him and Loreen together. Maybe not tonight, but definitely at a future time. I couldn't be happier about what's ahead for them.

"Kendall?" I hear faintly from beside me. It's Courtney. Jason's helped her to her feet.

"Hey. Welcome back."

She stares down, then bravely meets my gaze. "Ummm . . . thanks. You know. For that."

"That's what I do, Courtney," I say with a smile.

Jason leaves her side and wraps me in his arms, pressing me close to his chest. I can hear the rapid beat of his heart, as if he's been on a carnival ride himself. I guess we all have been tonight.

Miss Evelyn spreads her hands out, like she's feeling for rain inside her house. "The air in here has never been so light. It's as if an anvil has been lifted off my heart. There's no static in the air. No pinpricks on my neck. It just feels . . . normal."

Loreen blinks extra-hard. "It was Fair's presence looming over this property. He was a downer for anyone living in this house."

"Do you think that's why you and Dad fought so much, Mom?" Stephanie asks.

"I know it is," Loreen interjects.

Miss Evelyn nods. "Maybe so."

Taking Evelyn's hand, Loreen says, "I think you should call Joel and get together. Talk like you've never talked before. Be honest with each other. Get to the heart of the anger that was between you."

I have to add, "This could be a salvation for your marriage." I glance at Stephanie. "For your whole family."

Stephanie bursts into happy tears and hugs both Loreen and me, as does her mother.

"Well, wha'd'ya know?" I say.

"What's that?" Celia asks.

"I'm a ghost huntress, a matchmaker, *and* a marriage counselor."

Courtney laughs and smiles at me.

Yeah . . . this house—and all in it—is at peace.

CHAPTER TWENTY-TWO

LIKE I DO AFTER ANY SUPER-INTENSE ghost investigation, I sleep like the dead—ha-ha . . . get it? The dead . . . never mind—Sunday morning, not waking up until well past noon. (Oops! Father Mass is going to notice my absence in the Moorehead section.)

After a near thirty-minute shower and an extensive blow-drying session, I slip on my jeans and my most comfy T-shirt. Celia sent a group e-mail out to everyone saying we were doing evidence review at Becca's house. Jason's giving me a ride over.

Dad's at the office—yeah, on a Sunday—and Mom's working on a science-fair project with Kaitlin in the den when I hear the tires of Jason's Jeep crunch on our gravel drive.

"You heading out?" Mom asks.

"Going to Becca's to look at what we captured last night."

Mom blinks hard. "Did you get enough rest? I know . . . that sort of thing tires you out."

"I did. No worries."

I hear the *tink-tink* of the horn and I run over to kiss Mom on the forehead. "Love ya! Mean it!"

Outside, Jason steps from the driver's side and comes around to open my door for me. He lays a soft kiss on my lips before he shuts me in.

When he retakes his seat behind the wheel, I ask, "To what do I owe this honor?"

His eyes sparkle against the bright November afternoon. "Trying to be a gentleman."

"You always are, Jase. You're the best." I choke on my words. Not because they're not true, but because it's incredible that this amazing guy has stood by me through all of this stupidity.

He stares at me with those powerful blue eyes of his until I almost feel like he's the psychic one, reading my thoughts and emotions.

His fingers glide into mine; his thumb brushes the top of my hand. "I know I've been hard on you about all the investigation stuff."

"I know it's been—"

"Shhhh!" he says quietly. "I've been selfish and demanding in wanting a girlfriend who wants to hang out and do things just with me. What can I say? It's what I was used to. And I wasn't understanding enough about what you've been going through."

"Jason, it's been really—"

This time, his hand moves to cover my mouth. "Damn,

Kendall. Shut it, will ya?" he says with a hearty laugh. "I'm, like, baring my soul here. Guys don't do shit like that."

I smile underneath his palm. I let him finish.

"The investigating is important to you and even though I've been skeptical, I enjoy being a part of it with you. What happened last night was . . . whoa—I don't know how to put it in words. Even though I didn't see what you saw, or experience what you were going through, I could almost empathize with this awakening thing. I could see that *you* believed in what was going on. That you really helped that dude find peace. That you reunited him with the love of his life . . . in death. It was unlike anything I've ever observed." He stops for a sec and brushes his knuckles under his chin like he's reliving everything. "You did something useful, even when it meant it might suck out all of your energy. And you helped Courtney, despite the fact that she's a roost-ruling bitch. That's classy, Kendall. Not everyone would have done what you did for her. She owes you."

He takes a deep breath and sort of holds it.

I wait a moment. "My turn?"

"Yeah," he says, his eyes sparkling.

I lean across the stick shift and take his face in my hands. I plant the fattest, wettest kiss on his amazing lips and then pull back. "You are *the best* boyfriend I've ever had."

His eyebrows rise. "Aren't I the *only* boyfriend you've ever had?"

"Semantics," I say, using Father Mass's word.

This time, Jason kisses me. The kind of kiss that makes me crinkle up my toes inside my Timberlands.

"This weekend," I say. "You and me. No one else."

"Not even Emily?" he asks.

"Sorry she's been so aggressive with you."

"She's protective of you."

I shake my head. "I don't need protection from you."

Jason kisses me again. And again. And again. *Mmmm* . . .

We'll eventually get over to Becca's.

Taylor's exuberant smile nearly lights up the room. "I outdid myself, I must say."

"These pictures definitely don't suck," Celia notes.

We're spread out all over Becca's den with bags of Doritos, Tostitos, and Cheetos sustaining us through our evidence review.

"The temperature analysis I did throughout the night indicates areas with drops in degrees at the same moments that both you and Loreen were feeling the presence of the entity," Celia reports in a very scientific manner.

"That's amazing."

Taylor's digital images show mists and formations and shadows of a figure. The infrared picked up what we all think was Major Fair, and there's plenty of documentation of the windows banging and doors flying open. Even though Miss Evelyn and Stephanie were there, this will make one hell of a reveal if they'd like to go over it with us.

"The longer we do this," Celia says, "the better our evidence gets."

"It's *véritablement stupéfiant!*"

Becca grimaces. "English, Tillson! English!"

"Truly amazing," she says with an innocent grin. "What do you have, Becca?"

"The mother lode of EVPs. I'll play a few."

Feeling the need to reach out to her, I say, "You know, you've done an amazing job with all of this. I can't tell you how proud I am and how much help you've been."

She beams up at me. Not her usual don't-give-a-damn Goth-girl grin, but a genuinely warm, friendly smile. "That means a lot to me, K."

"You betcha," I say. I'm really glad to have her as a friend and to know she's not still upset with me for—

Wait. What's going on?

My left temple quivers slightly, as if a blood vessel has gone majorly insane underneath the surface. I freeze in place. I count to ten. I take a deep breath. Something is . . . here . . .

While Becca's cueing .wav files up on her software, I try to ignore the psychic sensations that are starting to swell within me. I'm getting the same sneaking feeling that I got the last time I was here. Something is calling to me, despite how hard I'm trying to ignore it.

I'm kind of busy right now . . . can you come back another time?

Nothing responds, so I hope I've dispelled the curious spirit.

"Listen to this one," Becca says, unaware of my inner struggle. *"Leeeeeeeeft for deeeeeeeeeeeead."*

"Cool beans," Celia says. "'Left for dead.' That's a clear one."

"It sure is!" Taylor says enthusiastically. "I got chills hearing that."

"What about you, Kendall? Pretty clear?" Becca asks.

I nod, only half listening. I move my eyes about the room, trying not to draw attention to myself as my friends are fascinated with the EVPs. Besides, I know what happened last night. I saw the major with my own eyes. I don't need further convincing. I do, however, need to know who's trying to contact me right now.

Please help us.

My heart hammers away; the blood is rushing to my head and making me dizzy. I have to hold it together. Maybe I'm just a little weak and overly sensitive after the connection with Major Fair last night.

Becca's playing another EVP. "Sounds like it says, 'You can see us.'"

"Us? Like more spirits?" Taylor asks.

"That's an old house," Celia says. "Lots of spirits around there, more than likely. Right, Kendall?"

She knocks me on the arm. "Huh? What?"

"There are probably other spirits in the Crawford house, 'cause it's so old."

"Oh, sure," I say, not really listening.

Celia kneels in front of me. "Are you all right?"

I hear a distinct whisper in my left ear.

Must heal her.

A lump forms in my throat, making it hard for me to utter anything coherent.

Celia's eyes are dark with concern. "Kendall? You're not, like, channeling anything, are you? You're not ready for that."

Shaking loose from my trance, I say, "No, no, it's nothing like that. It's . . ." I plead with Becca with my eyes. She looks toward the door to the trophy room and then back at me.

Her gaze tells me no, but then she says, "Someone's here?"

The voice whispers to me again in such an affectionate, tender way. It's like I'm sitting on a fluffy cloud of trust and comfort. I repeat what I'm told, although I have no idea what it means. "Granny Gama's here?"

Celia and Taylor exchange glances. "Who's that?"

Becca's mouth falls open.

I struggle with the pronunciation. "Gran-Gomma? No, it's definitely Granny Gama . . . Gahhhhma. Like *mama* with a *g*. Does this mean anything to any of you?"

"No clue," Becca says flatly. Then she hands two sets of headphones over to Taylor and Celia. "Y'all mind giving a second listen to this sound file for me? I may not have caught everything."

"Sure."

Becca carefully lifts herself off the floor, goes over to the trophy room, and motions for me to follow along. I don't say a word; I do as I'm told.

Once we're inside the dark, dusty room, Becca closes the door and bursts into tears. Huge, chubby drops roll out of her overly black-lined eyes; silent sobs rack her as she tries to stop the emotional overdrive churning through her system, which I sense as well. Charcoal eyeliner and mascara traces gush down her pale white cheeks, leaving tracks of sorrow in their wake.

She wipes at her face with the back of her hand, making everything worse. I pull a Kleenex from my pocket and gently dab her face.

"Talk to me, Becca."

She gulps for air, struggling to get out the words. "Gr-gr-gr-granny Gama was my—"

"Grandmother," I finish, already knowing the answer.

"When I was a little girl, my daddy wanted me to say, 'Hi, Granmama,' but it came out as Granny Gama. It stuck."

I smooth out the smear under her left eye. "I think that's sweet."

"Sh-sh-she was the world to me." Her hands fly up to cover her face, and her crying increases. "It's all my fault."

"What's your fault?"

A whispery image of a tiny woman slowly materializes in front of me. Her hair is dark and pulled up in a bun. Wrinkles smudge around her eyes and stretch over her cheeks. Her eyes are the same as Becca's. A fiery twinge clutches at my heart.

Definitely experiencing some coronary probs here. No doubt about it, since I've had it before with other spirits. Regardless, I pull my fist against my chest as if the sensation is overcoming me for real.

"Granny Gama had a massive heart attack. It took her before she even hit the ground," I say.

Becca lowers herself to the floor and puts her knees to her chest. Her tears have subsided some, but the emotional slash is still there.

"Please tell me what was your fault."

She blinks. "I'm responsible for her death."

"What?"

"No, child," her granny says.

"After my mother left, when I was five years old, Granny Gama raised me. Dad worked all the time—still does—and she was the one who cooked and cleaned and got me to school. She's the one who enrolled me in tap, ballet, gymnastics, and baton. She paid for all of it with her Social Security check because she knew I was obsessed with beauty pageants." She sniffs hard and wipes her nose with her hand. "Granny was at every single pageant. Front row, center, cheering me on." Becca gestures to her trophy cases. "She had these shelves made specially. And we celebrated each award and crown as I won them. I knew I was going to grow up to be Miss Georgia and then Miss USA or Miss America. I was *that* determined."

"So what happened?" I ask.

"Same thing that happens with any obsession. It became my life, to the detriment of everything else. Granny told me I was getting too big for my britches and that I didn't think my shit smelled." She stops and laughs sarcastically. "Well, she was right. I was gorgeous and I didn't mind flaunting it. I had such an attitude. I mean, I look back and I can see where people might think it was simply confidence in my abilities. It was more than that, though. Soon, I was out practicing more hours than I spent at home. I took every dance class I could. I worked hip-hop and aerobic moves into my routine. More, more, more. It wasn't enough."

"Becca," I say, trying to get her to focus. "How is Granny Gama's death your fault?"

She takes a staggered breath. "B-b-b-because for all she did for me, I couldn't do *one* thing for her."

"Stop, precious," her granny says. "Don't let her go on."

"She has to go on," I say. "This has obviously festered for too long." To the point that the multitalented beauty queen Rebecca Asiaf had turned into a Goth girl named Bulldozer Becca to remake the image she had of herself.

Becca buries her dark head into her folded arms. "I killed her."

"How?"

"It was the day before a pageant and she was finishing up an outfit for me. She could sew sequins and pearls and fringe like a pro. She asked me to pick something up for her. No big deal. Just a quick errand. I didn't do it, though. I was so caught up in myself and winning the next crown, practicing longer hours, that the store closed before I could go. So what, I'd get what she needed tomorrow." Becca looks up at me. "There was no tomorrow for her."

"What happened?"

"Granny was in the kitchen making dinner for Daddy and me when she had a heart attack. I got home just when it was happening. I rushed to her and held her, asking what was wrong. All she could do was fumble around in the pocket of her housecoat."

"Pills," Granny says. "I was looking for my nitroglycerin."

Suddenly, the whole scene plays out for me in my mind's eye. "Oh no . . . the errand?"

"I was supposed to pick up her prescription." Becca sniffs. "I didn't know it was that important. I didn't know she had heart problems enough to demand emergency pills."

"How could you know, precious," Granny says. "I never told you."

I place my hands on Becca's arms, trying to let Granny's love flow to her. "You didn't know. Not even your dad knew."

Tears shining in her eyes, she says, "No, he didn't."

"You didn't kill her, Becca. It was a mistake."

"I shouldn't have let my prescription run out," Granny tells me.

Becca lets out a silent scream of pain that I feel in my bones.

"I let her down. I couldn't take two seconds from my important life to go to the drugstore and get her pills. There aren't words to describe the guilt I've been living with."

But I understand. Her ache ebbs across the gap between us to wash me in her sorrow.

"Is that why you dyed your hair and pierced yourself and hide behind the black makeup?"

She nods her head. "I don't deserve to be looked at admiringly anymore. I'm a freak who killed her grandmother. I'll keep piercing body parts to punish myself for the pain she went through."

"Oh, Becca . . ." I glance at the apparition that watches with such concern. "Speak to her. Let her hear you. Use my energy if you have to."

Granny smiles. "You tell her for me, child."

I listen to the woman, so full of love for the granddaughter she raised.

"Becca, Granny Gama is here and she wants you to know that she's so proud of you. You had nothing to do with her death. She had a weak heart and had had 'episodes' early in the week. She knew she needed her medicine and shouldn't have put the responsibility on you."

"I let her down."

"No, you didn't."

"She's still here, though. She's not at rest. Not at peace."

"Yes, I am," Granny says. "I just check in on my precious every now and then. I'm so proud of her grades and how she helps her father, and I know she's going somewhere with her music."

I relay this to Becca, who sits up and listens. "Really, Granny Gama?"

"Tell her I'd forgive her, but there's nothing to forgive."

My voice catches before I can repeat everything. "She says that she died in the arms of the person she loved the most."

"Oh my God." Becca puts her hands to her heart. "I loved her sooooo much. I still do!"

"Tell her I love her too," Granny says. Then she moves forward and lays a see-through hand against Becca's cheek. My friend startles, like she can feel the touch.

"I miss her more than she can ever know," says Becca.

"I know, Becky."

A tear slips down my cheek; I'm missing my own grandmother. "She wants you to continue being you and doing what makes you happy. Most of all, she wants you to forgive yourself and live life to the fullest, like she did."

Becca cries again, only this time, it's happy tears. "I will, Granny Gama! I promise."

And then the spirit vanishes—just like that.

Becca slumps against the door and reaches out for the used Kleenex I've been holding. "Holy crap. Where did that come from?"

"She came when she thought you needed her the most."

Blowing her nose, Becca says, "That was remarkably intense."

"Welcome to my world," I say, laughing.

She wipes at her eyes again. "Don't tell Celia and Taylor anything. We'll just tell them I'm on my period or something."

"Whatever you say." Then I add, "So much for not investigating in your house, huh?"

Becca takes my hand. "It wasn't an investigation, Kendall. It was an intervention. I think you just saved me."

"Anything for a friend. And you're one of my best."

Chapter Twenty-three

On Monday afternoon, I approach physiology class with great trepidation, not knowing what I'm in for with Courtney. Will she have returned to her old ways, calling me Ghost Girl and sneering at me over our project? Or will she cut me some slack and see that I'm just a teenager like her, trying to fit in and survive high school? No matter how much I try to tune in to the energy around me, I can't predict what's going to happen.

My purse vibrates, alerting me to a text message. It's from Celia.

>Where were u @ lunch?

>Mom took me to The Loft.

The Loft is a cute little bistro-type place in the Square. Mom thought it would be fun to sneak me out of school for some girls' time. It was a blast to hang with her and eat the smoked Gouda and spinach omelet that was absolutely to die for—nummsies.

>Sweet! U'll never beeleeve CL.

I sigh hard and move my thumbs over the tiny keyboard.

>Got her bitch back on?

>No. Invited me and TT to sit w/her.

>Serious?

>As a heart attack.

>Almost 2 class. Talk l8r!

I walk into Ms. Pritchard's classroom, full of students milling about before the late bell sounds. I make my way over to my seat and try to calm the nerves that have sprung to life inside of me.

Soon, Courtney bounces in, clinging to Jim Roach's arm. She's all smiles and laughs, and the sullen pallor is gone from her cheeks. She seems well rested and . . . back to her popular self. *Oh, boy.* With a wave to Jim, she eases down the aisle between desks, stepping over Sean's still-cast leg. She sits right next to me.

"Hey," she says, not making eye contact.

I bite my bottom lip. "Hey."

Courtney pulls out a book and notepad from her Prada messenger bag and then picks through a plethora of pens before selecting a specific blue uni-ball.

All right. This is stupid. Why am I shaking like a leaf? What do I think she's going to do, draw on me? I have nothing to fear but fear itself. Course, Franklin Delano Roosevelt never dealt with the likes of Courtney Langdon.

Here I go. "Are you . . . okay? You know. From Saturday?"

She waves her hand in the air, as if dismissing everything

that happened at Stephanie's. "Everything's fine. I'd rather we not ever discuss that. Like, ever."

I sit up tall. "Umm, sure. I just thought . . ."

Thought what? That she'd apologize for the last two months of torture? That we might be friends somehow? That she might actually thank me, now that she's not under the influence of a spirit or exhausted after expelling it? I guess some people just never change.

Then Courtney knocks the earth off its axis. She withdraws a report; it's sheathed in a clear cover, black binding, and a nice vinyl backing. The best work from the Radisson Staples down the street. She plops the report on my desk, then claps her hands together like it's first-and-ten.

And she actually smiles at me.

"What's this?"

"So I had some time on Sunday and I thought I'd put together all of our notes on the piglet."

I thumb through the report and see that all of our forms are filled out, as well as the discussion questions on our findings during the dissection. What is this? Courtney finished our project on her own. "This is . . . amazing."

She tosses her long hair over her shoulder. "I thought so too. We're totally going to get an A on this project. Did you see the charts I did in the back, where we cataloged everything? Nothing like a little extra effort, huh?"

I hand it back to her. "I can't take credit for this. You did all the work."

She frowns; her perfectly plucked eyebrows form a V on her head. "We both did the work. I just put it all together. No big."

"But you did everything."

Courtney passes the report over to me again. Her eyes tighten and she focuses on me. "No, Kendall. *You* did everything."

I don't have to be a psychic to understand the meaning of her words. This is Courtney's way of thanking me for helping her. She's, like, making that grand gesture without having to goo or gush over it.

"Oh. Oh! Well, you know. I do what I do," I say with a half smile.

"You do what you're destined to do," she adds. Then she lays her hand on mine and kind of squeezes. It's not an eternal bond of friendship and we'll never be BFFs; however, an understanding passes between us, like a whispered secret.

My skin heats and my nerves finally relax. "Thanks, Courtney. We're gonna be just fine."

Right before class starts, she leans over and says, "So RHS homecoming is in a week."

Intrigued, I say, "I've heard." I don't think she'll necessarily be on the homecoming court, after her last couple weeks of performances and disappearances at school.

"I'm having a hay ride after the pep rally and bonfire on the Thursday before the game." She hesitates for a minute and then clears her throat. "You and Jason should, like, come along with us. Okra's bringing his guitar, and we'll roast corn on a spit and just hang out."

The pounding of my heart picks up, only not in anxiety this time. Instead, it's the adrenaline rush of being asked to do something fun with one of the popular girls in school. Of fitting in. Of belonging. "Yeah. We'd like that."

She adds, "Of course, Celia, Clay, Taylor, Ryan, Becca, and that weird guy she dates can come too."

"Dragon," I say.

"What?"

"His name is Dragon."

"Oh. Right."

"He's a good guy. You'd like him if you got to know him," I say, referencing myself at the same time.

Courtney smiles. "Sure, why not. The more, the merrier."

And just like that, everything seems like it's going to be okay for the new girl at Radisson High School. I've never been more relieved.

"It sounds like 'all's well that ends well,'" Loreen says to me after school.

"Ahhh, a woman after my Shakespearean heart."

"I've been learning from you."

I plop down on Loreen's sofa and scarf down one of her homemade brownies. "No one's more relieved than I am that Courtney's back to normal and isn't treating me like dog-doo, let me tell you what."

Loreen throws her hands up. "That reminds me! I have a present for you to give to her."

She turns to rummage through a shipping box and then pulls out a bright red T-shirt. She flips it around to face me, and I almost gag laughing at the slogan: "333—Only Half Evil."

I hold my middle tightly. "That is the funniest frickin' thing I've ever seen. I've got to have one of those for every member of our team. And you'll let me actually buy them."

Loreen tosses it at me and waves me off. "Thought you'd like it. Tell Courtney to wear it with her cheerleader uniform. And no more tackling opposing players."

"Although we did win that game," I note.

Loreen and I laugh together for a minute, and it feels good. Better than good—fantastic! For the first time since I moved to Radisson from Chicago, I'm just Kendall again. I'm not a psychic. I'm not a freak. I'm not Ghost Girl. I'm not an insomniac or a disrespectful child. I'm just a girl with a boyfriend and good friends—and a peculiar hobby. We do good things for people who need us, and we'll help even more in the future.

"But don't ever forget how special your gift is, Kendall," Loreen says, interrupting and reading my thoughts.

"I know."

She pats me on the leg. "I was very proud of the way you handled yourself through all of this ordeal with Courtney. Especially the other night at the Crawfords'. It was very grown-up of you. You could have just left that girl to her own devices, but you stepped up."

I pick at a brownie crumb on my left boob. *What a slob!* "I didn't feel grown-up. I felt cornered and bullied and sad and grateful, all at the same time."

"I know, sweetie," she says. "I can't tell you how impressed Evelyn was with you."

"She was?"

Loreen's smile spreads wide. "She called me this morning and told me that she contacted her ex, Joel, and they had a wonderful conversation. She said they haven't been that relaxed with each other in years. Evelyn wants to meet up with him and talk about reconciling."

My hand covers my mouth as I gasp. "That's phenomenal. Oh my God, how awesome will that be for them and for Stephanie?"

"It's all because of you, Kendall."

I don't know what to say. Imagine that, I'm speechless.

"I had an idea too," Loreen adds.

"What's that?"

"Why don't you hang out a shingle, so to speak, here at my shop? You can do tarot cards and psychic readings and whatever else you want to do."

"Are you for real?" Whoa. That would be—well, it would be some extra scratch in a teenager's pocket! "I have to ask my parents first."

"Of course you do."

The phone rings. "Divining Woman," says Loreen. She pauses for a moment and then smiles into the phone. "Well, thanks, Massimo. That would be nice. Sure. Sure. See you then." She hangs up the phone and barely dares to meet my gaze.

"What was that all about? You and Father Mass having an actual calm convo?"

"More than that."

I lift an eyebrow at her.

"He sort of asked me to dinner," Loreen says, a deep crimson blush staining her cheeks. "You don't mind, do you?"

"Mind? I think it's awesome!" Not to mention I already picked up on the tension between the two of them. It'll be good for Loreen to get out and socialize a little bit.

"Only thing," I say with a frown, "don't wear one of your sayings T-shirts. You do own, like, grown-up clothes, don't you?"

She laughs hard. "I won't embarrass myself, Kendall. I promise, I clean up real nice."

I hug her hard, knowing how lucky I am to have her in my life. "Well, I better get going. I want all the dirty details."

With a smirk, she says, "Well, maybe not all of them."

"Thanks, Loreen. Love ya! Mean it."

At home, I burst in to see Mom shucking ears of corn over our kitchen garbage can. Kaitlin barrels through in full lacrosse garb, tracking grass into the dining room.

"Change clothes now, Kaitlin!" Mom shouts out.

The back door opens and Dad walks in. He plants a kiss on my forehead and then grabs an apple from the bowl on the table. "Hey, kiddo. How's everything?"

"Great, Dad."

"David, don't eat too much. We're having barbecued chicken, corn on the cob, and coleslaw," Mom says.

"Why, Sarah, I do believe you're becoming Southern."

We all laugh together and then Dad grows serious. "I'm sorry I've been so preoccupied at work lately," he says to me. "I wish I could have gone to Atlanta with you and your mom. I knew you were in good hands though." He blows a kiss across the room. Mom winks at him.

"It's okay, Dad. You're wicked busy, I know. I haven't felt slighted at all."

He adjusts his glasses. "I'm extremely proud of you, though. You're accepting all of this change in your life like a real trouper."

"Thanks, Dad."

While I've got them both together, I tell them about Loreen's idea for me to do some readings at her store. Mom wipes her hand on a dishtowel and thinks for a moment.

Dad takes a bite out of the apple and says, "So, Sarah?"

Mom comes around the counter and sits at the kitchen table. "Sure, Kendall. If that's what you want to do."

"I think it could be fun. Especially since Loreen will be there with me."

"I really like her," Dad says. "She's got character."

Mom looks at him funny, but then says, "It's great that you have her as a mentor. I just want you to continue to be safe and careful."

306 — GHOST HUNTRESS

"I will, Mom."

She waggles her index finger at me. "The minute something demonic or evil or anything like that happens to you, you have to tell me and immediately stop what your—"

I stop her with a hug. "Don't worry about me, Mom."

"I'm your mother. It's in my nature to worry."

Dad shakes his head and laughs. "My girls . . ."

I'm the luckiest girl in the world. I have plenty of people guiding me: Mom, Dad, Loreen, Father Mass, my friends, and even Emily . . . although she hasn't been around lately. She'll come around when she's ready. She always does.

My cell phone rings. It's Jason.

I take a deep breath and smile. Now it's time for the "u + me" time!

Epilogue

I AWAKEN WITH A START, my throat dry and aching. My heart is thumping in my chest like Flea banging it out on the bass for the Red Hot Chili Peppers.

And speaking of red hot . . .

I throw the covers off me, realizing I'm tangled up in the sheets and drenched from head to toe in a sticky sweat. It's not even warm in here, but something has my adrenaline pumping and my body attuned to the static charge in the air.

Rubbing my eyes as they adjust to the dark room, I try to recall what I was just dreaming. Something strange and almost sinister. A mishmash of images flashing at lightning speed through my brain. A psychotic slide show that I can't stop long enough to decipher.

I sit up with a start and catch my breath.

Emily is sitting at the foot of my bed, staring at me.

"Emily, where have you been?"

"I've been around."

Has she? "What are you doing here now?"

She's paler—okay, I realize she's a flippin' ghost, but still—than usual. "Tell me about the dream, Kendall."

"My dream . . . yeah." Slowing my rapid-fire pulse, I try to halt the crazed reflections in my mind. Concentrating even as I'm still trying to wake up, I stare ahead at Emily's whitish silhouette in the dark of my room.

Then everything clicks into place; the dream feels almost like a memory of sorts. Only whose? Certainly not mine.

"I, umm, I think I was seeing you when you were alive or something like that."

The picture in my mind morphs into the scene. It's Emily. She's young and happy and alive. I can't tell the time period, but it's not too long ago since she's wearing jeans and clothes that could easily fit in with today's fashion. She's driving in the rain. Wait, no, she's the passenger. There's a guy driving. He's really cute, and I can tell that he totally digs her. They're holding hands and listening to . . . the Commodores—whoever they are.

"Tell me, Kendall."

"You're alive, Emily. In my dream. And so happy." Then, suddenly—*flash! Bang!* A collision. An explosion. Twisted steel, crunching metal, and flames. Fire everywhere. Burning out of control. My pulse is sprinting out of control as I recall this image, my blood pressure rising with each challenging breath. "Oh God, Emily! What happened? The guy . . . he's . . ." He's slumped over the steering wheel. No pulse. "He's dead? And you?" I shift my eye to view the image more. Emily's stuck in the car as it burns around her. Blood cascades down her pretty face and onto the shirt covering her bulging belly. "Holy shit! You were pregnant in my dream! I was there, and the baby was starting to come, so I called to my mom, 'cause she's a nurse, you know? But then it started raining so hard and I couldn't get to you. And you were bleeding so bad."

Tears stream down my face as I remember the dream. "I see myself moving toward the car to help you, but when I get to the door, it won't open. Crap! It's stuck. I look through the window to see how you are. But something morphs in the image. It's not the inside of a car at all. You're not there. I am, instead. Not in the car, but I'm on the floor of a house in a heap. Did I trip? Am I listening for something? No . . . I'm not . . . moving. There's so much pain. So much. Searing and hot and stabby all over." I lift my hands to my mouth, remembering what happened just before I woke up in a sweat. "Oh God, Emily. In the dream, I'm bleeding. Like, wicked bad. Jason's with me and he can't do a thing. Celia and Taylor are crying. Becca is screaming. What happened? Where are we?"

I gulp down the inflammation in my throat. Never have I had such a vivid dream. Okay, well, maybe when I dreamed about Jason Tillson before I ever met him. And that one came true. I gasp sharply and spout out, "What does this mean, Emily?"

"It's just a dream, Kendall."

"Like hell it is. Tell me!"

She lowers her eyes, not meeting my gaze. "I've tried to stop this, but I can't."

"Stop what?"

A sigh escapes her. "Your visions."

"It was just a dream," I say in a harsh whisper.

Emily focuses her stare at me. "No, it wasn't."

"What do you mean?"

"Kendall," she says. There's a dramatic pause, then: "You've just witnessed my past."

Startled, I want to reach out to her. "You were killed in an awful car wreck? All that blood and the fire and—"

She shakes her head. "I've tried to block you from seeing it."

"But the part about me in that house on the floor, bleeding? Like it was a life-or-death situation. What was that?" Every muscle in my body is tense, awaiting her response.

"I'm still trying to stop that part," she says.

I can't take any more. "What are you talking about?"

"Kendall, you've just seen your future."

To be continued . . .

Disclaimer

The thoughts and feelings described by the character of Kendall are typical of those experienced by young people awakening to sensitive or psychic abilities.

Many of the events and situations encountered by Kendall and her team of paranormal investigators are based on events reported by real ghost hunters. Also, the equipment described in the book is standard in the field.

However, if you are a young person experiencing psychic phenomena, talk to an adult. And while real paranormal investigation is an exciting, interesting field, it is also a serious, sometimes even dangerous undertaking. While I hope you are entertained by the Ghost Huntress, please know that it's recommended that young people not attempt the investigative techniques described here without proper adult supervision.

BIBLIOGRAPHY

Terminology and descriptions pertaining to Kendall's psychic awakening, skills, and abilities from Maureen Wood, psychic/intuitive/sensitive/healer/Reiki master.

Kendall's aura reading references come from www.reiki-for-holistic-health.com/auracolormeanings.html.

Kendall's and Courtney's dissection project directions and information from www.hometrainingtools.com/articles/pig-dissection-project.html.

Information on CT scan procedures and equipment from www.radiologyinfo.org/en/info.cfm?pg=bodymr&bhcp=1.

General information about exorcisms and the Episcopal Church from en.wikipedia.org/wiki/Exorcism.

Georgia history can be found at www.georgia encyclopedia.org/nge/Article.jsp?id=h-641.

Traditional exorcism prayer from www.byzcath.org/.

Shakespeare quotes from www.enotes.com/shakespeare-quotes/.